Sarah Mallory was born in the West Country and now lives on the beautiful Yorkshire Moors. She has been writing for more than three decades—mainly historical romances set in the Georgian and Regency period. She has won several awards for her writing, including the Romantic Novelists' Association RoNA Rose Award for *The Dangerous Lord Darrington* and for *Beneath the Major's Scars*.

Also by Sarah Mallory

The Scarlet Gown
Never Trust a Rebel
A Lady for Lord Randall
The Duke's Secret Heir
Pursued for the Viscount's Vengeance

The Infamous Arrandales miniseries

The Chaperon's Seduction
Temptation of a Governess
Return of the Runaway
The Outcast's Redemption

Discover more at millsandboon.co.uk.

THE TON'S MOST NOTORIOUS RAKE

Sarah Mallory

MILLS & BOON

First published in Great Britain 2018
by Mills & Boon, an imprint of HarperCollins*Publishers*
1 London Bridge Street, London, SE1 9GF

Large Print edition 2018

© 2018 Sarah Mallory

ISBN: 978-0-263-07483-3

MIX
Paper from
responsible sources
FSC™ C007454

This book is produced from independently certified FSC™ paper to ensure responsible forest management. For more information visit www.harpercollins.co.uk/green.

Printed and bound in Great Britain
by CPI Group (UK) Ltd, Croydon, CR0 4YY

For TGH, as we stand on the edge
of another great adventure.

Chapter One

'Molly! Molly!'

She held her breath, balanced in her leafy eyrie and peeping down at the path below her. Edwin would never think to look up into a tree. Her brother did not think girls could climb trees. He was four years older and at school now and he did not think girls could do *anything*. True, her skirts had been a hindrance in scrambling up into the branches and Mama would be sure to scold her when she saw the tear, and Papa might beat her for it, too, and make her learn another tract from the Scriptures, but it would be worth it. She would wait until her brother had passed beneath her, then jump down behind him. That would give him a scare.

'Molly, where are you?'

'Where the *devil* are you?'

The voice had changed. It was no longer Edwin

and suddenly she was no longer six years old and hiding in a tree. She was in a dark place, bruised and bleeding, and waiting for the next blow.

'Molly. *Molly!*'

It was a dream. Only a dream. She shook off the fear and panic, clinging to the fact that it was her brother's voice dragging her from sleep. She opened her eyes, but remained still for a moment to gather her thoughts. She was safe here. It was the vicarage garden and she was lying on a rug beneath the shady branches of the beech tree.

'So there you are, sleepyhead.'

She sat up, rubbing her eyes. 'I beg your pardon, Edwin. I came out here to do some sketching and I must have fallen asleep.'

'Well, if you will go off at the crack of dawn to help out at Prospect House.' He threw himself down beside her on the rug, grinning at her and looking far more like the errant elder brother she had grown up with than the sober Reverend Edwin Frayne, vicar of the parish. 'There is no need for you to visit more than once a week, you know. Nancy and Fleur are very capable of running the place.'

'But I like to help when I can and today is market day when they sell the surplus from the dairy and the kitchen garden. There is always so much for them to do to pack up the dog cart, deciding on a price for the eggs and butter, and—'

He threw up a hand, laughing. 'Enough, enough, Molly. You do not need to convince me. You are a grown woman and may do as you please.'

'I know they could cope without me,' she conceded, smiling. 'However, today will be the last of those early mornings. With the days growing shorter I shall go to the house on a Tuesday. We will prepare all we can in advance so that Fleur and the others have only to pack up the cart in the morning.'

'If you must.'

She reached for his hand. 'I like to do it, Edwin. I like to help. It makes me feel necessary.'

'You are very necessary, my dear. You are necessary to my comfort, keeping house for me here.'

She took his hand and squeezed it, wanting to say how grateful she was that he had taken her in when she was so suddenly widowed, but the memories that stirred up brought an unwelcome lump to her throat and she did not wish to embarrass either of them with her tears, so she pinned on a bright smile and asked him where he had been.

'I called upon our new neighbours at Newlands.'

'Oh.'

Edwin spread his hands, 'I could not ignore them, Molly, you must see that. And I admit I was pleasantly surprised. Sir Gerald is really most gentleman-like. He was most accommodating.'

'One would expect him to be, to a man of the cloth.' Molly bit her lip. 'I beg your pardon, Edwin, I know one should never listen to gossip, but from everything I have heard, Sir Gerald Kilburn and his friends are everything I most despise…'

She tailed off and Edwin looked at her with some amusement.

'You must learn not to attach too much importance to the gossip our sister writes to you. She has inherited our father's abhorrence of anything frivolous. Sir Gerald and his guests all seemed very pleasant. He introduced me to his sister, too. Miss Kilburn is to keep house for him here. She has with her an elderly lady who is her companion. Their presence and that of other ladies suggests this is not a party of rakish bucks intent upon setting the neighbourhood by the ears.'

'Not all of them, perhaps,' said Molly darkly. 'But Louisa wrote to warn me that one of the party is sure to be Sir Gerald's oldest and closest friend, Charles Russington. Even you will have heard of his reputation, Edwin. Louisa says the gossip about the man is no exaggeration. He is the most attractive man imaginable and no lady in town is safe.'

'If the fellow is so attractive, perhaps it is *he* who is not safe from the ladies.'

'Edwin!'

'I beg your pardon, I did not mean to be flippant, but I think you are making too much of this. Yes, I have certainly heard of Beau Russington, but I did not see him today.' He grinned suddenly. 'If the fellow is as rakish as they say, then perhaps he is coming into the country for a rest! No, no, do not rip up at me for that, my dear. Forgive me, but I think you are too quick to judge. It is our Christian duty to give these people the benefit of the doubt, at least until we are a little better acquainted with them. And we shall soon know what our neighbours think of the newcomers. Sir Gerald told me they plan to attend Friday's assembly at the King's Head. His party comprises five ladies, excluding the elderly companion, and six gentlemen, so just think how that will liven things up!'

Molly was still digesting this news when Edwin coughed.

'I thought we might go this time. Just so that you might meet the Newlands party, you understand.

Miss Agnes Kilburn is a quiet, well-mannered young lady, about your age, and your situations are quite similar. I think you might get on very well.'

Molly said nothing, but her doubts must have been plain in her face, for Edwin said earnestly, 'I really should like you to meet her, my dear.'

She narrowed her eyes, a sudden smile tugging at her mouth. 'Why, Edwin, I do believe you are blushing. Have you taken a liking to Miss Kilburn?'

'No, no, of course not, we have only met the once.' His ears had turned quite red, which only increased Molly's suspicions. He said, 'I am merely concerned that we do not appear unfriendly. And I thought you would prefer that to my inviting them here.'

'There is that,' she agreed. 'Very well, we shall go. I admit my interest has been piqued. In meeting Miss Kilburn, at least.'

'Molly.' Edwin tried to look stern but failed miserably. 'I will not have you making Miss Kilburn feel awkward.'

'No, of course not,' said Molly, her grey eyes twinkling. 'I shall be the very soul of discretion!'

Molly decided that if she was going to attend the assembly then she would need some new gloves, since she had noticed at their last outing that her old ones were looking decidedly shabby. Thus, on the morning of the assembly, she sallied forth to the high street to make her purchases. Hebden's was by far the most popular shop for the ladies of Compton Parva. The business had begun as a haberdasher, selling everything one might require for sewing such as ribbons, thread and needles, but as the number of families in the area increased, the business had expanded to include such necessary items as ladies' bonnets, scarves, reticules, stockings and gloves. The shop was now run by Miss Hebden, who had inherited the business from her parents, and when she saw Molly, she came immediately to serve her.

'Ah, Mrs Morgan, good day to you,' she greeted Molly with her usual cheerful smile. 'How may I help you today?'

'I need a pair of white gloves, but I can wait, if you have other customers.'

'No, no, those ladies are shopping together and Clara is looking after them very nicely. She does not need me always looking over her shoulder.'

'She has settled in well, then?'

'Oh, yes, indeed, very well. She is a quick learner and not afraid to ask if there's something she don't know.' She turned slightly away from her assistant and lowered her voice. 'I admit I was a little reluctant, when you first suggested I should take her on, but she's a good girl, very polite, and the customers like her, which is important.'

Molly smiled. 'I am very glad.'

'Yes,' Miss Hebden continued. 'And she's company, too. In fact, I have grown very fond of her.' She hesitated, then said in a rush, 'I think what you are doing at Prospect House is a very fine thing, Mrs Morgan, taking in those poor girls and giving them a second chance. What Clara has told me about her last employer, trying to take advantage of the poor maid and then turning her off without a character when she refused—well, it makes my blood boil, so it does. And him a gentleman, too, so she says. There's some wicked folks in this world, Mrs Morgan, and that's a fact.' For a moment, Miss Hebden's countenance was unusually solemn, then she gave herself a little shake and smiled. 'But I mustn't keep you talking all day, ma'am. It's white gloves you want, isn't it? Now, then, let me see… Yes, here we are. You are in luck, it is the very last pair. We've had quite a run on them this week and on ribbons, too. Everyone wants to look their best for tonight's assembly, I shouldn't wonder. I understand the new owner of Newlands intends to be there, with his friends, so everyone will be out to impress them.'

Molly stifled the urge to say that she did not wish to impress anyone. More customers came into the shop at that moment, so she paid for her gloves and left. She felt a little spurt of indignation that the arrival of a fashionable gentleman and his friends could arouse such interest in the town. Well, she for one would not give them another thought.

Alas for such hopes. Molly had not gone a hundred yards when she met up with Mrs Birch and Lady Currick, two highly respected matrons of Compton Parva. Since each of them had a daughter of marriageable age, Molly was not surprised when they told her they would be attending that evening's assembly.

'All of Compton Parva will be there,' remarked Mrs Birch, nodding sagely. 'Everyone is agog to see the new owner of Newlands. Have you met him yet, Mrs Morgan? No? Ah, then we have the advantage of you.'

'Yes,' averred Lady Currick, interrupting her friend. 'Sir William lost no time in visiting Newlands and invited them all to join my little card party last night. Was there ever such a man! Not a word to me until it was too late. I asked him how he thought I would accommodate another eleven guests, which, of course, he could not answer. But somehow I managed to squeeze in another table and it passed off very pleasantly, did it not, Mrs Birch? What a pity you were not able to join us, Mrs Morgan, for you could then have met the whole party.'

'I vow I was a little in awe of them to begin with,' said Mrs Birch, 'but I needn't have worried, they were all so pleasant and obliging. Sir Gerald is a most engaging young man, very genial and even-tempered, despite his carrot-coloured hair! And wait until you see the ladies' gowns, Mrs Morgan. London fashions, one can tell at a glance.'

Molly listened in good-humoured silence while the ladies went into raptures over the cut and quality of the various gowns and giggled like schoolgirls over the handsome gentlemen, saving an especial mention for Beau Russington.

'Oh, now there is a handsome gentleman,' said Lady Currick, sighing. 'One can quite understand why ladies are constantly throwing themselves at him. He is so very tall and with such an air of fashion about him!'

'And those *eyes*, ma'am.' Mrs Birch sighed gustily. 'So dark and intense, and that way he has of fixing his gaze upon one, as if you were the only person in the room. La, I think if I were not a happily married woman I might succumb to the beau myself!'

'Indeed, I think you are right, my dear, I have always had a soft spot for a rake, even one as notorious as Beau Russington.' Lady Currick gave another little giggle before becoming serious. 'But with so many personable young men in town, and all of them renowned for being a little *fast*, we must be sure the girls are properly chaperoned. No more than two dances, if any one of these gentlemen should ask them to stand up.'

Molly stared at them. 'You acknowledge the gentlemen to be libertines, yet you will allow your daughters to dance with them?'

'Why, of course, my dear, it would be a great honour to stand up with a fashionable gentleman. And I have no worries that they might attract the gentlemen's attention beyond the dance, for I think Mrs Birch will agree with me that our girls cannot hold a candle to the fine ladies staying at Newlands. But you will see for yourself, Mrs Morgan, if you are coming to the ball this evening.'

The ladies strolled off and Molly went on her way, wondering if it was too late to cry off from tonight's assembly, but it was not really to be considered. She would be obliged to meet the Newlands party at some point, so it would be best to get it over.

It was with the feeling of one doing an onerous duty that Molly went upstairs to change later that evening. She had no intention of dancing at the assembly and she chose to wear her grey satin gown with a demitrain, but when she tried to add a lace cap to the ensemble, Edwin protested, saying it made her look like a dowd.

'Nonsense, it is perfectly proper for a widow of my age.'

'Anyone would think you were forty rather than four-and-twenty,' retorted Edwin. He added, 'Covering your head like that is the sort of thing Father would have approved. He was ever the puritan.'

That made her laugh. 'That is certainly a strong inducement to me to remove it.'

'Which is my intention, little sister! Now, go and take that thing off.'

Molly capitulated, realising that her brother was very much displeased, and ten minutes later, she presented herself in the drawing room again, her unruly dark curls almost tamed by a bandeau of white ribbon.

The public entrance to the King's Head assembly rooms was at the top of a flight of stairs, leading up from the yard. When Molly and Edwin arrived, the Newlands party were about to go in, and Edwin would have hurried Molly up the stairs to meet them, but she hung back.

'There can be no rush, Edwin, and I would like to take off my cloak and tidy myself first. Even that may take some time, though; I so rarely come to these dances that I can already see several of our acquaintances waiting to speak to me.'

'Very well, go and talk to your friends, my dear, and I shall meet you in the ballroom.'

Molly happily sent him on his way and went off to the cloakroom to change into her dancing shoes. She tried not to dawdle, acknowledging her reluctance to meet Sir Gerald Kilburn and his guests. The presence of a party of fashionable gentlemen and ladies in Compton Parva was bound to cause a flutter and, while the young ladies present this evening had the advantage of their parents' protection, her girls, as Molly called the inhabitants of Prospect House, were very vulnerable.

Molly had set up Prospect House as a refuge for young women who had lost their reputation and had nowhere to call home. Some were of humble birth, but many were young ladies who had been cast on to the streets and left with no means of supporting themselves. Molly provided them with food and shelter, and in return, her 'girls' helped out in the house and on the farm attached to it. Molly tried to find them suitable work and move them on, but she knew there would always be more destitute young women to take their place.

Molly had worked hard to overcome the doubts and prejudice of the townspeople, but she knew that such a house would attract the attention of rakes and libertines, who would see its inhabitants as fair game. Molly was afraid that some of her younger charges were still innocent and naive enough to succumb to the blandishments of a personable man and that could have catastrophic consequences, not only for the young woman, but also for the refuge itself. In the five years since she had set it up, Prospect House had become self-supporting, but its success relied upon the continuing goodwill of the local townspeople.

She was thus not inclined to look favourably upon the newcomers, and when she went into the ballroom and saw her brother chatting away in the friendliest style to a group of fashionably dressed strangers, she did not approach him. Surmising this must be the party from Newlands, Molly moved to a spot at the side of the room and took the opportunity to observe them.

Sir Gerald was soon identified, a stocky young man with a cheerful, open countenance and a shock of red hair. Molly guessed it was his sister standing beside him. The likeness between the two was very marked, although Agnes's hair was more golden than red, and in repose, her countenance was more serious. Her glance quickly surveyed the rest of the party. She had no doubt the local ladies would be taking note of every detail of the gowns, from the uncommonly short sleeves of one lady's blossom-coloured crape to the deep frill of Vandyke lace around the bottom of Miss Kilburn's gossamer silk. By contrast, the gentlemen's fashions appeared to be very much the same—dark coats with lighter small clothes and pale waistcoats—but Molly was obliged to admit that she was no expert on the finer points of male fashion.

There was one figure, however, who stood out

from the rest of the gentlemen. It was not merely his height, but a certain flamboyance in his appearance. His improbably black hair was pomaded to a high gloss and brushed forward to frame his face with several artistic curls. His countenance was handsome, in a florid sort of way, with thick dark brows and lashes that Molly thought suspiciously dark. His lips, too, appeared unnaturally red, even from this distance. The points of his collar hid most of his cheeks and the folds of his cravat frothed around his neck. His black tailcoat was so broad across the back and nipped in at the waist that she suspected the shoulders were padded. He was gesticulating elaborately as he talked and the ladies around him appeared to be hanging on to his every word. Molly's lip curled in scorn.

'So *that* is Beau Russington.'

'I beg your pardon?'

The startled voice at her shoulder made her look around. A tall gentleman in a plain blue coat was regarding her. She did not know him, but recalled seeing him talking to Mr Fetherpen, the bookseller, when she came in.

'Oh, dear, I did not mean to speak aloud.' She smiled an apology. 'The gentleman over there, holding forth to the group standing before the mirror. He has been described to me as an—' She stopped herself from saying *an infamous rake*. That would be most impolite, and for all she knew the man at her side might well be one of the Newlands party. 'As a leader of fashion,' she ended lamely. She saw the amused look on the stranger's face and added quickly, 'That is what the epithet *beau* denotes, does it not?'

'It does indeed, ma'am.' The stranger looked across the room. 'You refer to the exquisite in the garish waistcoat, I presume?'

'Yes.'

'That fribble,' he said, a note of contempt in his voice. 'That painted fop.'

'Yes,' said Molly, glad to discover he shared her opinion.

'That is *not* Beau Russington, madam. It is Sir Joseph Aikers.'

'Not?' She looked at the stranger in surprise.

He gave a slight bow. *'I* am Russington.'

'You!' Molly's first impulse was to apologise profusely, but she held back. It was not her intention to pander to any man. Instead she gave a little gurgle of laughter. 'I thought you were a book salesman.' His brows shot up and she explained kindly, 'I saw you talking with Mr Fetherpen, you see. And our assemblies are open to everyone, as long as they have a decent set of clothes.'

Had she gone too far? She saw the very slight twitch of his lips and was emboldened to look up at him. There was a dangerous glint in his dark brown eyes, but that thought was nothing to the danger she perceived as she studied him properly for the first time. He was tall, certainly, but well proportioned with broad shoulders and a powerful frame. His black hair was too long to be neat and curled thickly about his head and over his collar. In repose, she thought his lean face might look saturnine, but with that smile tugging at the corners of a mobile mouth and his dark eyes laughing at her beneath their black brows, a bolt of attraction shot through Molly and knocked the air from her body.

Quickly she turned away. Lady Currick had in no way exaggerated this notorious rake's charms and Molly felt a stab of alarm. If *she* felt this way, what effect might he have on her girls?

'A book salesman?' he murmured, dashing hopes that he might have walked off. 'I suppose I should be thankful I was not talking to the butcher.'

Another laugh bubbled up inside Molly, but she resolutely stifled it and with an incoherent murmur she hurried away.

* * *

Oh, heavens, was there ever anything so unfortunate? Molly moved quickly around the room, smiling but not stopping when Lady Currick beckoned to her. That lady would have seen Molly talking to Mr Russington, but Molly was not ready to discuss it. She would dearly like to go home, but that would only cause more speculation. Instead she made her way to Edwin's side, bracing herself for the introductions she knew he would be eager to make.

Her nerves were still raw, but she achieved a creditable appearance of calm as her brother presented Sir Gerald and his friends to her. They were all genial enough, clearly willing to be pleased by the provincial company in which they found themselves. Even Sir Joseph, the painted fop, bowed over her hand and paid her a few fulsome compliments.

Molly made her responses like an automaton, her thoughts still distracted by her recent encounter with Mr Russington. However, she forced her chaotic mind to concentrate when Sir Gerald presented his sister. Agnes Kilburn was handsome rather than pretty, and during their short conversation, Molly gained the impression that she was an intelligent, thoughtful young woman. In any other circumstances, Molly would have been delighted to make her acquaintance, but she had no wish to give Sir Gerald and his friends any reason to spend more time than necessary in Compton Parva.

Suddenly Molly was aware of a tingling down her spine and she heard a deep, amused voice behind her.

'Ah, Mr Frayne, will you not introduce us?'

'I'd be delighted to do so! Molly, my dear, may I present Mr Russington to you? M'sister, sir. Mrs Morgan.'

Steeling herself, Molly turned, her smile pinned in place. She could not recall putting out her hand, but within moments he was bowing over her fingers. It was ridiculous to think she could feel the touch of his lips through her glove. That must surely be her fancy, but she did not imagine the little squeeze he gave her hand before releasing it.

'Mrs Morgan and I, ah, encountered one another a little earlier.'

She thought angrily that he might expect her to apologise for her mistake, but when he lifted his head and looked at her there was nothing but amusement in his dark eyes. A faint smile curved his lips and she felt the full force of his charm wrap around her.

She could hear music, but it took her a moment to realise the sweet strains were the sounds of the musicians striking up for the first dance. She was vaguely aware of Edwin leading Agnes Kilburn on to the dance floor, but for the world she could not tear her gaze away from Beau Russington's laughing eyes.

'Would you do me the honour of dancing with me, Mrs Morgan, or does that privilege fall to your husband?'

She felt dangerously off balance and his amusement ruffled her. It was as if he was aware of her agitation.

She said coldly, 'I am a widow, sir. And I do not dance tonight.' She moved towards the empty chairs at the side of the room. When he followed her, she said crossly, 'Surely, Mr Russington, you should dance with some other lady. There are plenty without partners.'

'Ah, but none to whom I have been introduced. Besides, the dance is now started. I shall have to wait for the next.'

When she sat down, he took a seat next to her. Could the man not take a hint?

'Pray do not feel you need to remain with me,' she told him. 'I am sure there are many here who would prefer your company.'

'I am sure there are,' he agreed, not at all offended.

Her agitation disappeared, ousted by a desire to shake him from that maddening calm.

She said, 'When I was a child, Mama had a house cat, a very superior being that had the unfortunate trait of always making for the visitor who liked him least. You are displaying a similar trait, Mr Russington.'

'You liken me to a cat?'

Molly hid a smile. She murmured provocatively, 'A tomcat, perhaps.'

A tomcat?

Russ glanced at the lady beside him. She was fanning herself as she watched the dancing and looking quite unconcerned. Did she realise what she had said, at the insult she had just uttered? Of course, she did. From their first exchanges he had had the impression that she was trying to annoy him. Well, perhaps not at first. Not until she had known his identity. He wished now he had not spoken, but when he had heard her speak his name and had seen her looking with such contempt at Aikers, he had not been able to help himself.

He remembered how she had turned to him, a smiling apology upon her lips and in her frank grey eyes. Then, when she realised who he was, the look had changed to one of unholy amusement and soon after that, sheer dislike. He was used to ladies fawning over him, or teasing him in an attempt to gain his attention. Never before had one been so openly hostile. A tomcat! He felt a momentary shock, until his sense of humour kicked in and he laughed.

'I fear a longer acquaintance with you will do my self-esteem no good, madam!'

'No good at all,' she agreed affably.

She rose and, with a nod of dismissal, she left him. Russ watched her walk away, noting the proud tilt of her head, her straight back and the soft, seductive sway and shimmer of her skirts as she glided across the floor. Perhaps it was a ruse to pique his interest. Perhaps he might indulge the widow in a flirtation. After all she was pretty enough, although nothing like the ripe, luscious beauties that he favoured.

He decided against it. Compton Parva was a small town and she was the reverend's sister. In his experience it was better to dally with dashing matrons who could be relied upon to enjoy a brief liaison without expecting anything more lasting, and then, when the time came to part, they would do so amicably and with never a second thought. No. Much better to leave well alone.

Edwin and Molly strolled home from the King's Head once the dancing had ended. They had decided against using the carriage for such a short journey and the full moon and balmy summer night made it a pleasant walk, but for Molly the enjoyment was dimmed as she waited for the inevitable question from her brother.

'Well, sister, what thought you of Miss Kilburn?'

Molly was cautious. 'She appeared to be a very pleasant girl, although we did not have an opportunity to speak a great deal.'

'You would have had more if you had not insisted upon spending all your time with the old ladies such as Lady Currick.'

'Edwin!'

'Well, you must admit, Molly, you are young enough to be her daughter.'

'But I could hardly sit with the young ladies who were waiting for partners. It was embarrassing to watch them all making sheep's eyes at the gentlemen.'

'You might have stayed with the ladies from Newlands,' he suggested mildly. 'Then you might have had more opportunity to become acquainted with Miss Kilburn.'

'Perhaps, but these things are never easy at a ball.'

Edwin patted her hand, where it rested on his sleeve. 'Never mind. All is not lost, my dear, we have been invited to Newlands for dinner next Tuesday. I am going fishing with Sir Gerald during the day, but I will come home to fetch you for the evening.'

Molly's heart sank, but before she could utter a word he continued, 'I know you usually visit Prospect House on Tuesdays, but if you take the gig, you will be back in plenty of time to change. And you will have saved yourself a tiring walk.'

'Well, that is the clincher!' She laughed. 'Especially since I tell you that I am *never* tired.'

'There you are, then. It is settled, you will come!'

She heard the satisfaction in his voice and said nothing more. It was clear that Edwin wanted her there and, after all the help he had given her, how could she refuse?

Chapter Two

Molly had never visited Newlands and as Edwin's carriage rattled along the drive she leaned forward to catch a first glimpse of the house. What she saw, glowing golden in the sunlight, was a rambling stone house in a mix of styles. Its previous, ageing owner had not used it for years, so she could understand the excitement that had erupted in the town when Sir Gerald bought the hunting lodge. The gossip had started several months earlier, when workmen had descended upon the property. Word soon spread that Sir Gerald was a bachelor of substantial means who was planning to bring a large party to the house at the end of the summer. Molly's sister, Louisa, soon provided even more information, writing to inform her that Sir Gerald was a familiar figure in London and numbered amongst his acquaintances many of the fashionable rakes and Corinthians who flocked to the capital each Season.

Now those fashionable acquaintances were here, staying only a couple of miles from the town and far too close to Prospect House for Molly's comfort. Beside her, she heard Edwin chuckle.

'You look disappointed, Molly. Were you hoping Newlands would be so ugly and uncomfortable Sir Gerald and his friends would quit it within the month?'

'Something like that.'

'Do not fret, my dear,' He patted her hands. 'Sir Gerald has made it very clear he and his party are here for the sport. Why else would he have bought a hunting lodge?'

'But if the area's hunting, shooting and fishing do not live up to the party's expectations, might not Sir Gerald and his louche friends look elsewhere for a little entertainment? And a house full of what they would consider to be "fallen women" is certain to attract their attention.'

'Now you are being unreasonable,' exclaimed Edwin. 'You cannot deny that at last week's assembly the gentlemen from Newlands behaved impeccably. You have no reason to think ill of them.'

'I have Louisa's letters,' replied Molly darkly.

'Louisa has nothing better to do with her time than pass on salacious gossip, for the most part untrue or exaggerated. Come, Molly, you are being unfair to Sir Gerald and his friends. When people are disparaging about the inhabitants of Prospect House, you tell them that one should not make hasty judgements, yet here you are doing just that.' Edwin squeezed her fingers, pressing home his point. 'I am sure our new neighbours will have no interest at all in Prospect House, and if they do…' He spread his hands. 'You cannot keep your charges locked away for the duration of Sir Gerald's visit, my dear.'

'I know that,' she admitted, as the carriage pulled up before the house. 'But even if the gentlemen have no designs upon them, I very much fear one or two of the girls might find the presence of such handsome and fashionable gentlemen in Compton Parva…distracting.'

'My dear, if they are ever to make their way in the world again then they will have to learn to withstand the attractions of personable gentlemen.'

'Of course.' Molly clasped her hands together. 'But you saw how the ladies at the assembly reacted. Such fashionable young bucks, with all the glamour of the town clinging to them, are particularly attractive to susceptible young women.'

Edwin laughed. 'Do you really believe that, Molly?'

She thought of Beau Russington with his dark looks and careless charm and felt her stomach swoop.

'Oh, yes,' she whispered, her mouth suddenly dry. 'I really do.'

Sir Gerald and his friends were waiting for them in the drawing room. With the exception of Mrs Molyneux, Miss Kilburn's aged companion, they had all been present at the assembly where introductions had been made. As greetings were exchanged, Molly took the opportunity to study the company. She had been reassured at the assembly to see that Mrs Sykes and Lady Claydon were homely matrons, while Agnes Kilburn and the Misses Claydon had soon been at ease and mixing with the young ladies of the town. They were all very lively, but not at all the dashing sirens she had feared. This second meeting appeared to confirm her view, which was a relief, and she turned her attention to the gentlemen. Their host, Sir Gerald, was the most genial looking of them all, while Sir Joseph and Mr Flemington were the most flamboyant in their dress. But there could be no doubt they were all very fashionable—the cut of their clothes, the number of fobs and seals and the intricacies of their cravats had made them stand out at the recent assembly.

All except Beau Russington. She had been too agitated at their first encounter to appreciate why he was considered a leader of fashion, but here, in the elegant drawing room of Newlands, she had the opportunity to make a calm appraisal of the man. It did not take her long to realise that although he was not as showily dressed as his friends, his style was far superior. At least to her inexperienced eye. There was a simplicity to his dress, but nothing shabby in the superb cut of his clothes. Not a wrinkle marred the perfection of the dark evening coat stretched across his broad shoulders. It fitted him so well she wondered how many servants it had taken to ease him into it.

A plain white waistcoat was buttoned across his chest and she refused to allow her gaze to linger on the close-fitting breeches that sheathed narrow hips and powerful thighs. She quickly raised her eyes to take in the snowy neckcloth, intricately tied and with a single diamond winking from amongst the exquisite folds. The study of his cravat took her eyes to the countenance above it. A lean face, darkly handsome with a sensuous curve to the mouth. At that moment, as if aware of her scrutiny, the beau turned to look at her and her cool assessment came to an abrupt end.

Even from the other side of the room she felt the power of his gaze. Those dark, almost-black eyes skewered her to the spot and caused her pulse to race. Not only that, excitement flickered deep inside, like flames licking hungrily at dry tinder. She looked away quickly, shocked to realise that he had awoken sensations she had never wanted to feel again.

Sir Gerald was addressing her and she forced her mind to concentrate on his words. She exchanged pleasantries with his sister and then joined in a conversation with Mrs Sykes and Lady Claydon while the gentlemen discussed the day's shooting until dinner was announced.

Molly found herself seated at Sir Gerald's right hand, with Sir Joseph Aikers beside her. Mr Russington, she was relieved to see, was sitting opposite her brother at the far end of the table. She did not think she would have enjoyed her meal half as much if the beau had been sitting beside her. Sir

Joseph might be a fribble and a painted fop—as some people so cruelly described him—but Molly soon discovered he was exceedingly good-natured and assiduous of her comfort, ensuring her glass was filled and that she had her pick of the succulent dishes on offer.

The food was excellent and the conversation interesting. No awkward subjects were broached and Molly began to relax. These were cultured, educated people who knew how to set a guest at ease. Perhaps she had been magnifying the dangers they posed. Just as that thought occurred to her, Edwin laughed and she glanced down the table towards him. After his day of sport, her brother was clearly upon easy terms with the gentlemen. Mr Russington was looking her way and he caught and held her gaze. Molly's heart began to race again. She felt trapped, like a wild animal, in thrall to a predator. With an effort, she dragged her eyes away, realising the danger was all too real. At least where one man was concerned.

Her appetite was quite gone and she was relieved when Miss Kilburn invited the ladies to withdraw. Molly intended to sit with Lady Claydon and Mrs Sykes, but when they reached the drawing room

Miss Kilburn and the Misses Claydon were determined that she should perform for them.

'Your brother was eager that we should hear you play upon the pianoforte, Mrs Morgan,' explained Miss Claydon, opening the instrument and beckoning to Molly to sit down. 'He told us you are most proficient and that you sing, too.'

'Such praise,' murmured Molly, vowing to give Edwin a trimming as soon as they were alone. 'I am very much afraid I shall disappoint you.'

Harriet Claydon gave a trill of laughter. 'I doubt that, ma'am. Judith and I are both hopeless, despite Mama insisting that we have the best of teachers.'

'Sadly that is very true,' agreed Lady Claydon, shaking her head. 'We spent a fortune upon their education and they can neither of them do more than play a few simple pieces. Miss Kilburn, however, is very accomplished.'

Molly drew back in favour of her hostess, but Miss Kilburn was quick to decline.

She said shyly, 'We should very much like to hear you play, Mrs Morgan.'

Molly took her place at the piano. Perhaps it would be as well to play now, before the gentlemen came in. She played a couple of short pieces and, when urged to sing, she rattled off a lively folk song, before concluding her performance with an Italian love song. Her audience were generous in their praise, but when she could not be persuaded to play more, Agnes Kilburn took her place and Molly retired to sit with the older ladies, relieved that she was no longer the focus of attention.

She hoped that might be the case for the rest of the evening, but it was not to be. When the gentlemen came in, the conversation turned towards Newlands.

'Many of our friends were against my purchasing such an out-of-the-way place,' said Sir Gerald cheerfully. 'Including the beau here. Ain't that right, Russ?'

'I was.' Mr Russington moved a little closer to the group. 'After all, there are good places to hunt that are much closer to London.

'Aye,' declared Mr Flemington, coming up. 'These provincial towns can be the very devil for entertainment. Not Compton Parva, you understand,' he added hastily, with a bow towards Edwin and Molly. 'The assembly at the King's Head last week was as good as any I have attended outside London.'

'Well, I do not regret my choice,' declared their host. 'It may be a long way north, but what is a few days' travel, compared to the sport that is to be had here? No, I am delighted with my new hunting lodge and glad now that I did not allow myself to be dissuaded.'

Edwin laughed heartily. 'Did you expect to find only savages in Knaresborough, Kilburn? I admit I had the same reaction from my friends and acquaintances when I accepted the living here. But I am very much at home, you know. And I vow it provides some of the best riding in the country.'

'Yes, I grant you, if your taste is for rugged grandeur,' put in Sir Joseph Aikers, waving one hand. 'You cannot deny the weather here is less clement than the south. And the mud.' He gave a comical grimace that made his companions laugh.

'In the main we are very favourably impressed,' declared Mrs Sykes. 'It is true the journey was a trifle wearisome. But Kilburn has made the house very comfortable and the townspeople of Compton Parva are most welcoming.'

'We are relieved to have Newlands occupied at last and not only for the enlargement of good society,' Edwin told her with a smile. 'It provides occupation for local people and business for our tradesmen. That must always be welcome.'

'There is one thing that surprised me,' remarked

Lady Claydon. She hesitated and glanced towards the pianoforte, where her daughters and Miss Kilburn were engaged in singing together. 'I had not expected to find a house here for females of a *certain order.*'

'My wife means the magdalens,' declared Lord Claydon. 'I admit I was surprised when I heard of it—one usually associates Magdalene hospitals with the larger cities. But I suppose small towns have the same problems, what? It's a way of keeping that sort of female off the streets.'

Molly stiffened, but Edwin caught her eye and gave a slight shake of his head.

'You refer to Prospect House' he said calmly. 'It is a refuge for unfortunate women who have suffered at the hands of men. It is not a house of correction.'

'However, it is a little disturbing to think there is a need for one in Compton Parva,' remarked Mrs Sykes.

'The sad fact is we need more of these places,' said Edwin. 'Since Prospect House opened its doors, it has always been full, taking in residents from far and wide.'

'Ah,' cried Mr Flemington, rolling his eyes, 'So it is not that this area has more than its fair share of Lotharios.' He cast a laughing glance around at the gentlemen standing beside him. 'At least, not until now!'

There was much good-natured protest from his auditors and Mrs Sykes rapped his knuckles with her fan, telling him to behave himself.

'This is no laughing matter,' she said. 'I would assure Mr Frayne that we are great supporters of the Magdalene houses. After all, someone has to help these poor women and show them the error of their ways.'

'Error of their ways?' Molly was unable to keep silent any longer. 'None of the women in Prospect House are prostitutes, ma'am, although that might have been their only way to survive had they not been taken in. However, I admit it was set up on the *precepts* of the original Magdalene hospital,' Molly added, 'to provide a safe and happy retreat for women of all classes.'

Molly knew her words would bring the attention of the group upon her, but it could not be helped. She sat up very straight, holding her head high. A couple of the gentlemen had raised their eye-glasses to regard her and Beau Russington, too, was watching her, but Molly ignored them all.

'Do you mean there is no attempt to reform

them?' asked Lady Claydon, her brows rising in surprise. 'Is this not merely pandering to vice?'

'The women at Prospect House are the *victims* of vice, ma'am, not perpetrators,' Molly told her. 'Some have been seduced, others come here to escape seduction or because their reputations have been ruined by men who sought to use them for their own ends. As for reform, they are taught suitable skills in order that they may support themselves.'

'You appear to be very well informed about the business, Mrs Morgan,' remarked Mr Russington.

'I am,' said Molly, tilting her chin a little higher. 'I set up Prospect House.'

Her words brought a flutter of gasps and exclamations.

'Oh, good heavens,' murmured Mrs Sykes, fanning herself rapidly.

Molly kept her head up, prepared to meet any challenge, but she could see no condemnation or disapproval in the faces of those around her. Some of the gentlemen looked amused, the ladies merely surprised and then, to her relief, she heard Edwin's cheerful voice.

'Yes, and I am very proud of my sister. She purchased the property, provided a small annuity to fund it and then set up a committee of local people, knowing it was important to have the goodwill of the town if the house was to survive.'

'Most commendable, I am sure.' Lady Claydon responded faintly.

'It is proving a great success,' Edwin continued. 'They have a small farm which provides most of their food and any surplus of eggs, butter and the like is sold at the weekly market.'

'Quite an enterprise,' declared Sir Gerald. 'You must allow me to contribute to your fund, Mrs Morgan.'

'Thank you, sir.' Molly smiled, warming to him, until in the next breath he suggested they should all visit Prospect House to see it for themselves.

'I am afraid not,' she said quickly. 'With the exception of the doctor, they admit only women to the house. All deliveries and callers are directed to the old farmhouse.'

'But a house full of women, that is quite a temptation.' Mr Flemington sniggered. 'To, ah, uninvited guests.'

'We have seen to it that they are well protected,' replied Molly. 'Their manservant, Moses, is a fearsome fellow. A giant. He has orders to keep all unwelcome callers at bay.'

Her fierce stare swept over the gentlemen.

'Well, well,' declared Sir Gerald, breaking into the awkward silence. 'Shall we have some dancing?'

The gentlemen jumped up with alacrity and began to move back the furniture from the centre of the room and roll up the carpet. Hoping to atone for making everyone feel uncomfortable, Molly immediately offered to play. This was robustly contested by Mrs Sykes and Lady Claydon, who both expressed a willingness to perform this duty and persuaded Molly that as a guest she must take her turn on the dance floor.

'Now, now, Mrs Morgan, I hope you are not going to say you do not dance tonight,' said Lady Claydon, moving towards the pianoforte. 'Lord Claydon does not dance, since his accident, and if I play for you all, everyone else has a partner. Is that not splendid?'

'And as our guest, the honour of leading you out falls to me,' declared Sir Gerald, coming up. He held out his hand. 'Come along, let us show the others the way!'

Molly felt her heart sinking. She had not expected that there would be any impromptu dancing, but a very quick calculation told her there were just enough gentlemen and ladies to make six couples, if one excluded the pianist and Lord Claydon, with his bad leg. It would look odd, therefore, if she refused to dance, for that would leave only one gentleman without a partner. She had not even the excuse that she was not dressed for dancing, because her green muslin evening gown with its moderately flounced hem would not be any hindrance at all. She accompanied her host to the floor, pinning her smile in place.

Sir Gerald's good humour was infectious and Molly's smile became genuine. She loved to dance, although she did not indulge in the amusement very often, and she was soon lost in the music. She skipped and hopped and turned as the lively, noisy, country dance progressed. They began to change partners and Molly was moving from one gentleman to another and another, and by the time she was standing opposite Mr Russington her smile was wide and brilliant. As they joined hands and began to skip down the line she looked up into his face. He caught and held her eyes, a glinting amusement in his own, and in that moment everything changed. She could hear the piano, the other dancers clapping in time, but it was as if she and her partner were in a bubble, contained, connected. Her mind was filled with images of him pulling her close, holding her, kissing her, undressing her…

The familiar patterns of the dance saved her from humiliation. She danced like an automaton, moving on, smiling at her next partner, on and on until Sir Gerald claimed her once more and the dance was ending. She joined the others in applauding, but inside she was in a panic. Everyone was changing partners for the next dance. From the corner of her eye she saw Beau Russington looking at her. She could not dance with him. Would not! Quickly she grabbed Edwin's hand.

'Pray dance with me, brother. It is an age since we stood up together.'

'Dance with you?' Edwin sent a quick look over her head. 'Oh, I was hoping to ask Miss Kilburn to stand up with me again.'

'Please, Edwin.' She hoped her tone was not too beseeching, but she clung to his hand, and after a moment, he capitulated.

For this dance she had only the smallest contact with the beau as the dancers wove in and out of one another. It was a mere touch of the fingers and this time she was prepared. As they crossed one another she was careful not to meet his eyes, but just his presence made her body tingle. Every part of her was aware of him, as if there was some connection between them, and it frightened her.

When the music ended Molly made her way to the piano, where Lady Claydon was leafing through the sheet music.

She said, 'My lady, I know the music for "The Soldier's Joy" by heart. I beg you will allow me to play.'

'Oh, but surely you would prefer to dance, my dear. You so rarely have the opportunity.'

'I think I sprained my ankle a little in the last dance, ma'am, and would prefer to rest it for a while, but that would leave a gentleman without a partner, and besides, my brother would fuss so if he knew of it.'

Lady Claydon was immediately full of sympathy. That made Molly feel a little guilty, but they exchanged places, Lady Claydon going off to join in the dancing, and Molly's guilt eased a little when she saw how much the lady was enjoying herself.

She remained at the piano for two dances, then Miss Claydon suggested 'Dancing Hearts' and Molly was obliged to search through the sheet music. She had just found the piece when Beau Russington approached and that nervous flutter ran through her again.

'Would you not prefer to dance, Mrs Morgan? I am sure one of the other ladies would play for us.'

Without looking at him she waved her hand towards the music. 'No, no, I am quite content, thank you. I am not familiar with the steps of this dance.'

He leaned closer. 'I could teach you.'

Her mouth dried as, inexplicably, her mind filled with images that had nothing to do with dancing. It was his voice, she decided. It was too low, too deliciously seductive.

'No. I—that is, I turned my ankle in that first dance and prefer not to dance again this evening.'

'Ah, I see. So you do not trust yourself to dance? I quite understand.'

His tone suggested he did not believe her and Molly felt guilty colour rushing to her cheeks. She busied herself with straightening the sheet music on the stand, trying to concentrate on the notes she would have to play, and after a moment he walked away.

'Well, if he understands that I do not want to dance with *him*, then so much the better,' she muttered, running her fingers over the keys. 'And if he is offended enough to leave me alone then that is better still!'

She played two more dances, which were very well received, then Sir Gerald announced that refreshments awaited everyone in the dining room. There was a general move towards the door and as Molly got up from the piano, she found Beau Russington beside her.

'Allow me to give you my arm, ma'am.' When she drew back he added, 'It is best you do not put too much weight upon your foot.'

'My—oh. Oh. Yes.'

He offered his arm, and as her fingers went out he grasped them with his free hand and pulled them on to his sleeve.

'I am perfectly capable of walking unaided,' she told him, panicked by his firm grip.

'But what of your ankle, Mrs Morgan?'

'It is well rested now, thank you.'

'I think you are afraid of me.'

'And I think you are teasing me.'

'Well, yes, I am. Your reluctance for my company is intriguing.'

'It is not meant to be. A gentleman would be able to take the hint.'

He sucked in a breath. 'Cutting. You do not consider me a gentleman, then?'

'Oh, no,' she said with deceptive sweetness. 'I know you for a rake, sir.'

If she had hoped to offend him, she was disappointed.

'Do you think you are being quite fair to me, madam?'

'Oh, I think so. Your reputation, and that of your friends, precedes you. And it is not mere gossip, I assure you. The information comes on good authority and from more than one source.'

Molly felt exhilarated by the exchange. She could not recall speaking so freely to any man before.

'The devil it does!'

She laughed and was immediately aware of the change in him. Through the fine woollen sleeve beneath her fingers she could feel the muscles tighten. And she suspected she had angered him. When he spoke his voice was soft, smooth as silk, cold as steel.

'But all this is hearsay, madam—what do you really know of me?' They had reached the hall and with practised ease he whisked her away from the crowd and into the shadowy space beneath the stairs. 'Well, Mrs Morgan?'

He had turned her to face him, his hands resting on her shoulders, very lightly, but she found it impossible to move. Even in the shadows, his dark eyes glowed with devilish mischief. She had the strangest feeling that invisible bonds were wrapping around them, tightening, forcing her closer. She could feel him, *smell* him, a musky, spicy, lemony scent that she wanted to breathe in, to close her eyes and give in to the desire burning in her core. She fought it, curling her hands until the nails dug into her palms, using the pain to stop her from reaching out and pulling him towards her. To stop herself surrendering, as she had done once before to a man. A rake who had taken everything and left her to suffer the consequences. Desire was replaced by panic and she fought it down, struggling to keep the terror from her voice.

'You go too far, sir. I beg you will let me go.'

His hands tightened. 'Are you afraid I might kiss you?'

I am afraid I might not be able to resist!

'You would not dare.'

Russ felt her tremble, saw the uncertainty in her eyes and knew she was weakening.

He murmured softly, 'But you said yourself, madam, I am a rake and rakes are very daring.'

Her eyes widened, he saw the pink tip of her tongue flicker nervously across her lips and for a moment he was tempted to carry out his threat. To pull her close, capture that luscious mouth and kiss her into submission. Then he saw the apprehension in her gaze and something more, a fear that was not warranted by the threat of a mere kiss. She was terrified.

What the devil were you thinking of, Charles Russington? Are you such a cockscomb that you think no woman should be able to resist your charms?

He took his hands from her shoulders and stepped away. This was no way to treat a lady.

'You are right,' he said. 'I beg your pardon for teasing you.'

The look of terror had lasted only a moment and it was now replaced by anger. She glared at him.

'I would expect nothing else from a libertine.' Her voice was shaking with fury as she put up her hands to straighten the little puff sleeves of her gown that had been flattened by his grip. 'Your disgraceful behaviour proves that the reports I have heard about you do not lie. The sooner you and your…your *friends* remove from Compton Parva, the better!'

With a toss of her head she turned and hurried away. Russ watched her go, but he made no move to follow her back into the laughing, chattering throng that was slowly making its way into the dining room. He knew he had been wrong to tease her, but she had made him angry and he had forgotten himself. His lip curled in scorn. The great Beau Russington, famed for his sangfroid, his charming manners, had allowed his temper to get the better of him.

He raked his fingers through his hair. Damn the woman, she should not have this effect on him. Why, she was not even his type—too small and dark for one thing, and a sanctimonious reformer to boot. No, his original instinct had been right. *Leave well alone!*

Two days of rain followed the dinner at Newlands and Molly was relieved that the bad weather deterred visitors. She thought—hoped—no one had seen that brief interchange with Beau Russington, but had no wish to discuss the evening with anyone, not yet, when she was still so unsettled.

On Thursday she took the carriage to make her

belated visit to Prospect House, thankful for the inclement weather. The house and its farm were situated on the opposite side of the valley to Newlands and she knew Sir Gerald and his guests rode out frequently beyond the bounds of the park, but it was much less likely that they would do so in bad weather.

Prospect House was a stone-built dwelling standing tall and square on the landscape. It had belonged to a gentleman farmer who had built himself this house in a style more fitted to his dignity and it now boasted large sash windows and a pedimented front door. The new dwelling had been built at a suitable distance from the old farmhouse and separated from it by the stables and a kitchen garden.

Prospect House was now home to ten women of various ages and stations in life. They tended the house and garden with the help of one man-servant, who also looked after the farm. It had taken Molly years of hard work and determination to turn Prospect House into a successful and self-sufficient refuge, and as the carriage turned in through the gates she felt an immense pride in the achievement.

The door was opened to her by Moses, the only

male servant, whose size and somewhat bovine countenance belied a sharp intelligence. He had worked at Prospect House all his life, and when Molly bought the property, she had kept him on, recognising that his knowledge of farming would be invaluable. This had engendered Moses with a fierce loyalty to his employer and made him protective of the house and its female residents. Molly greeted him cheerfully and made her way to the office at the back of the house. The pretty blonde poring over the accounts glanced up as the door opened and flew out of her chair to hug her.

'Molly! I did not expect you to come here in all this rain.'

'But as patron I must call at least once a week to see how you go on, although I was certainly not going to *walk* here.' Molly laughed and returned the hug. 'But, Fleur, I am interrupting you.'

'Not a bit of it, I had just finished totting up the money we took at market yesterday and I am pleased to say we sold everything, which was a surprise, given the heavy rain.'

'I am glad of it and only sorry I did not come over to help you—'

'There is no need to apologise, Molly, we tell you time and again that we can manage.' Fleur took her arm. 'Come along into the drawing room, and we will take tea.'

Molly accompanied Fleur out of the office, reflecting that the happy young woman at her side was a far cry from the frightened girl she had taken in all those years ago. Fleur Dellafield was a childhood friend of Molly's. She had grown up to be a beauty, but when her widowed mother had married again, life had become a nightmare. She had been thrown out of her home after thwarting her stepfather's attempts to ravish her. Molly had found her, destitute and starving, and brought her to the newly opened Prospect House. She had settled in well and shown such an aptitude for organisation that Molly had been delighted to make her housekeeper. She had protested at the time that Fleur was too pretty to languish for long at Prospect House, but Fleur had been adamant.

'I met plenty of gentlemen at my come-out in Bath,' she had told Molly. 'I found none of them more than passable, and after what happened with my step-papa, I have no wish to meet any more. No, Molly, I want only a comfortable home and to be *needed*.'

So Molly had installed Fleur as housekeeper and seen Prospect House flourish. Now, as they entered the drawing room and she saw the welcoming bowl of fresh flowers on the highly polished drum table, Fleur's words came back to her.

'I like to come here, Fleur,' she told her friend. 'I like to feel I am needed.'

'Then do, please, call as often as you like, for there is always something to be done!'

Fleur tugged at the bell pull and a few moments later a maid in a snowy cap and apron entered. Molly smiled at her.

'Good day to you, Daisy. How are you?'

'Very well, ma'am. Thank you kindly.' The maid dropped a curtsy, her cheerful face creasing into smiles. 'Between Miss Fleur and Miss Nancy, I am learning how to run a household and to cook.'

'And your son?'

'Ah, Billy is doing very well, thank you, ma'am, although he don't much like his lessons.' She gave a sigh. 'Twice this week I left him practising his letters and he escaped through the window.'

'He does prefer to be working out of doors,' remarked Fleur. 'He is a great asset in the garden and Moses says he has an ability with animals.'

'Perhaps we should let him help out on the farm more,' suggested Molly. 'Although I think it imperative that he learns to read and write, at least enough to get by.'

'Then I shall tell him that if he works for an hour at his lessons every morning he may spend the rest of the day helping Moses,' said Fleur. 'Will that be acceptable to you, Daisy?'

'Very kind of you, Miss Fleur, and more than we have a right to expect.'

'Nonsense, you have worked very hard since you have been here and we would like to help you and Billy to find a home of your own. Now, perhaps you would be kind enough to fetch tea for Mrs Morgan and myself, if you please.' Fleur waited until the door had closed behind the maid before sighing. 'I wonder if we did the right thing, taking in Daisy Matthews and her son. We have none of us any experience of ten-year-old boys.'

'But where else would they have gone? Daisy's employer had thrown them on to the streets upon discovering that Billy was her natural child. And Edwin tells me the vicar who applied to us had tried to find them another home, with no success at all.'

'It is such a cruel world,' said Fleur, her kind face troubled, but then she brightened. 'However, Daisy is quick to learn, and I am already looking about for a suitable position, although I fear Billy may not be able to go with her. However, if all else fails he can stay here and help Moses.'

'A very sensible idea,' agreed Molly, 'but we can make no decisions until we have procured a position for Daisy. Which reminds me, I was in Hebden's on Friday last and saw Clara at work. You will be pleased to learn that Miss Hebden is delighted with her, so I think we may write that down as another success. Now, you must tell me how everyone else goes on here.'

Molly listened carefully while Fleur made her report. It did not take long and they had finished their business by the time Daisy returned with the tea tray.

'Which means we may now please ourselves what we talk of,' declared Fleur, preparing tea for her guest. 'And I very much want to know what you think of our new neighbour at Newlands.' Molly did not reply immediately and Fleur shook her head at her. 'You cannot think that we would remain in ignorance,' she said, handing her friend a cup of tea. 'Everyone at the market this week was talking of Sir Gerald and his friends. I would like to know your opinion.'

Molly made a cautious reply. 'They are all extremely fashionable.'

'They spend a great deal of time in London I believe,' remarked Fleur. 'Six men, I understand. Are all of them libertines, do you think?'

Molly was surprised into a laugh. 'Good heavens, Fleur, that is very blunt. Why should you think that?'

'Nancy told me.'

'Ah, of course.'

Molly sipped her tea and considered the woman who was now cook at Prospect House. Nancy, or more correctly Lady Ann, was the youngest daughter of an eccentric and impoverished earl who had tried to force her into a marriage with a man old enough to be her grandfather. Molly should have remembered that she was still in contact with one of her sisters, a terrific gossip, who kept her well informed of the latest London scandals.

'So, Molly, tell me what you think,' Fleur prompted her.

'Edwin thinks them all very gentlemen-like.'

'But you, Molly. What do you think?'

With her friend's anxious blue gaze upon her, Molly could not lie.

'I suspect one or two of them might have a...a

roving eye.' She saw Fleur's look of alarm and hurried on. 'They know of Prospect House, of course, but there is no reason to think they will call here. I gave them to understand you were very well protected.'

'That is all very well, but we cannot remain within the bounds of Prospect House for ever!'

'No, indeed, and I see no need for you to do so, as long as you never go out unaccompanied. These are gentlemen, Fleur, they would not force their attentions upon an unwilling female.'

'Would they not?' Fleur gave a little shudder. 'That has not been our experience.'

Molly was silent, remembering the loud voices, the blows, the pain. Fighting back the memories, she said quietly, 'The horrors we experienced happened in private, at the hands of men with power over us.'

'But Nancy says Sir Gerald and his friends are known for their wildness.' Fleur turned an anguished gaze upon Molly. 'We both grew up in one small market town in Hertfordshire and now live in just such another. You were married at eighteen and I have never been further afield than Bath. What do we really know of rakes and libertines and the fashionable world?'

Molly sighed. Fleur was right and it was useless to ask Edwin for advice. He insisted upon seeing the best in everyone. Unlike their father, she thought bitterly. He had only seen the worst in everyone, especially his youngest daughter. The truth, she suspected, was often somewhere in between. She put down her cup.

'Come along,' she said, rising. 'Let us go and talk to Nancy. She knows far more about these things than we do.'

They made their way down to the kitchen where they found the earl's daughter beside the kitchen table, sitting in a most unladylike pose with her feet up on a chair. Nancy was large, loud and brash, but she had a heart of gold and a surprising flair for cooking. She had explained to Molly that she had learned the skill from her father's French chef, a tyrant with a soft spot for a child so ignored and unloved by her parents that she might disappear to the kitchens for days on end without question. Now Nancy ruled the kitchen at Prospect House and was something of a mother hen to all the residents. She greeted Molly and Fleur cheerfully and invited them to join her at the table.

'I don't suppose you want more tea,' she said,

swinging her feet to the floor and turning to face them.

'No, thank you,' said Fleur, disposing herself gracefully on a chair. 'We have come to talk to you about the people at Newlands.'

'More especially the gentlemen,' added Molly, taking a seat beside Fleur. '*My* sister has already hinted that they were…er…gentlemen of fashion, and I understand yours has sent you similar information.'

'Yes, only in far less mealy-mouthed terms,' said Nancy, not mincing matters. 'Sir Gerald Kilburn's set are infamous in town. Young men with too much time and too much money and spend both on flirtations, affairs and outrageous wagers.'

'Oh, heavens,' murmured Fleur.

'But Newlands is a hunting lodge,' said Molly. 'Sir Gerald told Edwin they are here for the sport.'

Nancy gave her a pitying look. 'Sir Gerald's party will be made up of rakes and Corinthians. They regard pursuing women as *sport*. But you have met them, Molly. What is your opinion?'

'They all appeared very amiable. Two of the gentlemen are accompanied by their wives, and Lord and Lady Claydon have also brought their daughters. Miss Kilburn acts as hostess for her brother and she has brought a companion, to give her countenance.'

Nancy shrugged. 'Perhaps we are misinformed, then. But rich, idle men are always a threat to women. Who else is in the party, what single gentlemen are there?'

'Apart from Sir Gerald?' Molly tried to sound unconcerned. 'There is Mr Flemington, Sir Joseph Aikers and Mr Russington.'

'Kilburn's closest cronies,' exclaimed Nancy. 'I remember them all from when I was in town. Flemington and Aikers were notorious womanisers even then, at least my father would not countenance them making me an offer, but that may have been more to do with their station than their reputation. He was determined that I should marry an earl at the very least.'

'And Mr Russington?' asked Molly, tracing a crack in the table with her finger.

'Ah, yes, the beau.' Nancy rested her chin on one hand, a smile on her lips and a faraway look in her eyes. 'He is more notorious than all the rest. I remember him very well. He and Kilburn are of an age, I believe. They must be, what, eight-and-twenty now.'

'The same age as yourself,' put in Fleur.

Nancy nodded. 'They came to town after my come-out. My sister tells me Russington is a friend of Brummell, although unlike Mr Brummell, he is also a noted sportsman. A Corinthian rather than a dandy.' She cast a mischievous glance across the table. 'We danced once, at Almack's, you know, I remember it because he is taller than I! And so handsome. All the ladies were in love with him, but he soon earned a reputation for being danger-ous, because any woman who threw her cap at him was likely to be indulged in a wild flirtation. Wise mamas keep their daughters out of his way now, but it may be that Kilburn has Russington in mind for his sister. I believe he is exceedingly wealthy.'

Fleur shuddered. 'He sounds exceedingly dan-gerous, if he is so very attractive. What did you think of him, Molly?'

'I?' Molly gave a little laugh, playing for time. 'I had very little to do with him.'

'Was he one of those gentlemen you said had a *roving eye*?'

She did not know how to answer Fleur's ques-tion. She had not noticed the beau's dark eyes on anyone but herself and then with devastating effect. Just the thought of it sent a shiver along her spine.

'I am not sure the beau needs one,' said Nancy,

meditatively. 'From what my sister says he does not need to look about him. Women fall over themselves to gain his attention.'

Molly gave a little huff of despair. 'Oh, how I wish Sir Gerald had never come to Newlands!'

'Too late for that now,' said Nancy, 'they are here and we must deal with it. We must make sure the others are aware of the dangers.' She began to list the girls on her fingers. 'Daisy is hopefully too old to attract the attention of these gentlemen. She has Billy to look out for, too, which should make her wary. Elizabeth and Bridget are young and pretty, but as the daughters of gentlemen they already know what a dangerous combination that is and will be anxious to avoid repeating the mistakes that led to their being cast out of their homes. Marjorie is near her time now and her condition should make her safe from any unwelcome advances. That only leaves the two housemaids. They are still young and silly enough for anything. I shall keep an eye on them and make sure they do not step outside without Moses or one of us to accompany them. I shall also ask Moses to inspect that all the doors and windows are fastened at night.'

'Perhaps we should get a dog.' Fleur suggested.

'That is a good idea.' Nancy agreed. 'I shall tell

Moses we must have a guard dog, although knowing his soft heart he is likely to bring back the first mongrel he sees that needs a home. In the meantime we must all be vigilant to keep the girls safe from predatory men.' She sat up straight, folding her arms across her ample bosom. 'As for you, Fleur, you must *always* take one of the girls with you when you go to market, for with your golden hair and blue eyes, you are quite the prettiest of us all and the most likely to attract the attentions of a rake, especially such a noted connoisseur of women as Beau Russington.'

Molly was aware of a little stab of something that felt very much like jealousy and quickly pushed it aside. She did not want the beau's attentions, so why should she be jealous? It made no sense at all.

'You flatter me, Nancy,' said Fleur, blushing. 'And I really do not wish to attract any man's attention, or unwelcome advances.'

'They will not harm you, Fleur,' said Molly, catching her friend's hand. She frowned and added grimly, 'I shall not allow them to harm anyone here.'

Chapter Three

Despite her brave words, Molly came away from Prospect House knowing there was very little she could do to protect its residents. It was unlikely that any of the gentlemen would actually come to the house, but it was very possible they would see the girls when they went into town to fetch supplies or to sell produce on market day. However, when she mentioned her worries to Edwin, he was sanguine.

'I believe your charges have little to fear from the gentlemen at Newlands,' he told her. 'There is enough sport to be had to keep them hunting, shooting or fishing for weeks, and apart from the assemblies there is little to bring them into Compton Parva. Why, it is quite possible they will never set eyes upon your girls, as you call them!'

With that Molly had to be satisfied. Since Edwin

had no wife to help him, she took it upon herself to visit the sick and distribute clothes and food to the poor of the parish. This, combined with her role on various committees, including that of Prospect House, kept her busy most days and she was able to put her worries about the Newlands party out of her head until the following Sunday.

When she accompanied Edwin to the morning service at All Souls, Sir Gerald and some of his guests were already occupying the box pew allocated to Newlands. She spotted Mr Russington's tall figure immediately, but Sir Joseph and Mr Flemington were absent.

The residents of Prospect House were amongst the last to arrive. They were all most soberly dressed, with the ladies heavily veiled, and they were accompanied by Moses and little Billy Matthews, scrubbed and dressed in his best coat. The whole party slipped into their usual seats at the back of the church and, although they quickly settled down for the service, Molly found it difficult to concentrate. She rebuked herself for her inattention and told herself there was no reason at all why Sir Gerald or his friends should have occasion to look back at Fleur and her companions, but she did not relax until the service was over and the Newlands party had gone out without sparing a glance for the rest of the congregation. She hovered at the church door and watched them exchange a few words with Edwin and only when they had climbed into their carriages and driven away did she turn her attention to her friends.

'Everything is well at the house,' Nancy told her, in answer to Molly's anxious enquiry. 'We have had no unwelcome visitors and Moses has found us a guard dog.' Her eyes twinkled. 'He brought home the prettiest little terrier! Not a mastiff, I know, but he has a good bark, which is what we need, and Moses tells me he will be useful for keeping down the rats in the barn.'

Molly laughed. 'He sounds perfect.'

'Why not come back with us and you can see him for yourself?'

'I would love to do so, but I am helping with the Sunday school today, and tomorrow I have promised to call on Mrs Calder at Raikes Farm. Edwin tells me she has not been well and asked me to visit her. No matter, I shall see this new addition on Tuesday, when I come over to help you prepare everything for the market. If the weather is as fine as today, I shall walk.'

'And you will bring your maid?'

'Of course. I intend that Cissy shall go everywhere with me from now on, whenever her other duties allow. Having recommended that you must all be circumspect, I must lead by example!'

Alas for such good intentions. On Monday, when Molly went below stairs to collect the basket of food for Raikes Farm, she found that the upper housemaid, who also acted as her dresser, was in tears, having received word that her mother was very ill.

'Then you must go to her immediately,' Molly decided, quickly revising her plans. 'Gibson shall take you in the gig. He is waiting for me at the door now.'

'Ah, no, ma'am, I couldn't possibly,' sniffed Cissy, mopping her eyes with her apron. 'You and the master is too good to me already, taking me in, and me without a reputation—'

'Nonsense,' said Molly briskly, handing Cissy her own handkerchief and shepherding her up the stairs. 'Reverend Frayne and I know very well that you were too young to be blamed for what happened to you. But I hope you know better now than to walk out into the gloaming alone with a young man.'

'Aye, I do, ma'am, and it won't ever happen again, I promise you. I am much wiser now.' She managed a watery smile. 'And the baby is doing very well.'

'You have no regrets about sending him to live with your sister and her family?'

'Oh, no, because I wants to become a lady's maid and I can't do that if I have my baby with me, so I was very happy when my sister offered to have him. No, he is very happy where he is. They quite dotes on him.'

'I am very glad of it,' said Molly, 'and you are proving to be a very good dresser, Cissy. As soon as we can find another housemaid to take your place, I shall promote you to my personal maid.'

She cut short Cissy's effusive thanks and instructed her to run up and fetch her cloak. 'I will tell Gibson there is a change of plans and he is to take you to your mother. And you must remain with her at least until tomorrow. Promise me.'

'Very well, miss, if you say so, but what will you do about delivering your basket?'

'Mr Frayne shall drive me to Raikes Farm in the carriage.'

Having seen the maid off, Molly went in search of her brother, only for him to tell her that he had made other arrangements.

'My old college professor is on his way to Ripon and is breaking his journey at Compton Magna to-night,' he said. 'He has invited me to join him at the White Hart for dinner.'

His face clouded when she explained she had sent her maid off in the gig and he immediately suggested he could cancel his engagement, but Molly stopped him.

'No, indeed you must not do that,' she said, smiling. 'You will be passing the turning to Raikes Farm on your way, so if you set off a little earlier you can drop me off there. Now, please do not argue, Edwin. It promises to be a fine afternoon for me to walk back. I do not intend to stay above an hour and it is barely two miles from here cross-country, so I shall be back in good time for dinner.'

The arrangements having been agreed, Molly collected her basket and set off with her brother in the carriage. The inclement weather had not let up for the past week, but at last the skies had lifted and although the sun only showed through intermittently, there was every promise of a fine afternoon and evening.

Molly's visit to Raikes Farm was much appreciated. Mrs Calder was the wife of a hard-working farmer and the young family had been struggling to cope while their mother was ill. They fell with delight upon the basket of food, with its bread and pies and cakes. Molly soon ascertained that Mrs Calder was on the mend and after spending an hour talking to them all, she set off to follow the footpath back to Compton Parva.

The sun was peeping in and out of the clouds, but there had been so much rain over the past week that the footpaths were thick with mud. Molly did not mind. She had taken the precaution of wearing serviceable boots and she would be able to change as soon as she reached the vicarage, so she strode away from the farm, determined to enjoy her walk.

The highway to Compton Parva followed a circuitous route, but the footpath was much more direct, ascending between enclosed pastures until it joined the stony cart track running along the ridge. A solidly built drystone wall ran along one side of the track and separated the farmland from the moors that stretched upwards to the skyline. To avoid the thick, glutinous mud that covered large sections of the lane which had not yet dried out, she walked along a narrow grassy strip at the side.

The view from here was unrivalled. Looking across the valley and the road that ran through Compton Parva, she could see the lane leading to Prospect House, while directly ahead was the dark green mass of Newlands's Home Wood. At this distance she would see immediately if anyone was riding out from the Park, but all was quiet and she knew she would shortly be cutting back down towards the town, so she had little fear of meeting anyone while she was alone and unprotected. She gave a little sigh. Before Sir Gerald and his rakish friends had appeared, she had never worried about walking unaccompanied in the town or in the surrounding countryside. Now she was aware of the constant danger.

As if summoned by her thoughts, her eye caught a movement on the lane ahead of her. Someone was approaching from the opposite direction. The gentle curve of the lane meant she could not see the figure clearly above the walls, but she could make out it was a man, carrying a long staff. Most likely a farmer, checking his stock. A shepherd, perhaps, looking for a stray sheep.

Distracted by trying to peer into the distance, Molly missed her footing. Her boot slipped off the uneven grassy bank, and she lost her balance.

Her left foot flew forward, but landed awkwardly amongst the stones of the rutted lane and she gasped as the impact jarred her ankle. The next moment she found herself measuring her length along the ground.

Bruised and shaken, Molly pushed herself up, feeling very cross. Her skirts and spencer were filthy and she suspected that her face, too, had not escaped the mud. As she tried to stand a sharp pain shot through her ankle and she fell back. She took a couple of moments to compose herself, then struggled to her feet, but one tentative step was enough to tell her that the pain was too severe for her to walk unaided.

She hobbled to the wall and leaned against it, considering what she should do. The farmer, or shepherd, had by this time reached the junction and turned to follow the footpath down to the road in the valley bottom. A glance each way along the cart track showed her that it was deserted. She might sit there all day in the hope of someone driving past. Molly bit her lip, knowing she had no choice but to shout out and ask the only other person within sight for help.

She called, then called again. The man stopped and she waved to attract his attention. He started back up the path, but it was only as he turned into the lane that Molly realised he was no farmer, despite the long staff he held. As he strode along the lane towards her she could see the embroidered waistcoat and the tight-fitting buckskin breeches he wore beneath his country jacket and his mud-spattered top boots had the cut and fit only obtained from a first-class bootmaker. With a sinking heart she raised her eyes and looked into the lean, handsome face of Beau Russington.

It took Russ a few moments to recognise the bedraggled figure leaning against the wall and he was aware of a most reprehensible feeling of satisfaction. So the widow who had so plainly shown her dislike of him, who had been so contemptuous, now needed his help.

'Mrs Morgan.' He touched his hat, all politeness. 'How may I be of assistance?'

Her cheeks were flushed with a mixture of annoyance and chagrin.

'I think I have sprained my ankle.'

'Indeed?' He could not help it, his lips twitched. 'Possibly fate is paying you back for your using the excuse the other night. I should be flattered that you were prepared to go to such lengths to avoid dancing with me.'

She bit her lip and glared at him, but he noticed she did not deny it.

She said icily, 'I thought, perhaps, if you would lend me your staff, I could manage to walk home.'

'Don't be ridiculous.' He rested the staff against the wall and came closer.

'Wh-what are you going to do?' She shrank back, putting her hand out as if to hold him off.

'I am going to carry you.'

'B-but you can't.' She looked horrified.

'Oh, I think I can. You do not look to be too heavy.'

'But I am covered in mud. Your clothes—'

'The mud will certainly test my valet's skills,' he agreed, scooping her up into his arms. 'However, we must risk that.'

'And it is too far,' she protested.

'Flack is waiting with my curricle at the bottom of the lane.'

'What about your staff?' she objected as he began to walk.

'I will send someone back to collect it later.' He settled her more comfortably in his arms and set off towards the footpath. They had only gone a few yards when he stopped and looked down at her. 'I think you will be more comfortable if you allow yourself to lean against me,' he said. 'And you might want to put your arm about my neck to support yourself.'

Her cheeks flamed, but one dainty hand crept around his collar.

He grinned. 'That's better.'

She did not reply, neither did she look at him, but Russ did not mind. He was enjoying himself, bringing the haughty widow down a peg or two. That might be an ignoble and unchivalrous sentiment but it was damned satisfying. After all, he was only human.

The curricle was soon in sight and Flack showed no surprise when Russ came up with a woman in his arms, merely watching in wooden-faced silence as Russ deposited his burden on the curricle seat. She winced as her foot touched the boards and he frowned.

'We had best ascertain the damage to your ankle. May I?'

She did not protest, but pulled her skirts aside to reveal her footwear. As Russ untied the laces, he reflected wryly that he was more in the habit of removing satin slippers than serviceable half-boots, but such thoughts disappeared when he looked at her ankle.

'I do not think you have broken any bones, but it is already swelling,' he muttered. 'We must get some ice upon that as soon as we can.'

Molly was beginning to feel a little faint, and she clung on to the side of the curricle as the beau jumped up beside her and they set off at a smart pace along the road, the groom swinging himself up into the rumble seat as the vehicle shot past him. Her ankle was throbbing most painfully and she was content to sit quietly as the curricle bowled along, but when it slowed and turned off the main road she sat up, saying urgently, 'This is not the way to Compton Parva.'

'No. I am taking you to Newlands.' He glanced at her. 'Do you have any ice at the vicarage?'

'No, but—'

'We need to reduce the swelling, and thus the pain, as quickly as possible. Newlands has an ice house. Not only that, but it is considerably closer.'

Molly was silenced. She knew she was not think-ing clearly and all she wanted was for the pain in her ankle to be over. She gave a sigh of relief as they reached the door of Newlands and made no demur when her escort lifted her into his arms to carry her indoors. Miss Kilburn was crossing the hall as they entered and as soon as she realised the situation, she sent a footman running to fetch some ice before instructing Mr Russington to follow her upstairs to one of the guest rooms. However, when she directed that Mrs Morgan should be laid upon the daybed by the window, Molly was roused to protest.

'No, no, my clothes are far too dirty.'

She was dismayed to find her voice broke upon the words, but no one remarked upon it. Agnes pulled a cashmere shawl from the back of a chair and spread it over the couch.

'No one will worry about a little dirt, ma'am, but you shall lie on this, if it makes you feel better. Oh, goodness, you are looking very pale.'

'Shock,' said the beau, removing Molly's gloves and beginning to chafe her hands. 'Perhaps we might find a little brandy.'

'Yes, yes, of course.'

Agnes hurried away and Molly thought she should protest at being left alone with a gentleman who was no relation, but she did not have the energy to complain and the way he was rubbing warmth into her hands was so comforting she did not want him to stop, so she lay back against the end of the daybed, watching him from half-closed eyes, thinking idly that it was quite understandable if ladies threw themselves at such a man. He was very attractive, in a dark and rather disturbing sort of way...

Molly knew she must have drifted off to sleep, because the next moment, she felt a glass pressed gently against her lips and heard a deep, soothing voice urging her to drink. She became conscious of being cradled against a man's chest. The smooth softness of a waistcoat was against her cheek and when she breathed in her senses were filled with a heady mix of citrus and spices and something very male. There was something familiar about that scent, but at the moment she could not place it.

Obediently she took a sip from the glass and coughed as the sharp and fiery liquid burned her throat. She struggled to sit up and immediately the strong arm around her shoulders released her. For the first time she saw Agnes Kilburn standing on the other side of the daybed, looking down at her with concern. Molly was relieved at her presence and even more so when she looked back to

Mr Russington, kneeling beside the daybed, and realised he was in his shirtsleeves.

His eyes were full of amusement, but also understanding.

'I beg your pardon for removing my coat, ma'am, but it had picked up rather a lot of mud from your clothes, and I did not want to rub that into you.'

Molly murmured a faint thank you and looked past him as a footman hurried in.

'Ah, the ice at last,' exclaimed Agnes. She removed the bucket of ice and towels from the servant and brought them over. 'Mr Russington, will you see to it, if you please? You have much more experience in these matters than I. That is, if you do not object, ma'am?'

'I think Mrs Morgan might prefer you to remove her stocking,' the beau remarked. He smiled at Molly and held out the glass to her. 'You might like to finish drinking your brandy, for it may hurt a little.'

Molly was relieved that he turned away while Agnes began to untie the garter and roll the stocking down over her damaged ankle. Cautiously she sipped at the brandy. He was right, it did hurt, but she was also mightily embarrassed. She had never liked to be the centre of attention and now she sought for something to distract the gentleman from what was going on behind his back.

'It was fortunate for me that you were walking on the moor, Mr Russington,' she said at last. 'Although I am curious as to why you had left your curricle at that particular spot.'

'I have formed the habit of walking the moors every day before breakfast. There are golden plover up there, did you know? I have been watching them. It was not possible to make my usual walk this morning, so I stopped off on my way back to Newlands. No doubt you thought my only interest in birds was in killing them. For sport.'

She flushed guiltily. 'I did not think that at all, sir.'

'There, it is done,' said Agnes.

Molly was relieved that the soft words brought an end to their interchange. The beau turned his attention back to her ankle and she clasped her hands about her glass, biting her lip as he used towels to pack the ice around her foot.

'It is exceedingly swollen. Are you sure it is not broken?' Agnes asked him.

'I inspected it earlier, when I first came upon Mrs Morgan, and I am sure it is merely sprained,' he replied. 'However, if you would feel happier we will send for the doctor.'

Molly quickly disclaimed. 'I am sure I shall be well again very soon,' she assured them. 'Although I may have to trouble you for the use of your carriage, Miss Kilburn, to take me home. My brother has gone off to Compton Magna and will not be back until very late, if at all tonight.'

'Then it would be best for you to stay here,' said Agnes. 'We will send a carriage to the vicarage to tell them what has happened and to bring your maid— You look distressed, Mrs Morgan, have I said something amiss?'

'No, no, it is merely that I gave my maid the evening off.'

'Then on no account can you go home,' declared Agnes. 'You must stay here, where we can look after you.'

In vain did Molly protest. Shy, quiet little Agnes Kilburn proved immovable.

'There is no time to fetch your clean clothes before dinner, so you shall dine here,' she told Molly. 'And afterwards, if you feel well enough, my maid shall help you change and you can be brought downstairs to rest on a sofa in the drawing room. I know everyone will want to assure themselves that you are recovering well and the evening will pass much more quickly in company, do you not agree?'

Molly did not have the strength to withstand such common sense. With Edwin out for the evening, and Cissy looking after her mother, she knew there was no argument she could put forward that would not sound ungrateful.

'Very well, then. Thank you, Miss Kilburn. You are too kind.'

'Call me Agnes, please,' said her hostess, smiling. 'And, if I may, I shall call you Molly.'

'Then it is settled,' said Mr Russington, picking up his coat. 'We will leave you in peace now, ma'am, and I shall return after dinner to carry you downstairs.'

'I am sure that will not be necessary, sir,' said Molly swiftly. 'I might be able to walk by then, or, if not, one of the servants—'

'Oh, but I insist,' he interrupted her, his eyes teasing her in a way that made Molly want to hit him. 'As your rescuer, I think I have earned that privilege.'

He followed Agnes out of the room and Molly was alone. She felt exhausted, and not a little homesick, despite the undoubted comfort of her surroundings. She glanced at the small table beside her with its glass of water, the vinaigrette bottle in case she should feel faint and the little hand bell that Agnes had urged her to ring, should she require anything at all.

She closed her eyes, allowing her thoughts to drift. Nothing could have exceeded Agnes Kilburn's kindness, but Molly could not help thinking that she was in the lion's den. The people in this house stood for everything she detested: wealth, privilege and a lack of moral restraint that she could not condone. But even as the idea formed she rebuked herself for being unfair. Sir Gerald had not brought a party of single gentlemen and their inamoratas to Newlands. The ladies were all perfectly respectable and if any of the gentlemen had a reputation for loose living, it was up to the mothers of Compton Parva to protect their offspring from these dangerous individuals.

Molly stirred restlessly. It was one of those dangerous individuals, Beau Russington, who had come to her aid that afternoon and she had come to no harm. Now that she was alone with time to reflect, she realised that what disturbed her most was that when the beau had lifted her into his arms—as if she weighed nothing!—she had not felt at all afraid. In fact, she admitted now with great reluctance, she had never felt safer. Not that *that* made the man a jot less dangerous!

'So, Russington, you have been rescuing damsels in distress.' Joseph Aikers helped himself to more brandy before pushing the decanter towards his neighbour.

'I could hardly leave her sitting in the lane,' said Russ, refilling his own glass. 'It was fortunate that my curricle was nearby.'

He kept his tone neutral. The ladies had withdrawn and Gerald had dismissed the servants, so there were only the gentlemen left in the dining room and Russ knew from experience that at this stage of the evening the conversation could easily degenerate, and somehow he did not want Molly Morgan to become the object of any lewd discussion.

Flemington gave a coarse laugh. 'I'd wager the beau would have preferred to find a pretty young gel languishing at his feet. I saw a few that I wouldn't mind trying at the assembly last week.'

Gerald met Russ's eyes as he took the decanter from him.

'Seducing innocents has never been the beau's

way,' he remarked. 'He's like me—too afraid of the parson's mousetrap.'

There was general laughter at that, but it was Lord Claydon who answered.

'I know you young bucks think yourselves awake upon every suit,' he said, shaking his head in mock severity. 'But let me warn you that one day you will find yourselves in the suds and I hope when you finally make a fool of yourself that you have the sense to choose a good woman.'

Gerald chuckled. 'I am not sure a *good* woman would suit the beau.' He grinned at Russ. 'If I thought that, I'd have suggested m'sister as a match for you, my friend, but your roving ways would break her heart and I would have to call you out.'

'Then it is fortunate for everyone concerned that Agnes and I regard each other as siblings,' Russ told him. 'You may be assured, though, that when I do eventually decide upon a wife, my…er…*roving ways*, as you call them, will be at an end.'

A ripple of laughter went around the table and cries of disbelief.

'Is that why you have remained single for so long, Russington?' called Sykes from the far end of the table. 'It can't be for lack of opportunity.

Your lineage is impeccable and your fortune is so vast you have the pick of the *ton*.'

'Aye, you lucky dog,' cried Flemington, the suspicion of a sneer in his voice. 'You can have any woman you want for a bride.'

'But I do not want any woman,' drawled Russ. He lifted his glass and stared at it, as if inspecting the contents. 'If, *if* I marry, it must be based on mutual affection and respect. A marriage of true minds, as Shakespeare calls it. Nothing less will do.'

'Ha, you are searching for a mare's nest,' declared Sykes, reaching for the decanter. 'Believe me, it doesn't exist. You'd be advised to give up such daydreams and find yourself a good-natured woman who will make you a comfortable wife.' He gave a shrug. 'Mrs Sykes wasn't my first choice, nor was I hers, but we have rubbed along very nicely for the past twenty years, which is more than many couples can boast.'

'Sound advice,' agreed Claydon. 'Best to leave love well out of it, my boy. Look what happened to your own father, hardly out of mourning before a beautiful woman got her claws into him. Never seen a man so besotted. Pity it wasn't mutual. She almost ruined him.'

'Quite.' Russ's fingers tightened about his glass as the familiar pain sliced into him, but he said lightly, 'I want a wife who will love me for myself, not my fortune.'

'And if you don't find her?' asked Gerald.

'Why, then, I shall continue to enjoy my bachelor life.' He drained his glass. 'Which reminds of a promise I have made. If you will excuse me, gentlemen, I offered to carry Mrs Morgan down to the drawing room.'

'Oh, ho!' cried Sir Joseph. 'Stealing the march on us with the widow, are you, Russington? I wouldn't have thought she was your type.'

Russ paused at the door to look back, unsmiling.

'She is not at all my type, as you so crudely put it, but she is safer in my arms than anyone else's, because she has made no secret of the fact that she detests me.'

Mindful of propriety, he went to find Agnes and ask her to accompany him when he collected the invalid, but when he entered the drawing room, he found that Molly was already downstairs and resting on a sofa. He had to admit she was looking very much better, dressed in an evening gown of lavender silk trimmed with silver lace and with a fine silk shawl thrown over her feet.

'So, you are here before me, Mrs Morgan.'

He was surprised that he should feel so unaccountably annoyed, as if he had been denied some treat. It was a ridiculous idea and it exacerbated his temper even further, but he forced himself to speak cheerfully. Her bright smile was equally false.

'Yes. I managed to walk downstairs, with help from Miss Kilburn.'

His brows snapped together. 'That was rather reckless of you, ma'am.'

'I did not wish to inconvenience anyone.'

'It will be more of an inconvenience if you have further strained your ankle! If you will permit me to check?'

'No!' Her hands came down quickly on the shawl. 'I assure you there is no need. I am quite well.'

'Fie, Mr Russington,' cried Mrs Sykes, coming up, 'Would you be so indecorous as to expose a lady's ankle in public? Come away, sir. Mrs Morgan assures us she is quite well and needs only to rest, is that not so, my dear?'

'Yes, it is.'

She was looking up at him, her grey eyes defiant, and Russ hesitated. He wanted to argue, but at that moment the rest of the gentlemen spilled noisily into the room.

'I pray you will go away, sir, and not draw any further attention to me.'

Her words were quiet but heartfelt, and he moved away. Gerald and the others descended upon the widow to enquire after her health. Mrs Sykes went to sit near Molly, and Russ was drawn into a discussion about the following day's shoot, but all the time part of his mind was racing.

Had she walked downstairs rather than have him carry her? He could hardly believe it. He had known women to throw themselves at his feet, feigning an injury to gain his attention, but never one so determined to reject his help. Ungrateful creature!

He turned to glare across at the petite figure reclining on the sofa. As if he could have designs upon such a thin drab of a woman. He recalled that moment under the stairs, when he had been tempted to kiss her, but that meant nothing. It was merely the result of too much wine. True, there was something appealing about her elfin face, but her mouth was far too wide for beauty and those unruly curls would not stay beneath her bonnet. They had tickled his chin as he had carried her down the hill this afternoon. Damned annoying that had been, too!

And her eyes, a cool grey with an unsettlingly direct gaze. What man would want that? He preferred cerulean blue, or deep chocolate brown. Eyes that a man might drown in. He tried to name one of the beauties of his acquaintance, as evidence of this assertion, but could think of none. Russ shook his head. What did it matter? He dragged his mind back to the conversation, agreed that if the weather was fine tomorrow, they might enjoy an afternoon's shooting, and kept his back resolutely turned towards the sofa for the rest of the evening.

However, when the tea tray was brought in, he could not refuse Agnes's request that he carry a cup across to Mrs Morgan. She watched him approach, such a wary look upon her countenance that his bad mood evaporated and he could not help the smile tugging at his mouth.

'Am I that alarming, Mrs Morgan?'

She relaxed a little. 'No, of course not, but I feared you might be going to scold me again.'

'I would not dare,' he murmured, handing her the cup. 'You have made your opinion of me perfectly clear, Mrs Morgan.' Everyone else had moved towards the tea table, so there was no one to over-hear him. 'You likened me to a tomcat, if I recall correctly.'

Her chin lifted a little at that. 'I was trying to convince you that I did not desire your attentions.'

'As you did when you feigned an injury rather than dance with me the other evening. Although I rather think you have been paid back for that little deception, do not you?'

She looked away, spots of colour staining her cheeks. 'It was not just you. I did not wish to…to dance with anyone else.'

'Why was that? You seemed to enjoy your first dances.'

'I have already told you. The reputations of the gentlemen staying at Newlands are well known in Compton Parva. I have no wish to encourage such persons.' She met his eyes, but only for an instant. 'I am extremely grateful for your assistance today, sir, but one such act is not enough for me to make a sound judgement of your character.'

'I think your judgement of my character has al-ready been formed,' he retorted, nettled.

Molly's spirits dipped as she watched him walk away, but she rallied them immediately. It should not worry her that the gentleman did not like a little plain speaking. If he ignored her in the future, then that would be a good thing. And if he and his friends thought Compton Parva too dull for them and decided to quit the area, that would be even better!

She finished her tea and put the cup down on the little table Agnes had thoughtfully placed within easy reach. The party was now seated around the room and cheerful conversation flew back and forth. She was grateful for their efforts to include her, but she felt very tired and her ankle was throbbing most painfully. The clock chimed midnight, but no one seemed in the least inclined to bring the evening to an end. Molly was just wondering if she could attract her hostess's attention and ask for help to retire, when the beau rose from his chair.

'I fear we have fatigued Mrs Morgan with our chatter.'

'Goodness, yes,' exclaimed Agnes. 'You are looking very pale, ma'am. How thoughtless of me not to notice sooner. We must get you to your room.'

'Allow me.' Before Molly had realised his intention, he had lifted her into his arms, the silk shawl still wrapped around her skirts. He said, 'Perhaps, Agnes, you would have someone light our way with a candle?'

'Really, there is no need,' Molly protested, but with no conviction at all.

'Do not fret, Mrs Morgan,' said Sir Gerald, opening the door for them, 'You are perfectly safe and you must not deny Russ the chance to show how chivalrous he can be!'

He called to a hovering footman to precede them up the stairs, bade Molly a cheerful goodnight and shut the door on them. Molly swallowed, uncomfortable with the silence.

'I am sorry to give you so much trouble, sir.'

'Think nothing of it, ma'am.'

He paused on the stairs to shift her more comfortably in his arms and she slipped one hand around his neck, her head dropping against his shoulder. Suddenly she felt too tired to fight. When they reached the guest room they found a maid dozing in a chair. She jumped up as they came in.

'Miss Agnes has instructed me to wait on you, ma'am. I'm to fetch you anything you need.'

'First, light the rest of the candles,' the beau ordered. 'I need to see what damage Mrs Morgan has done.'

He put Molly down upon the daybed and pulled the shawl away. For the sake of propriety she had managed to put on silk stockings and a pair of lilac satin slippers, but although she had fastened the left shoe very loosely about her ankle, the bruised flesh was already pushing against the ties.

'Go and fetch more ice,' he commanded the maid. 'Immediately.'

He sank to his knees beside the sofa and began to loosen the ribbons.

'I really thought it would do no harm,' she murmured, watching him. 'I made sure I did not put my full weight upon it.'

'No, you merely hobbled along the corridor and down a full flight of stairs.' She gave a little gasp as his fingers touched her skin and he said quickly, 'Forgive me. Did I hurt you?'

'No more than I deserve,' she said contritely. 'You must think me very foolish.'

'Yes,' he retorted. 'And obstinate. You should never have walked downstairs. Risking your health to avoid me. The utmost folly.'

Gently but quickly he removed both her shoes and dropped them on the floor. Molly held her breath as he pushed her skirts above the knee and began to unfasten the garter. Then his hands stilled.

'I beg your pardon, I—'

'No, no, go on.' Her voice was little more than a

croak and she tried to clear her throat of whatever was blocking it. 'The…the stocking needs to be removed for you to examine my ankle.'

'Yes.' He was staring at her leg, his voice devoid of all emotion. 'Of course.'

Molly sat very still, clutching the sides of the daybed as he dropped the garter on the floor and reached for the stocking top. The throb of her ankle was eclipsed now by her racing pulse. Her heart banged painfully and erratically against her ribs as his fingers brushed her skin. No man had touched any part of her leg since…

She blocked out the thought. She would not succumb to the fear and panic that came with those memories. She would not.

Molly sank her teeth into her lip and forced herself to watch as he began to roll the silk over her knee. Her fear was subsiding, replaced by the thought that no man had touched her with such tenderness. Ever.

Not even the love of her life. The man who had sworn to love her until death.

Her hands slid protectively over her stomach, but her thoughts could not be distracted from the man beside her. She looked at his dark head, studied the handsome profile while his long fingers moved gently down her leg and another emotion began to grow inside her. A warmth, a yearning that tugged at her loins. He had reached her ankle. Molly sucked in a breath, anticipating pain, but he stretched the stocking wide before easing it with infinite care over the swollen joint.

'There.'

His eyes were fixed on her foot as he dropped the stocking on the floor and she noted that his breathing was ragged and uneven.

'Should you not remove the other stocking, too?' She was shocked to hear herself suggest it. 'That you may better compare the ankles,' she ended lamely.

'No, no need for that. It is quite clear where the damage lies.' He pulled the skirts more decorously over her legs and gave an impatient huff. 'Where is that girl with the ice?'

'I doubt there was any in the house at this late hour,' said Molly, desperate to keep talking. 'They will have had to go to the ice house and that could be some distance away, most likely in the park. It is most likely locked, too—'

'Stop it, for heaven's sake!'

'I beg your pardon?'

'You are prattling because you are afraid of me.

You have no reason to be nervous, Mrs Morgan. I assure you. I have no designs upon your virtue.'

'No. Of…of course not.'

'Respectable widows are not my type.'

Molly flinched. 'You make that sound like an insult.'

'It was intended merely as the truth. I thought it might set your mind at rest to know that I do not seduce every woman I meet.'

'It does. Thank you.'

The door burst open and the maid hurried in.

'Here you are, sir, another bucket of ice. An' I beg your pardon for taking so long, sir, but we had to send out to the ice house for it.'

Just for an instant the beau's eyes met Molly's, a glinting smile in their black depths.

'That is what we thought,' he said gravely. 'Come along then, girl, bring it here.'

Ten minutes later Molly's ankle was once more soothed by an ice pack. The beau gave instructions to the maid before turning back to Molly.

'Under no circumstances are you to put your foot to the floor again tonight, madam. Do you understand me? The maid will help you with everything and now you have both seen what I have done, you can pack it with fresh ice in the morning, if the swelling has not reduced. Is that clear?'

'Yes. Thank you, sir.'

'Then I will bid you goodnight.'

'Mr Russington!' Molly held her hand out to him. He took it, his brows raising a little. 'You are wrong, sir,' she said. 'You are wrong to think my evasive actions are aimed solely at you. I have learned to be wary of all gentlemen.'

He stood, looking down at her for a moment, his face unreadable, then with an almost imperceptible nod, he went out.

Russ closed the door of the guest room and walked slowly to his own chamber. He was not sure he believed Molly Morgan wanted to keep all men at bay. She had seemed happy enough during that first dance, but Gerald was the host and it would have been difficult for her to decline. A wry smile twisted his lips. If he doubted her veracity, might she not doubt his, when he claimed he had no designs upon her virtue? And with good reason.

Twice he had carried her in his arms, and he was well aware that beneath the layers of demure clothing, her body was slim but well formed. Yet it was peeling off the stocking that had confounded him. He had started innocently enough, concerned only that she might have done more damage to her ankle, but rolling the silk down her leg and revealing the soft skin beneath had been strangely arousing. For a brief moment his imagination had run with the idea of undressing her for his own pleasure.

The thought had been fleeting, but the widow had noticed it. She had been tense, almost shaking and he cursed himself for frightening her. He had made it even worse by allowing his anger to show.

He frowned. The dashed woman brought out the worst in him. Over the years he had learned to keep his true thoughts and feelings hidden beneath a cool, polished exterior and created Beau Russington, the epitome of the fashionable gentleman. He was a friend of Brummell, a noted Corinthian. The men sought his company while the ladies sought his bed. He had heard himself described as society's darling, charming to a fault and renowned for his good humour.

So what was there about the little widow that unsettled him? Surely he was not so conceited as to be put out because she did not like him?

'Bah, it is of no consequence,' he muttered aloud. 'Tomorrow she will be gone from here and after that, if our paths should cross, we need spare each other no more than a nod in passing.'

His words were swallowed by the gloomy corridor, but the creak of boards as he reached his bedchamber echoed through the darkness like a laugh.

Chapter Four

By the next morning Molly's ankle was showing great signs of improvement. The swelling was
much reduced and, although she took breakfast in
her room, she was later able to go downstairs with
the aid of a stick. This had been thoughtfully provided by Lady Claydon, who assured Molly that
her husband always brought a spare with him.

The gentlemen had gone out, but she found the
ladies gathered in the morning room. They all
bustled around Molly, Agnes's companion, Mrs
Molyneux, insisting she should have the most comfortable seat and the Misses Claydon bringing over
a footstool for her use and asking what they might
do for her entertainment. She had barely made herself comfortable when the butler announced that
her brother had arrived.

Edwin hurried in, looking flustered. In one

breath he thanked Agnes for looking after his sister, enquired what had happened and apologised for not coming earlier. He turned to Molly to explain.

'I stayed in Compton Magna last night and did not receive your message until breakfast.'

'Then you saved yourself a night's unnecessary worry,' Agnes told him, smiling. 'You may see for yourself that Molly is recovering well.'

Edwin moved across to kiss Molly's cheek.

'What can I say? If only I had come with you to Raikes Farm.'

'You must not blame yourself because I was foolish enough to slip,' she told him, grasping his hand. 'A few more days' rest and I shall be as good as ever.'

'I hope you do not intend to rush off,' said Agnes, moving towards the bell pull. 'Gerald and the other gentlemen have ridden to Knaresborough to look at the castle ruins there. They will be gone all day so your company would be most welcome, Mr Frayne, and we are about to sustain ourselves with cake and a little wine.'

Lady Claydon spoke up immediately to agree and her daughters added their voices to the request that he should stay. Edwin looked at Molly.

'Well, sister, what do you say? Are you desperate to go home this minute?'

Molly shook her head and disclaimed. After everyone's kindness, how could she say she wanted to quit Newlands before the gentlemen returned? Especially when it was clear that Edwin would like to stay for a while. Besides, it was still early. The gentlemen would not be returning for hours yet. She sank back in her chair, content to let her brother enjoy himself.

She was very proud of Edwin and thought him ideally suited to his calling. Mr and Mrs Frayne had marked their son out for the church from an early age, but Edwin had inherited none of their father's harsh and intolerant religious fervour. He was honest and thoughtful, unfailingly kind and cheerful and at ease in any society, as she was now witnessing. The conversation was lively and entertaining, the wine and cakes brought in for their delectation could not have been bettered and the hours slipped by, until Molly heard the clock chime and gave a little gasp.

'Oh, heavens, Edwin. The time!'

'Goodness, is it four o'clock already? I had no idea. Perhaps, Miss Kilburn, you would summon my carriage. I should be getting Molly home.'

'Certainly, sir, but…' Agnes hesitated. 'Perhaps I might suggest Mrs Morgan should remain here another night? We should be delighted to have her stay.'

'Oh, no, I could not possibly trouble you any further,' said Molly. 'And it is no distance, we shall be home in no time.'

Agnes looked unconvinced. 'But the upset, Molly. After resting your ankle all day, are you sure you should be jarring and jolting it over these rough roads? I believe another night here would be most beneficial for you.'

Molly was about to insist that they leave when they were interrupted by the entrance of their host, which immediately caused a distraction.

'Gerald! I had not expected to see you for an hour or more yet. Is everyone back already?'

Agnes jumped up from her seat, but her brother waved her back. He was smiling and flushed from the fresh air, although Molly thought he looked a little distracted as he made his reply.

'No, no, they have all gone to Knaresborough, as planned, but my horse cast a shoe before we had gone ten miles, so I turned back.'

'And you are only now come in?' Edwin glanced at the clock. 'I trust you did not get lost.'

'Oh, no, nothing like that. I left my horse at the smithy and took the opportunity to explore a little. And as you can see—' he grinned, glancing down at himself '—I did not come in here until I had washed and changed out of all my dirt.'

He turned to Molly to enquire after her health and then joined his sister in pressing her to remain another night.

'And Frayne can stay for dinner, if he wishes,' he declared, turning his cheerful smile upon Edwin. 'I am not expecting the others to return until the dinner hour, so we have already agreed we shall not stand upon ceremony tonight, which means it will be perfectly acceptable for you to sit down to dinner as you are. And there is a full moon, too, Edwin, so you could safely drive home afterwards. And tomorrow, I will bring Mrs Morgan back to you in the barouche.'

'No, no.' Molly was suddenly alarmed. 'That is too kind of you, Sir Gerald, but we really must go.'

Agnes shook her head. 'I assure you it would be no imposition. After all, the guest room is already set up for you, so an extra night would make very little difference to us, but it could mean your ankle will heal all the sooner.'

'Do you know, I think you may be right, Miss

Kilburn,' said Edwin. 'And, Molly, perhaps you will be more inclined to remain when I tell you that your maid is not yet returned. She sent word that her mother is no better, so I gave her permission to remain with her another night.'

'Oh, poor Cissy. Of course, she must stay,' Molly agreed, her own worries forgotten.

'All the more reason for you to remain here, then,' Sir Gerald declared triumphantly.

Molly knew it would be churlish to argue and, when Edwin looked at her, she nodded her assent.

'Capital,' cried Edwin. 'I can only thank you most sincerely, Miss Kilburn, for your kindness towards my sister.'

Edwin was beaming broadly and Molly saw that Agnes, too, was smiling and there was a telltale flush blossoming upon her cheek.

Oh, good heavens.

Molly sank back in her chair and lapsed into silence. Not since his schooldays had Edwin shown such a strong preference for any young lady, so why now? And why had his interest fixed upon Agnes Kilburn of all people?

She was immediately ashamed of her uncharitable thoughts. She would be very happy for Edwin to fall in love and settle down. She must not let her selfish concerns get in the way if he and Agnes truly liked one another. But to remain at Newlands tonight, to be in the company of Beau Russington for another evening, how would she endure it? His presence unsettled her. She could not forget how easily he had carried her, how secure she had felt in his arms. When he was in the room her eyes wanted to follow him and if he looked at her she felt the heat rising through her body. It was not to be borne. She did not even *like* the man.

Oh, do not be so foolish, she told herself crossly. *He has told you that he has no amorous intentions towards you.*

Which should have put her at her ease, but instead made her feel very slightly aggrieved and a little unsure of her instincts, because last night, when he had removed her stocking, she had been so sure that he, too, had felt something.

Like a conceited schoolroom miss! And do not forget you have been wrong about a man before.

Molly shifted uncomfortably at the thought, which immediately brought attention back to her. Mrs Molyneux asked if her ankle was hurting and the eldest Miss Claydon offered to bring another cushion to place beneath her foot. She was at pains to reassure them, but she could barely bring herself to smile when Edwin came to sit beside her and murmured that he thought she was very wise to remain at Newlands until tomorrow.

It was not long until the gentlemen came back from their sport. They greeted Edwin with unfeigned bonhomie and were delighted that he was joining them for dinner. When Agnes announced that Molly was staying for a second night, they all agreed it was a wise precaution and appeared quite content with the decision. All except Mr Russington. Molly saw a shadow flicker across his countenance. It might have been dissatisfaction, but she thought it looked more like alarm. It was gone in an instant, but it raised her spirits. Perhaps he was not quite so indifferent to her, after all.

And, strangely, the fact that the thought pleased her shocked Molly most of all.

Dinner was an informal affair. Agnes offered to have a tray sent into the drawing room for Molly, but she insisted that she was well enough to join them, if Edwin would give her his arm. She was given a seat between Mr Sykes and Lord Claydon and nothing could have exceeded their kindness. The conversation ebbed and flowed, it was lively, but there was no hint of impropriety, and later, in the drawing room, there was nothing in the least alarming about the way the party entertained themselves.

Mr Russington and Lord Claydon spent the evening playing piquet while Molly was invited to make a fourth at whist with Mr and Mrs Sykes and Lady Claydon. The others gathered around the piano and took turns at singing duets. Sir Joseph and Mr Flemington flirted with the Misses Claydon. Mr Flemington's high-pitched giggle was annoying, but since neither his nor Sir Joseph's attentions were aimed at her, Molly could relax and enjoy herself.

She felt a slight pang of regret when Edwin went home, but when the party broke up, it was Agnes who accompanied her to her bedchamber and delivered her into the hands of her maid and Molly went happily to bed, thinking that perhaps, after all, she had been too prejudiced against fashionable society. Perhaps it was not all dissipation. At least, not when there were chaperons present. So, she reasoned, staying at Newlands exposed her to no danger at all.

She allowed her thoughts to wander back to Beau Russington, recalling him at the dinner table. He had been listening to something Edwin was saying, his gaze abstracted and his lean fingers playing with the stem of his wine glass. She remembered those same fingers on her skin, peeling away the silk stocking, and once again she felt the hot ache deep within. She curled into a ball and pulled the bedclothes around her a little tighter.

For her, the danger was not with society, she realised, but with one man.

By the time Agnes took Molly back to the vicarage the following morning in the barouche, they were firm friends. Molly was not surprised when Edwin came out of the house as the carriage drew up. He opened the door himself, following up his words of greeting by inviting Miss Kilburn to step inside and take a little refreshment.

'Yes, please do, Agnes,' Molly added her entreaty, knowing that her new friend's hesitation was from shyness rather than reluctance.

Edwin beamed when Agnes agreed and he handed her out of the carriage before turning to Molly and insisting that he carry her into the drawing room.

'We do not want to undo all of Miss Kilburn's good work,' he said, depositing her on the sofa.

'Now, Miss Kilburn, perhaps you will sit with Molly and make sure she does not move while I go and ask Mrs Rodgers to bring us some tea!'

Molly shook her head as he lounged out of the room.

'Really, there is no need for all this fuss,' she said to Agnes, who smiled.

'Gerald would be just the same, if I were in this situation. You know he was minded to cancel his ride today to escort us here.'

'And we were both adamant that it was not necessary,' said Molly. 'We are fortunate to have such caring brothers.'

'Have you always kept house for Mr Frayne?' Agnes asked her.

'For five years, since he obtained the living here at Compton Parva.'

Agnes's eyes widened. 'You were widowed very young, then.'

'Yes, before I was twenty. And you, Agnes—' Molly was eager to move the conversation away from that subject '—have you always kept house for your brother?'

'Oh, no, I have been living at the family home in Oxfordshire since our father died two years ago.' She saw Molly's sudden frown and added quickly,

'Out of choice. Gerald prefers to live in London, but I do not like the town.'

'I have never been there,' Molly confessed.

'But you were married very young. I wish I had done so.' Agnes gave a sad little smile. 'I was betrothed to a naval officer, a captain, soon after my come-out six years ago. His birth was impeccable and Papa agreed to the engagement, but insisted we wait a little. It was a sensible decision, my fiancé wanted to win a little more prize money with which to set up our own establishment, but it was not to be. He was killed in an action off the French coast.'

'Oh, I am so sorry!'

Agnes fluttered a hand, as if to ward off Molly's sympathy. 'That was four years ago. I am over it now, but I envy you your time with your husband, however short.'

'I pray you will not!' Molly saw that her vehemence had shocked Agnes and she continued more gently, 'What I mean is, we were only married for a few months. It was not a happy time.'

She broke off thankfully when Edwin returned. The conversation became general and remained so until Agnes took her leave an hour later. Edwin accompanied her to the door, and came back beaming.

'What a delightful young lady, is she not, Molly? So kind of her to bring you home herself. Perhaps, once you are better, we should hold a little dinner, invite the Newlands party to come here.'

Molly's response was non-committal. Despite her burgeoning friendship with Agnes, and her conviction now that the gentlemen at Newlands were not as dissolute as she had first imagined, she was still wary of forging closer ties with any of them.

Edwin had been adamant that Molly should rest until her ankle was quite recovered and threatened to summon the doctor if she disagreed with him. She therefore rested dutifully on the sofa until the Saturday, when she came down to breakfast dressed in her green walking dress.

'If I spend another moment indoors, I vow I shall scream,' she told her loving brother when he looked at her in surprise. 'I am going to visit Fleur and Nancy at Prospect House as soon as I have broken my fast. I shall take the gig and Gibson will be with me. He is quite capable of taking the reins should I go off in a dead faint.'

Edwin laughed at that. 'Your constitution is stronger than most, so I do not foresee such an event. No, I am content to have kept you resting for so long. Just remember that we are engaged to dine with the Curricks this evening and do not be late back!'

Fleur and Nancy came running out as the gig pulled up.

'There is no need for that,' Molly said, laughing as Nancy reached up to help her alight. 'I am perfectly well now, I assure you.' She glanced down at the little dog prancing around her feet. 'And this is your new guard dog.' She picked up the furry bundle, laughing as he squirmed in her hold and tried to lick her chin.

'Yes, this is Nelson.' Fleur chuckled. 'I fear he will not offer us much protection, however he is quite noisy when anyone arrives, so that is useful.'

Nancy took Molly's arm. 'But let us not stand out here in the wind. Come indoors, Molly. You must sit down and tell us how it happened.'

'Every detail,' Nancy commanded, as they made themselves comfortable in the drawing room and Daisy came in with the tea tray.

'It is nothing exciting,' Molly told them. 'I was

coming home from Raikes Farm on Monday when I slipped and sprained my ankle. Mr Russington drove me to Newlands and Miss Kilburn insisted I should stay for a few days. I hope you did not think too badly of me for not coming to help you on Tuesday and not a word of explanation.'

'Oh, but we knew about your accident by then,' put in Daisy, setting out the teacups.

'I suppose someone told you at the market.' Molly noticed the guilty looks upon the faces of her friends and she looked from one to the other, frowning. 'Fleur, Nancy?'

'Fleur met one of the gentlemen from Newlands on Tuesday,' Nancy explained. 'She was in the orchard as he came along the lane.'

'His stopped to ask directions,' said Fleur, two pink spots colouring her cheeks. 'He was most gentleman-like.'

'It was most likely Sir Gerald,' said Molly. 'He was back before the others, because his horse had cast a shoe.'

'Yes, we introduced ourselves.'

As the blush deepened so did Molly's frown.

'And there is more?' She saw Fleur's anguished look at Nancy and she said sternly, 'Tell me.'

'He and his friends came to our stall on market

day,' muttered Fleur. 'There was nothing untoward in their manner, Molly, I assure you. They were merely passing through the market, and he—Sir Gerald—recognised me.'

'So it was purely coincidence.' Molly looked sceptical.

'Let us look on the bright side,' offered Nancy. 'He sent a runner back in the afternoon to buy up the remainder of our produce.'

Despite her concerns, Molly laughed. 'He is certainly very brave, to be interfering in his housekeeper's business!'

The mood lightened and no more was said about the meeting until Molly took her leave. As she hugged Fleur, she warned her to be on her guard.

'You must not worry, Molly. I know better than to be taken in by any gentleman's fine words. Everyone thought my stepfather was the most charming man imaginable.'

Molly felt her shudder and held her closer.

'I cannot fault Sir Gerald as a host,' she said carefully. 'He was most amiable and obliging while I was at Newlands and I have no first-hand knowledge that he is anything but a gentleman. But he is reputed to run with a very fast set and some of them are at Newlands.'

'They are rich and single,' said Nancy. 'Such men think they have the right to do anything they wish, but they will not be welcome here. And we have our protectors. Is that not so, Moses?' she called to the giant, who had brought Molly's gig to the door, and he nodded back at her, grinning.

'Aye, Miss Nancy's right there, Mrs Morgan. I'll keep an eye out for them all, don't you fret about that.'

'And don't forget Nelson,' added Nancy, scooping up the little puppy. 'We shall train him to attack any gentleman who comes within a mile of Prospect House!'

That assurance kept Molly smiling as she drove away. Fleur was far too soft-hearted, but Molly knew she could trust Nancy and Moses to look after everyone at Prospect House.

Dinner at Currick Hall was Molly's first social engagement since her accident and her hosts were anxious to assure themselves that she was fully recovered. Having made her way unaided through the great hall and up the oak staircase to the dark-panelled reception rooms, she was able to reassure them on this point, but she soon realised that no small part of their interest was the fact that Beau

Russington had carried her to Newlands. The ladies were all eager to hear more of the rescue and all those who had not yet dined with Sir Gerald were keen to have the house described to them.

Molly did her best to comply, but she was relieved when dinner was announced and everyone prepared to file into the dining room. However, as she rose and shook out her skirts, the squire's daughter, Helen, a bouncy seventeen-year-old, told her in an excited whisper that Papa had a surprise for them.

'He has invited Sir Gerald and his party to join us later! We could not accommodate them all at the table, for it was arranged such a time ago, but Papa thought it would be a great shame not to ask them to come for supper and they have accepted!'

The squire came up, chuckling. 'What's that, Puss, have you been giving away my secrets? I hope you are pleased, Mrs Morgan. Nell here and the Misses Claydon hit it off very well at the recent assembly and she has been plaguing the life out of me to invite them back, so I mentioned the matter to Sir Gerald when I saw him earlier today and he has sent me word that they are all to come.'

'Is that not marvellous news, Mrs Morgan?'

Helen was almost hopping with excitement. 'Papa has said we may have a little impromptu dancing, too.'

'Well, we shall see. We shall see.' His twinkling eyes came to rest upon Molly. 'I have no doubt you'll be glad to see Mr Russington again, will you not, madam? I promise you all the ladies here envy you your good fortune in having such a hand-some rescuer.'

He went off, still chuckling, and when Edwin came up to take Molly in to dinner, she muttered angrily that she had become the talk of the town.

'It will pass.' He gave her fingers a reassuring pat. 'It will be eclipsed by other news soon enough.'

'I would not consider my spraining my ankle to be news in the first place!'

'No, it isn't. But being rescued by an arbiter of fashion is. The squire is right, every lady here is wishing it had happened to her.'

Molly gave a long sigh. 'Could we not make our excuses and leave as soon as dinner is ended?'

'No, of course not.' He laughed. 'Cheer up, Molly, everyone from Newlands will be pleased to see you are going on so well. And I confess I should not object to a little dancing this evening, although there is no need for you to join in, if you would rather not. You can say your ankle is paining you.'

It was on the tip of her tongue to retort that she had already used that excuse once, but then she remembered that Edwin knew nothing about that little episode. So she gritted her teeth and held her peace.

Currick Hall was a rambling old house going back at least two centuries and it lacked the spacious reception rooms to be found in more modern properties. The arrival of another dozen people caused a crush in the drawing room, but their host cheerfully assured everyone that once the servants had finished clearing all the furniture, save the pianoforte, from the great hall, there would be plenty of space for everyone, whether dancing or sitting and watching the proceedings.

The crush in the room made it very warm and Molly moved across to one of the deep window embrasures where she knew from experience the ill-fitting casements allowed in plenty of cold air. She stepped past the curtains to where the shadows were deepest. With her dark hair and deep grey gown, she thought she would attract least attention there. The draught from the windows was refreshing and she was happy to breathe it in, allowing the noise and chatter from the room to pass her by.

She was just thinking she should rejoin the crowd when she heard the rumble of masculine voices approaching. They came to a halt and she recognised the squire's genial tones, and the deeper voice of Mr Thomas, the mill owner, who had moved to the area ten years ago, but had never lost his lilting Welsh accent. They had not noticed her and she would have been happy to step out past them, but Mr Flemington's rather nasal voice made her shrink back even further.

'We enjoyed a fine day's shootin' yesterday. Ain't that so, Aikers? Although Kilburn's land is sadly out of condition.'

'But with good management, that will improve,' replied the squire. 'And even now I am sure it provides some good sport.'

Molly heard Mr Flemington's irritating giggle. 'Talking of sport, we were in town on market day and saw a couple of young women from the Magdalene hospital.'

'You mean Prospect House,' Mr Thomas corrected him. 'And it may well have been the ladies that you saw. They are not above selling their surplus from the farm.'

'Mr Thomas is on the committee,' put in the squire. 'I can assure you, gentlemen, it is a very respectable establishment.'

'Respectable, you say?' Molly could almost hear the leer in Sir Joseph Aikers's voice. 'By Gad, but they are dashed pretty, for all that. Wouldn't mind getting a little better acquainted.'

'Well, you won't do it,' Mr Thomas told him. 'They allow no gentlemen callers.'

'But what about at night?' said Flemington. 'Surely some of the younger fellows would want to try their luck, eh? And mayhap some of the older ones, too!'

'If anyone was to try such a thing, they'd be disgraced,' retorted Mr Thomas bluntly. 'Found out, they would be, you mark my words.'

The squire harrumphed. 'Such behaviour would be very much frowned upon, gentlemen, and in a small town like this, word would be bound to get out.'

'Aye, I suppose it would,' said Sir Joseph. He gave a laugh. 'Still, it might be worth an attempt.'

They moved off but it was some moments before Molly felt calm enough to leave the shadows. She was shaking with rage. All her effort, all her work to build up Prospect House into a respectable enterprise and it was scorned by a couple of rakehells. She should not be surprised. These were London ways—her sister, Louisa, wrote to her constantly about them.

She left the cool security of the window and went in search of Edwin. He was talking with a group of townsfolk, but as soon as she could draw him away, she told him everything she had heard. He tried to reassure her, telling her it was merely the foolish way men boasted to one another.

'You said Mr Thomas and the squire were quick to warn them off. I am sure nothing will come of it.'

'Are you? I am not. Oh, I wish these people had never come here!'

'Now, Molly, you must not think like that. Despite what your sister writes, the ladies are all most amiable, and as for the gentlemen, they have none of them acted with the least impropriety.'

She swung away from him, saying through her clenched teeth, 'Not yet!'

'Molly, Molly.' He gently caught her arms and turned her back to face him. 'I know you were hurt, my dear, but I pray you will not allow yourself to be prejudiced against all men.'

'It is not prejudice,' she told him fiercely. 'Sir Gerald came upon Fleur in the orchard last Tuesday and the very next day he and his—his *friends* were in the market. Do you tell me that was coincidence?'

'No, I say it was curiosity, nothing more. I spoke to Kilburn about his meeting with Fleur Dellafield and he was most complimentary, even respectful. You know my advice, Molly. You should judge a man's character by his actions.'

'Surely a man should also be judged by his words.'

He gave her a little shake. 'Can you honestly say that Kilburn, Sykes or Claydon have said or done anything to make you think them dissolute? And as for Russ, why, if he had not been on hand to bring you down off the moors and apply ice to your ankle so quickly, your injuries might have been a great deal worse.'

Russ. Even her brother called him by that familiar name now!

'Russ had no choice but to carry you to his carriage, Molly, and Agnes tells me it was he who tended your injury.' He paused and frowned at her. 'But tell me truthfully now, did he at any time offer you insult?'

Her eyes fell. 'If anything it was *I* who insulted him,' she confessed. She raised her head, rallying. 'But what of Mr Flemington and Sir Joseph? What of their outrageous comments just now?'

He shook his head at her. 'Remember what Plato says. An empty vessel makes the loudest sound. You may warn your ladies to be vigilant, but I think you will find that it was an idle boast.'

His attention was claimed by Mr Thomas, who wanted to discuss a point of theology with him. Molly waved him away with a smile, knowing he had done all he could to allay her fears. She wanted more time to think things over, so she avoided Agnes and everyone from Newlands and chose instead to sit with some of the matrons and discuss the rather tedious but much safer subject of their ailments.

Thankfully the announcement soon came that they should all make their way to the great hall for a little dancing and entertainment.

The squire came up to Molly. 'My dear Mrs Morgan, you are not to attempt the stairs without a gentleman to support you, especially in this crowd. Allow me.'

'Thank you,' she murmured. 'That is very kind.'

'Ah, but here is Mr Russington and in good time, sir! You will provide a much more agreeable escort for my young friend, I am sure! I pray you will give your arm to this lady.'

'I should be delighted.'

The beau held out his arm, all smooth urbanity, but it was all Molly could do not to whip her own hands behind her back out of the way.

'Of course, you would!' declared the squire cheerfully, unaware of Molly's reticence. 'Why, 'tis another opportunity for you to play Sir Galahad, what?'

The squire laughed heartily at his own joke as he walked away. Cautiously, Molly slipped her hand into the crook of the proffered arm and her escort led her towards the top of the stairs.

'Are you actually *touching* my sleeve?' he asked her. 'You may safely lean on me, you know. Perhaps you did not understand our host's reference to Sir Galahad.'

'Of course, I understood it.' She gave a little tut of indignation. 'Anyone would think you had rescued me from a dragon.'

'No, no,' he murmured. 'That would make me Saint George and I am no saint.'

'I can readily believe that,' she retorted.

'Although tonight, for you, I am on my best behaviour, basking in my new-found fame as a rescuer of helpless damsels.'

Molly gasped. 'Helpless—'

She glared at him. His glance was full of wicked amusement, but his mockery was not aimed at Molly. Rather it invited her to share the joke. Her anger suddenly felt ridiculous and a laugh bubbled up inside her.

'You are quite outrageous,' she told him, trying to sound severe.

'No, no. I am the epitome of chivalry. You heard the squire say so.'

'Nonsense.' She maintained a dignified silence as they began to descend the stairs, but it only lasted as far as the half landing. 'I have always understood Sir Galahad to be extremely pious. Something *you* are not!'

'You do not know that. I have been a soul of propriety since coming to Compton Parva.'

'Why did you come?' she asked him. 'We are a small town, full of bankers and tradespeople. Hardly the society you are accustomed to.'

'Kilburn invited me.' They had reached the hall by this time and he looked up as the scrape of fiddles sounded above all the chatter. 'Ah, so it will not only be the pianoforte accompanying the dancing this evening. Not quite such an impromptu hop, then.'

'We have some talented musicians in Compton Parva,' said Molly. 'I expect the squire requested that they bring their instruments as soon as Sir Gerald had accepted his invitation.'

Russ would have guided her towards the part of the hall that had been cleared for dancing, but Molly held back.

'It is not yet a week since I turned my ankle and I would rather sit out, sir.'

'Then I shall join you.'

'There is no need,' she said quickly.

'But I insist. There are plenty of gentlemen this evening, so I shall not be missed.'

Having heard several ladies gushing over his handsome figure and good looks, Molly did not agree, but she would not pander to his vanity by saying so. She took a seat at one side of the room, not too near to the roaring fire, and tried to look indifferent as he sat down beside her. For a while they were silent, watching the guests mill-ing around, some moving towards the seats at that end of the hall, others taking their places in the sets that were forming nearer the musicians. The squire's wife was looking very pleased to be partnered by Sir Gerald at the head of the first set, while further down the line, Edwin was standing up with Agnes.

'You know,' remarked Russ, following her glance, 'I believe we may be thrown into each other's company a great deal in the coming weeks. It would be as well if we were not always at daggers drawn.'

'Of course not. I can be perfectly polite when it is required of me.'

'Can you?' His quizzical glance made her look away quickly.

'Yes,' she replied, 'if you can assure me that you and your friends are here purely for the sport?' When he did not respond, she mustered her strength to continue as coolly as she could. 'It… it would be a gross outrage if you were to…to try to visit Prospect House.'

'Why the devil should I do that?'

'You might think that they are unprotected and… and I know what many people think of women who are obliged to take refuge there. It was one of your own party who called it a Magdalene hospital.'

'I cannot answer for the others, but I have no interest in chasing such unfortunate women, madam.'

'No, you do not have to pursue women at all, do you, Mr Russington? My sister tells me they fall over themselves for your attention.'

He said softly, 'But not you, Mrs Morgan.'

'Not in the least.'

She kept her head up and managed to hold his gaze. Until he smiled and those little demons danced in his eyes, sending alarm bells clamouring in her head.

'Good. Then to return to my original suggestion, I think we should we call a truce.'

Molly's thoughts were fixed on the sensuous curve of his lips and she was obliged to drag them back, rapidly.

'A…a truce?'

'You have left me in no doubt of your opinion of me, but I think it would be more comfortable for our mutual acquaintances—and your brother—if we could act in a civilised manner when we meet. What do you say?'

'I shall be perfectly civil to you. As long as you do not provoke me.'

'Ah. I thought there would be a caveat.'

'The matter is in your hands, sir,' she told him, feeling more confident of her ground now.

'Then there should be no difficulty.' He eased his long frame from the chair. 'Gerald says we should attend the morning service at All Souls tomorrow morning, ma'am, so no doubt we shall meet there. And we may even manage to be civil to one another.'

He gave Molly the neatest of bows and sauntered away, leaving her to stare after him. *Civil?* Was it civil to set her nerve ends quivering with indignation at his insupportable arrogance, his conceit?

But it is not merely his cool air of superiority that upsets you, is it? It is the fact that you find him undeniably attractive!

'He is a rake, a libertine. He has had mistresses by the score. He is everything you hold in abhorrence,' she rebuked herself sternly, using her fan not only to cool her cheeks but to hide the fact that she was talking to herself. 'He is also part of a group that threatens my friends at Prospect House. If nothing else should make you hate the man, Molly Morgan, it is that!'

Chapter Five

The idea that someone might attempt to gain access to Prospect House during the night remained with Molly, but by the time she reached home that night, it was far too late to send a note. She would speak to Fleur and Nancy at church the next morning.

The day dawned bright and sunny, so she remained near the lychgate, greeting her neighbours while she watched the road, waiting to see the ladies and girls from Prospect House walking to morning service.

The carriages from Newlands were amongst the first to arrive: Sir Gerald and Beau Russington in the chaise with Miss Kilburn, Lord Claydon and his family in a smart barouche and Mr Sykes driving up in his curricle with his wife sitting beside him. Molly's first thought was relief that Sir Joseph and Mr Flemington were absent, because after the conversation she had heard last night she did not think she could be polite to them. It was difficult enough to pin a smile in place to greet the beau. She managed it, but wished he would move on, instead of standing aside while she greeted the other members of the party, and as they strolled away he stepped closer.

'There,' he murmured, 'that was not so very bad, was it?'

His low voice and the smile in his eyes sent a delicious shiver through Molly and made her toes curl, but not for the world would she let him see how much he affected her.

She replied frostily, '*I* have no difficultly in being civil.'

His brows went up. 'What a corker. Admit it, your first thought, when you saw me approaching, was to scurry away and hide.'

It was so near the truth that Molly blushed, but she laughed, too, and shook her head at him.

'That may be the case, but it is very *un*civil of you to say so.'

'Odd, is it not, that we should be able to be so frank with each other? As if we were old friends.'

She looked up at him then. 'My dear sir, how on earth could you and I ever be friends?'

He smiled at her, a strange, arrested look on his face.

'The rake and the reformer? There have been more unlikely alliances, you know.'

He was smiling down at her and Molly's breath caught in her throat. The world tilted, as if every belief she held was suddenly in doubt.

'There can be no question of it in this case,' she managed at last.

She saw Nancy entering the churchyard and with no little relief she gave the beau a dismissive nod and turned to greet her.

'Thank heavens,' she said, holding out her hands. 'I have been waiting for you to arrive.'

'We would have been earlier, but for a little scare that Marjorie's baby was coming,' said Nancy. 'The signs passed off, but Daisy has stayed with her and Moses, too, ready to fetch the midwife if necessary.' She smiled and put her hand on Billy's shoulder. 'So we have this young man for our escort today.'

Molly smiled at Billy and took the time to exchange a word with the little maids, but it was only when, from the corner of her eye, she saw

Russ saunter away that she could at last bring her chaotic thoughts into some sort of order. She linked arms with Nancy as they walked towards the church door and quickly explained what she had overheard last night.

'Edwin says it is nothing more than bluster, but you must take care,' she ended, just as they reached the door.

'We have been taking care ever since they came to Newlands, my dear. Moses checks the locks and the shutters around the house every night.' Nancy signalled to the others to go inside. 'But I fear we may have a more pressing problem than night-time prowlers.'

Molly followed her glance and saw that Fleur was coming slowly up the path with Sir Gerald beside her. They were talking earnestly, Sir Gerald in no wise disheartened by Fleur's veil. Neither did he show any signs of self-consciousness when he saw Nancy and Molly waiting at the door. His greeting could not have been more cordial.

'Good morning to you, Sir Gerald,' Molly responded with equal cheerfulness, but shamefully less sincerity. 'The rest of your party are already inside.'

'Yes? Oh—yes. That is, they have gone on ahead

of me.' Another smile, a touch of his hat and he went in, leaving Fleur with her friends. Her veil might hide her blushes, but it could not disguise the defensive note in her voice as she explained they had met by chance at the gate.

'He was waiting for you.'

'Oh, no, Nancy, surely not—'

'How else could it be, when the Newlands carriages have been here for a good half hour? 'Tis a pity Moses did not come with us today—he would have put a stop to it.'

'Perhaps Sir Gerald had something to discuss with his coachman,' said Molly, taking pity on Fleur. She linked arms with them both, saying cheerfully, 'Come along, we had best take our places inside. Edwin will be wanting to begin!'

It was a bright morning and after the service the congregation gathered outside the church, exchanging greetings and catching up on gossip. Molly saw Sir Gerald edging away from his friends, but Nancy was already taking Fleur's arm and hurrying her and the rest of the girls down the path very much like a mother hen protecting her brood from a fox. She wished she could go, too, instead of having to wait for her brother, who was standing a little apart, deep in conversation with two of his churchwardens. Thus she could not escape Miss Kilburn's invitation for her and Edwin to join a little dinner party they were arranging the following week.

Molly demurred, saying that she must confer with Edwin, although she was well aware that the only reason he would decline would be if there was a previous engagement that could not be re-arranged. The Newlands party moved off towards the waiting carriages, the gentlemen tipping their hats to Molly as they passed. She acknowledged Russ's polite nod with a faint, distant smile and turned away immediately to greet Sir William, who was coming up with his wife on his arm.

'A good turnout, ma'am,' he observed. 'I am relieved. I did not want your brother blaming our little gathering last night for depleting his congregation.' He glanced towards the line of carriages. 'However, I note only two single gentlemen from Newlands came along today.'

Molly pursed her lips. 'No doubt the others consider the restoration of their bodies more important than their souls.'

'La, Mrs Morgan, that is too naughty of you!' Lady Currick laughed and tapped her arm. 'But it is to be expected from these young bucks, with their London habits. They carouse the night away and then sleep until noon! We must hope your brother can reform them.'

'We must indeed,' said Molly, forcing a smile. 'But one cannot expect a leopard to change its spots, you know.'

'Whoa, Flash.'

Russ brought the big grey hunter to a stand on the edge of a high ridge. He had no idea how long he had been riding, but a glance at the sun told him it was close to noon, so he must have been out for several hours. He had gone out early to try to shake off the unaccustomed restlessness that had come over him the past few days.

Perhaps he should go back to town. There were more entertainments there than at Newlands, but he knew that was not the answer. He had been growing bored with London life even before Gerald had invited him to come north. A shaft of self-mockery pierced him. He was regarded as a Corinthian, a top-of-the-trees sportsman and second only to Brummell as an arbiter of fashion. He had been indulged since birth, had more money than he could spend, the pick of society's beautiful women and yet, at eight-and-twenty, he felt that life had nothing new to offer.

He knew he should feel grateful. Most second sons had to find an occupation, usually the army or the church, but he had been blessed with a rich godmother, who had left him her entire fortune. He was equally blessed in the fact that along with the investments and estates, he had inherited reliable staff and an astute man of business, who between them looked after his interests, leaving him nothing to do but enjoy himself. But lately he had found all his usual amusements had begun to pall. He had no desire for self-destruction. Gambling to excess held little attraction, nor did he wish to drink himself into oblivion.

He gazed out over the countryside spread out before him. He had ridden down into the valley where Compton Parva nestled and up on to the moors on the far side, so now he could look back towards Newlands with its extensive grounds and woodlands, but even the prospect of more hunting did not excite him.

'Admit it,' he said aloud. 'You are bored. Bored with life.'

He allowed his eyes to travel down from Newlands to the valley below. The houses of Compton

Parva straggled along each side of the winding valley road, burgeoning around the town square and the vicarage. He could see tiny figures moving in the square and traffic on the road. Everyone was going about their business, seemingly happy and content. So why could he not be happy?

Perhaps he should marry. His brother, Henry, had made a prudent match just after their mother had died, and now lived in quiet contentment on his country estates with his large family. Perhaps a wife would help to fill the aching void that Russ had become aware of. But he had never met any woman who could hold his interest for more than a few months. And most of—if not all—the women who came into his sphere were more interested in his fortune than in him. His father had made the mistake of falling in love with such a woman and he was not about to do the same.

He had learned much from those early days, when his father had brought home his beautiful new wife, who doted on him only as long as he lavished a fortune upon her. That was why, apart from one or two close friends such as Gerald Kilburn, Russ kept everyone else at a distance. Always polite, always charming, he was equally at home riding to hounds or in the salons of society hostesses. He was accepted everywhere, acclaimed as an excellent fellow and a perfect guest, but he never forgot that he owed his popularity to his wealth. He was happy to oblige any pretty woman who threw herself in his way in a fast and furious flirtation, but when his interest cooled he would leave them without a second thought.

'So why is such a life suddenly not enough?' he muttered.

At the sound of his master's voice the big hunter pricked up his ears and sidled restlessly. Russ leaned forward to run a hand over the grey's powerful neck.

'I must be growing maudlin, Flash, and damned ungrateful, to have so much and yet want something more.' He gathered up the reins and touched his heels to the hunter's flanks. 'Come up, boy. Let's gallop off these fidgets, from both of us!'

Lady Currick might laugh at the idea of carousing rakes, but it did nothing to allay Molly's fears and early the following morning she drove to Prospect House. She found Moses and Billy at work on the flower beds outside the drawing-room window.

'Trampled, they was, ma'am,' Moses told her. 'In the night.'

Molly grew cold. 'Intruders!'

'Nay, ma'am, no one got in. I didn't hear any-thing, my room bein' at the back o' the house, but *someone* was prowling around last night.'

Molly hurried inside, her imagination running wild with horrid scenes, but she found Fleur in her office, calmly writing up her ledgers. When Molly expressed her concerns she giggled, but refused to say anything more until she had summoned Nancy to join them in the drawing room.

'I must not stay too long,' said Nancy. 'I have left Bridget making a potato pudding, but she will be at a loss to know how to dress the hog's head when it is boiled. But where is your groom, Molly? Surely you did not come alone.'

'The carriage horses needed shoeing and Gibson has taken them to the smith. And before you ask why I did not bring my maid, Cissy's mother is still ailing and I have sent her home again for a few days to look after her.' She waved an impatient hand. 'Tell me quickly now, what happened here last night.'

'Let us say we had visitors.' Nancy went on quickly, 'But the shutters were up and the doors bolted, so there was never any risk of them getting into the house.'

'Oh, heavens!'

'They were not housebreakers, Molly,' Fleur assured her. 'We could make out their white neckcloths and waistcoats quite clearly in the moonlight.'

'You *saw* them?'

'Oh, yes.' Nancy nodded. 'The first I knew of it was when Bridget came to tell me that she could hear someone on the drive.'

'And did the puppy not bark?' asked Molly.

Nancy shook her head. 'He is not yet fully house-trained, so Moses keeps him shut in the cellar at night. Shortly after Bridget had woken me, I heard gravel being thrown against the bedroom windows. Mine and Fleur's. I was thankful they did not make their way to the back of the house and disturb Marjorie, she is so close to her time now she is finding it difficult enough to sleep as it is! It was two of the men—I will not credit them with the label of gentlemen—from Newlands. We had seen them in the market, but we did not learn their names.'

Fleur said quickly, 'Nancy and I both saw them, Molly. It was definitely *not* Sir Gerald.'

Nancy nodded. 'It was the very tall, thin one.'

'Sir Joseph Aikers,' said Molly. 'And…and can you describe the other one?'

'He was much shorter,' said Fleur, 'but he had a horrid laugh.'

'Like a girl giggling?' Molly was aware of an inordinate amount of relief when Fleur nodded. 'That will be Mr Flemington.'

So Russ was not involved. Molly told herself it meant nothing, he might well be aware of this night-time escapade. For all she knew he might have suggested it to his companions.

'I saw their open carriage on the lane,' Nancy went on, her lip curling. 'Heaven knows how they managed to get to us without overturning it, for they were so drunk they could barely stand.'

'Why did you not fetch Moses to see them off?' asked Molly.

'That was not necessary, we saw to it ourselves.'

'Nancy! You did not go down to them!'

'No, no, nothing like that. It is best you do not know, Molly, for it was not at all ladylike.'

Nancy's eyes were positively sparkling with mischief now and a gurgle of laughter escaped from Fleur.

'We put up the window and told them to be off, but they were too drunk to do anything but fall about, crushing all the flowers, which made Nancy very angry, because we had worked so hard to plant them all in the spring.'

'So how did you get them to go away?' asked Molly, intrigued.

'Nancy suggested they should serenade her, under her window, so we persuaded them to move across to the little bay at the end of the house.'

'But that is the landing window,' said Molly, confused.

'I wanted them away from the flower beds,' muttered Nancy. 'Besides, that window juts out over the drive.'

'Is that important?'

'Oh, yes.'

'Oh, for heaven's sake,' said Molly, thoroughly exasperated. 'Tell me!'

'We waited until they were both singing their hearts out, then we emptied the contents of our chamber pots out of the window.'

Nancy and Fleur collapsed into giggles and, after struggling against it, Molly joined them, relieved of her worries, at least for a while. When Nancy had returned to the kitchens Molly went upstairs to visit Marjorie, who was embroidering a little gown for her baby, whenever it should appear. Then she went off with Fleur to speak with Moses about the harvest and talk to the other girls, who were collecting apples from the orchards.

However, when Molly set off from the house it was not Marjorie's imminent confinement, nor the excellent progress that occupied her mind, but last night's occurrence. Nancy might laugh at what had happened and say they were very well able to look after themselves with Billy and Moses to help, but Molly wondered if perhaps another manservant should be hired. Billy was only ten years old and, although he was very useful around the farm, he was far too young to be thought of as a protector.

Indignation welled up inside her as she slowed the gig to negotiate a tight corner. No protector had been needed before Sir Gerald and his friends came to Newlands! As if conjured by her thoughts, she rounded the bend to see Beau Russington sitting at the side of the road, his horse quietly cropping the grass close by. She pulled up the gig beside him.

'Are you hurt, sir?'

He rose gingerly. 'I think not. I was enjoying a gallop along this stretch of open grassland when the girth broke.' He began to brush off his coat. 'If I had been paying attention, I would not have been thrown.'

Molly had been so intent upon the man that she

had not noticed his horse was missing its saddle. A glance showed it lying on the ground a little distance away. She gave Russ another look. He appeared decidedly pale.

'I will take you back to Newlands,' she told him. 'Can you manage to tie your horse to the back of the gig? And I am sure we can find somewhere to put the saddle.'

Five minutes later they had set off, Molly keeping a steady but slow pace.

'I do not want to put your horse under stress,' she explained. 'Nor do I wish to subject you to more jolting than necessary.'

'Your concern is very comforting, Mrs Morgan.'

'I would do the same for anyone, Mr Russington.'

'There is no need to show hackle, madam, I was being quite sincere.'

'Were you?'

Russ observed her sceptical look and his lips twitched.

'I thought we had agreed to be civil to one another,' he remarked. 'That resolution did not last long.'

'As I told you, it was conditional upon you deserving civility.'

'Oh? And what is it I am meant to have done?' He twisted around so that he could look at her, resting his arm along the back of the seat. Several unruly dark curls were peeping beneath her bonnet and he was tempted to tug at one of them, but the frowning look upon her face gave him pause.

'Come, madam, to my knowledge I have done nothing to warrant your disapproval.'

'Not you, perhaps, but your friends.'

'Oh? Would you care to explain?'

'They…called, last night. At Prospect House. They were intoxicated.'

He frowned. He and Gerald had stayed up talking until gone midnight.

'Are you sure it was anyone from Newlands?'

'Oh, yes.' She threw him a swift, angry glance. 'The ladies—and they *are* ladies, despite what you might think!—recognised them. They remembered seeing them with Sir Gerald at the market. Once they had described them to me I knew it was Sir Joseph and Mr Flemington.'

'Damned fools!' He straightened in his seat. 'How much harm did they do?'

'Apart from the inconvenience, and unsettling everyone, very little. They trampled a flower bed.'

Watching her, Russ saw a sudden lightening of her countenance.

'What was so amusing, Mrs Morgan?'

He was surprised when she gave him a look brimful of mischief.

'Nancy and Fleur paid them well for their impudence.'

'Go on.'

'They emptied their chamber pots over them.'

Russ was silent for one stupefied moment, then he put back his head and roared with laughter.

'Well, that explains something,' he said, when at last he could command his voice. 'When I came downstairs this morning the valet was just coming out of Flemington's room with his master's clothes bundled in his arms and there was a distinct smell of the privy surrounding him.'

She shook her head. 'I beg your pardon. It is most improper that I should have told you.'

'It is most improper that they should be skulking around Prospect House at night!'

'Yes.' Her brow furrowed again and he felt a twinge of regret that she was no longer full of merriment. 'It was most reprehensible. And it could be very damaging. You see, Prospect House can only continue here if it keeps its reputation as a respectable establishment. Which is why this escapade of your so-called friends does not help at all.'

He wanted to tell her that they were no friends of his, nor were they long-standing friends of Kilburn, if truth were told. Aikers and Flemington had been on the town for years, but had only recently become friendly with Gerald. Russ had never liked them, but he gave a mental shrug. He was only a guest at Newlands, after all. He could do little about it. He glanced at her, suddenly curious.

'Why are you so passionate about Prospect House?'

'It is impossible not to be touched by the plight of the women there. Not that I expect you to understand that.'

'No?' He turned to look at her again, once more resting his hand along the back. 'I might understand better, if you were to explain it. Believe me, I have no ulterior motive, madam, only curiosity. You say some of them are ladies?'

'Fleur and Nancy's birth is equal to yours or mine, Mr Russington, but circumstances made it necessary for them to quit their homes.'

'Tell me about the others,' he invited, enjoying

the animation that lit her countenance when she spoke of these women.

'Well, there is Betty, a gentleman's daughter who was cast out of her home after being persuaded to elope with a plausible gentleman. He took her only as far as the next town, where he abandoned her, and when she tried to return to her family, they disowned her.'

'That is very sad, I agree, but what hope can you give her for the future?'

'She is well educated and I am not unhopeful of finding her a place. In a girls' school, perhaps. For now, she helps out in the charity school my brother has set up. And Bridget, who helps Nancy in the kitchens. She is the widow of a sailor. She was left destitute and found her way to us. Daisy and her son, Billy, were turned out when her employer discovered she was not married. Then there's Marjorie. She was earning her living as a seamstress until an encounter with a so-called gentleman. He promised her the earth and she believed him, until she discovered he had a wife and he left her penniless, alone and with child. Now she makes clothes for the house and for us to sell in the market. She also teaches the others how to sew.' She was at ease now and eager to tell him more. 'One of Marjorie's protégées now works for Miss Hebden, in the town. And a couple more are looking promising—two housemaids who were both thrown on to the streets after being seduced and have horrific tales to tell. One lost her baby and without a character she has been unable to find more work. The other, Ruth, left her newborn son at the foundling hospital—'

'In London!'

'Yes. She was affianced to a sailor, the father of her child, but after he had gone back to sea she discovered he had tricked her and had no intention of returning. Then she met another man, who promised her if she went with him they would go back for the baby. Instead he brought her here, to the north, and abandoned her in Compton Magna. Her intelligence is not high, but her needlework is exquisite. Marjorie has put a plan to me that I hope the committee might approve—once her baby is born we might set her up in a little shop in one of the bigger towns, such as Harrogate, which is becoming quite fashionable. Then the other two girls could live and work with her. We might even be able to have Ruth's baby returned to her.'

'Quite an ambition.'

'But not impossible. The girls are all hard-working and determined to improve themselves. They merely need a little help.'

She fell quiet and he prompted her with another question.

'Where do these women come from? How do you find them?'

'Some of them find us, but usually Edwin comes upon them through his work. Some, like Ruth, are displaced and the parish will not help them.' She sighed. 'It is much worse in the cities, of course, but even in a small town like Compton Parva there are many who need our help. Cissy, my own maid, for example, was seduced by a travelling man and abandoned. If Edwin had not agreed to employ her she would have had to leave the town.' Molly paused as she slowed the gig. 'Heavens, we are already at the gates of Newlands. I beg your pardon to have rattled on so. You must be thoroughly bored with my chattering about people you do not know.'

'Not at all.' Russ was surprised to find it was the truth. He added quietly, 'I understand now why you are so prejudiced against our sex, Mrs Morgan.'

'I do not think I am prejudiced,' she responded. 'There are very many good people in the world.

The townsfolk of Compton Parva, for example, are in the main very generous. I admit that I am cautious, although I hope I am fair-minded. I believe one should judge a man on his deeds.'

'But you judged the party at Newlands before you had even met us,' he challenged her. 'You know very little about Kilburn. Or about me.'

Molly kept her eyes fixed on the winding drive and did not speak until she had brought the gig to a halt at the steps of the house.

'I know you are a dangerous man, Mr Russington.'

'Dangerous?' He sounded genuinely surprised. 'What makes you say that?'

She turned towards him, determined to be honest. 'You are…a danger to women.'

Those sensuous lips curved upwards and she felt the devastating force of his smile.

'I could take that as a compliment.'

She had to fight the urge to smile back. 'I did not mean it so.'

He shook his head. 'I have never forced my attentions upon a woman.'

No, he would not have to, she thought, taking in the dark brown eyes, the curling black hair and the lean handsome face. He had the lithe grace of a cat, the body of an athlete. He only had to walk into a room for all eyes to turn towards him. She had seen it for herself, the way the ladies looked at him and not only the young, unmarried ones.

'Can you also be sure you have never broken a woman's heart?'

'I have never set out to do so. In most cases, the ladies fall in love with my fortune.'

The smile was still there, but it no longer charmed Molly. Now it was full of self-mockery.

She said quietly, 'Then I am very sorry for you.'

She knew she had surprised him. His eyes became dark and unreadable and she braced herself for some withering remark. It never came. Instead he looked over her shoulder and she heard the scrunch of footsteps on the gravel.

'I beg your pardon for keeping you waiting, ma'am, Mr Russington.'

Sir Gerald's butler was hurrying towards them, but he was overtaken by the master of the house demanding to know what had happened. The moment was lost and Molly could not be sorry—the mood between her and Russ had grown too serious.

'I took a tumble when the girth broke, Kilburn.

No harm done and Mrs Morgan kindly brought me home.'

Russ gave her a rueful smile and climbed down from the gig while Sir Gerald barked orders for the horse and the damaged saddle to be taken to the stables. Until this was done Molly could not drive off, but she refused Sir Gerald's invitation to step inside, explaining that she needed to get back to the vicarage.

'But surely you can spare five minutes,' Sir Gerald pressed her. 'You must give Russ the chance to thank you properly.'

She glanced at the beau, standing beside his friend and a laugh bubbled up. She said sweetly, 'Mr Russington will need to change out of his muddy clothes, Sir Gerald, and I really cannot wait while his valet restores him. I am sure it will take an hour, at least.'

Sir Gerald gave a shout of laughter, and Russ's lips formed the word *witch*, although his eyes were gleaming.

'Very true,' he said gravely. He reached out for her hand. 'We have one rescue apiece now, Mrs Morgan. Shall we cry quits?' He added softly, 'Shall we cry friends?'

Her fingers were wrapped in a strong, warm

grasp, his eyes were smiling at her. She felt no alarm, no fear, only comfort. She smiled.

'Very well, Mr Russington.'

'If we are truly friends you should call me Russ, but perhaps that would raise a few eyebrows.'

'It certainly would! Out of the question, sir.'

'Quite.' He released her hand, but their eyes remained locked for a moment longer, then he stepped away. 'Off you go, then, Mrs Morgan. I hope you reach home without further mishap.'

She set the gig rolling, urging the horse on until they were trotting away along the drive. She did not look back, but her heart felt lighter than it had done for weeks.

She had just made friends with a rake.

Chapter Six

'Of course, one cannot *really* be friends with a rake.'

Molly uttered the words to the darkness. She had pushed the thought to the back of her mind during the day while she attended to her usual household tasks but now, lying alone in her bed, her mind had returned to her conversation with Russ earlier that day. It was not the same sort of friendship she shared with Fleur and Nancy, and even Agnes, although they had not known each other for very long. But now that she and Russ had cleared the air she believed they could be comfortable together. He would no longer try to flirt with her and cause her heart to beat so erratically. Nor would he fix his eyes upon her and smile in a way that made her stomach swoop with pleasurable anticipation and set her body aching with desire.

She stirred restlessly. She had not felt that for years. Since she had been seventeen, in fact, when she had fallen in love with the handsome Irish soldier who promised to love her to eternity and beyond. Sadly, eternity had lasted only a few months. Since that idyllic summer seven years ago Molly had never experienced that same rush of pleasure, until Beau Russington had arrived with his engaging smile, his flashing eyes and dark looks.

Turning on her side, she snuggled her hand against her cheek and smiled sleepily. It was not Russ's physical presence that attracted her, it was his quick mind, the way they could talk together, laugh together. As long as he behaved himself, she could relax and enjoy his company.

And on this pleasing thought, she finally fell asleep.

Wednesday morning brought a brief note from Prospect House written in Fleur's elegant, flowing hand. Molly put down her breakfast cup with a little cry of surprise that had Edwin looking up from his newspaper.

'Fleur tells me she has engaged another man-servant.'

'She is perfectly entitled to do so,' remarked

Edwin, 'as long as the costs can be covered by the farm's income.'

'Easily, so there is no need to apply to the committee. I am very pleased, for I was going to suggest it, but it seems she has taken the initiative.'

'Who is the man? Does she say?'

Molly studied the note again. 'No, but she says she discussed the matter thoroughly with Nancy and, since he comes with excellent references, she has taken him on immediately. He is to sleep in the gatehouse.' She smiled across the table. 'It seems an ideal solution. He was most likely recommended to Fleur by Lady Currick or one of the other local families, but I shall find out all the details when I see Fleur this morning.'

'Oh, are you going to the market? I shall walk with you then, as far as the town square, for I have calls to make.'

Molly folded her napkin and set it down on the table. 'Very well, Edwin. I shall go and put on my pelisse and meet you in the hall when you have finished your breakfast.'

It was a crisp autumn morning and the town square was very busy. Molly parted from Edwin and made her way to where Fleur was busy selling a pot of honey to a customer. She was dressed in a sober gown and modest bonnet that covered most of her golden curls, but Molly thought she still looked exceedingly pretty. A shadow of anxiety dimmed her spirits for a moment until she saw that Daisy and Billy were also in attendance.

Fleur waved to Molly and left Daisy serving more customers while she moved to one side.

'You look busy,' Molly remarked, coming up. Fleur nodded.

'Business has been brisk. We have sold the last of the honey and most of the spare apples have gone, as well.'

'That is capital news!'

'Aye, ma'am,' said Daisy, taking advantage of the lull in customers to rearrange what was left of their produce. 'If this carries on, we shall be able to pack up and go home early today.'

Molly nodded. 'Tell me about your new manservant, Fleur. Is he a local man? Do I know him?'

'It is Jem Bailey, the brother of Mr Thomas's mill manager.'

'I thought he was working at Newlands.' Molly caught a look passing between Fleur and Daisy. 'Has he been turned off? Or…heavens, Fleur, have you offered him higher wages to entice him away?'

'No, no, he is to get the same wage he is on now.'

The blush on Fleur's cheek deepened and Daisy said brusquely, 'You had best tell her, Miss Fleur.'

'Tell me what?'

'Sir Gerald brought him to us yesterday.'

Fleur stopped and, following her glance, Molly saw Sir Gerald striding towards them. It was clear his gaze was fixed upon Fleur, but as he drew closer he saw Molly. He missed a step, then came over to her.

'Mrs Morgan.' He touched his hat.

Molly acknowledged him warily. 'I understand Prospect House is in your debt, sir.'

He glanced at Fleur. 'Mrs Dellafield has told you? Perhaps I should have spoken to you or some other member of the committee first, but I wanted to get matters settled as soon as possible. Jem is a good worker and very reliable. You may be sure I made thorough enquiries into his character before recommending him. Mrs Dellafield was reluctant to take him at first, but after the other night—' He shook his head, looking unusually solemn. 'I cannot tell you how sorry I am for what happened, Mrs Morgan. I was most put out to think that any guests of mine could behave so outrageously. I acted as soon as I learned of it from Russ—'

'Mr Russington told you what had happened?'

'Yes. On Monday, after you had dropped him off. I could see it was more than the fall from his horse that was troubling him and when I pressed him he told me about Aikers and Flemington's disgraceful behaviour.' A faint twinkle returned to his eyes. 'He also told me how the ladies dealt with the disturbance. It was well deserved, if you ask me. But you need not fear a recurrence of the incident, I sent them packing that very day and rode over to Prospect House to tell Mrs Dellafield. Not that I made any attempt to enter the house,' he added quickly. 'I am well aware that you have very strict rules about that.'

'He gave me tuppence to hold his horse while he went to find Miss Fleur in the orchard,' piped up Billy, ducking as his mother aimed a swipe at him and told him to hold his peace.

'Sir Gerald made a very handsome apology,' Fleur put in hastily.

Molly frowned at him. 'Are we to believe you had no suspicion of what your friends meant to do?'

'They are no longer friends of mine, Mrs Morgan. I explained to Fl—Mrs Dellafield that I have not known them that long, although I had seen them about in London. It is true that we kicked up a spree or two together in town, but only harmless fun. Nothing like the outrage they perpetrated the other night. And feeling somewhat responsible, I thought it my duty to do something about it.'

Molly was not wholly convinced, but, judging by the way Fleur was smiling warmly at Sir Gerald and telling him how obliged they were to him, it was clear that she was satisfied. The conversation went on, Sir Gerald declaring that he would not have had it happen for the world, Fleur responding with shy gratitude, until at last Molly interrupted them, bringing to Fleur's attention that the stall was now bare of produce and they could go home.

Molly quite pointedly dismissed Sir Gerald, then waited only to ascertain that they did not require her help to pack up their baskets before making her way back to the vicarage. Whatever she thought of Sir Gerald, there was no doubting his generosity in sending a reliable man to Prospect House. She was also grateful to Russ for informing Sir Gerald of his guests' nocturnal activities. She had not expected that. If he disapproved so much of their behaviour, perhaps he was not quite as rakish as his reputation painted him.

'I am sure his reputation is well deserved,' she

argued with herself, 'but he knows the value of not upsetting one's neighbours in a small town like Compton Parva.'

For the rest of the day she found herself wavering between wanting to see Russ and thank him for his intervention, and the thought that if Sir Gerald had set his sights on Fleur, he might want to rid himself of potential rivals. She discussed it with Edwin after dinner, but although he told her Sir Gerald was a splendid fellow and had acted just as he should, Molly knew that Edwin's views were coloured by his growing affection for Agnes Kilburn.

'I see you are still troubled,' he said, when it was time to retire. 'My dear, all you can do is to warn Fleur to be careful. She is a grown woman and is well aware of the risks posed by men like Sir Gerald.' He took her hands. 'Fleur is not you, Molly. You have decided not to trust any man again—'

'And with good reason!'

He squeezed her fingers. 'True, but Fleur must make her own choice.'

He was right, of course, but as Molly prepared for bed that evening she determined that she must spend more time at Prospect House and keep an eye on things for herself.

* * *

Molly had no opportunity to visit Fleur for the next couple of days because she was busy helping Edwin with his parish work and making charitable visits in the town, including a call upon Cissy's mother, who was still very weak from her recent illness. Knowing that her maid would like to spend a little more time with her ailing parent, Molly decided to give her the rest of the day off and walk back to the vicarage alone.

'I have only to call at the post office on my way home and I shall not need you until after dinner this evening, Cissy,' she said, gathering up her empty basket. 'But do be home before dark.'

'I will, ma'am, thank you.'

Molly set off from the little cottage, thinking that the day reflected her sunny spirits, which had been lifted still further by the pleasure she had seen in the old woman's face when she realised her daughter would be able to spend a few more hours at home. Molly felt a bubble of laughter welling up in her. If Edwin asked her to help with a subject for his sermon, she would suggest that this week it should be about the rewards to be gained from such little gestures of kindness.

The idea occupied her until she reached the centre of the town, when she spotted Mr Russington on the far side of the square. He was talking with several local gentlemen, but he excused himself and came across to greet her. When he turned to accompany her, Molly felt obliged to tell him there was no need.

'But I insist,' he replied. 'Unless you think it will do you harm to be seen walking with such a one as me.'

She laughed at that. 'I think my character will survive a short walk in your company, Mr Russington. In fact, I am pleased we have met.' She became serious. 'I wanted to thank you. For telling Sir Gerald what went on at Prospect House the other night.'

There was a pause.

'I mentioned it, yes. I did not expect Kilburn to be quite so angry about it. He is usually the most placid of men, but he ordered Aikers and Flemington to leave immediately.'

'Perhaps he is removing potential rivals.'

'That is a very cynical point of view, madam.'

'Experience has taught me to be cautious where men are concerned.'

'You are very world-weary, for one so young.'

'I am four-and-twenty.'

'You look younger.'

She disguised her blushes with another laugh. 'Do not be offering me Spanish coin, Mr Russington. There is nothing to gain by it.'

They had reached the post office and she stopped. He was looking down at her, a faint smile playing at the corners of his mouth.

'Now, why should you think I am trying to flatter you?'

'Because you are a rake, perhaps?' She could not help smiling back at him, surprised she could talk to him so easily.

'Even rakes should tell the truth to their friends, madam.'

He touched his hat and strolled away, leaving her to stare after him and remind herself yet again that one could never truly be friends with a rake.

The news that Marjorie had given birth to a lusty baby girl gave Molly the excuse she needed to visit Prospect House regularly over the next couple of weeks, and it soon became clear that Sir Gerald rode to the house almost every day, stopping to talk to Fleur if she should be out of doors. Little Billy spoke of him as a great gun and told Molly that Sir Gerald always let him look after his horse. When Molly teased Fleur about the number of tasks requiring her attention in the gardens, Fleur flushed, but Molly could not order her to remain indoors. When she mentioned it to Nancy, the cook was philosophical.

'You are not running a prison, after all,' she told Molly. 'And you cannot prevent Fleur from talking to Sir Gerald if she so wishes.'

Molly agreed and in the end all she could do was to warn Fleur to take care and beg Nancy and the others to look out for her. She felt a little guilty, cautioning Fleur against Sir Gerald when she herself was seeing much more of Russ and growing more at ease in his company. It was inevitable they should meet, she supposed, given the good weather. She was out of doors every day, taking the gig to Prospect House or walking in the town visiting her brother's sick or poverty-stricken parishioners. Once she met him when she was on her way to Raikes Farm with another basket of provisions and he dismounted and carried her basket for her.

'Shall I wait to escort you back?' he asked, when they reached her destination. 'I know your propensity for injury.'

She was no longer embarrassed by his reference to her turning her ankle and merely laughed at him.

'But it is not in the least muddy today. No, you must go on with your birdwatching, I do not need you.' She hesitated, giving him a speculative look and his brows went up.

'Well, Mrs Morgan?'

'I wondered if you would be free on Friday morning.'

His eyes narrowed suspiciously. 'Why?'

'I plan to go to Hobbs Lane that day. I want to find greenery from the hedgerows to decorate the church in readiness for Marjorie's baby to be baptised there. I was going to take Cissy, but she is even shorter than I am. Whereas you…'

He laughed. 'You think I might be useful? Very well, madam, I shall be there to help you!'

They parted, Molly feeling only a trifle guilty for issuing the invitation.

Friday dawned bright and when Molly informed Cissy of her plans for the morning, the maid suggested Molly's old primrose dimity would be most suitable.

'You don't want to risk spoiling one of your newer gowns if you are scrambling around the hedgerows, ma'am.'

It was a very sensible idea and Molly agreed, but

she voiced a protest when Cissy brought out the russet spencer of fine wool that Edwin had given her last summer. There was a matching hat to go with the little jacket, a frivolous little cap that allowed her dusky curls to cluster around her face and Molly objected that it was far too fine to wear upon such an outing.

'But you never wear it on *any* occasion,' Cissy argued. 'If it sits in the cupboard much longer, it will be quite out of fashion.'

Molly allowed herself to be persuaded and some twenty minutes later she sallied forth. Hobbs Lane was only a stone's throw from the church and she found Russ waiting for her as she turned off the main road. The sight of him in his blue coat and buckskins made her mouth go dry and she wondered if she should have brought Cissy after all, but only for a moment. They were well within sight of the busy road and besides, at this time of year, there was much to do in the house and Cook had asked if Cissy could help her in the kitchen, preserving fruits for the winter.

Russ touched his hat to her as she came up to him. 'Mrs Morgan.' He put his hand in his pocket and drew out a stubby knife with a curving blade.

'I borrowed this from the gardener at Newlands. Shall we begin?'

'I commend your foresight,' she said, the flutter of her nerves subsiding. 'By all means, let us make a start.'

They worked companionably and Molly was grateful for his help, the beau's height and long arms giving her more choice of greenery. He cut heavy bunches of scarlet rowan berries and long tendrils of ivy, before they moved on to a thick, late-flowering gorse, its vivid yellow flowers making a striking contrast to the dock, with its vibrant green leaves and red-brown seeds. They had almost finished when Molly became aware that the clouds were gathering and the threat of rain hung in the air. Russ filled her large basket until it was overflowing, then piled more ivy and dock leaves into her arms, saying he would carry the basket.

'Come on,' he said, glancing up at the lowering sky. 'We must hurry if we are not to be caught in a shower.'

They were in sight of the church when the first drops of rain began to fall and they ran the last few yards to the lychgate and up the path into the church, laughing and giggling like children. Molly dropped her burden on the empty table just inside the door, leaving space for Russ to put down the basket.

'Thank you,' she turned to him, still smiling. 'I could never have achieved so much without you.' She pulled off her gloves, the better to brush her damp curls from her face.

'You are missing most of them.' He pushed her hands away and she stood passively while he gently tucked the stray curls beneath her cap.

'There. That is better. Now, let me look at you.'

He turned her to face the great west window, his hands resting lightly on her shoulders. Until that moment she had felt comfortable, at ease, but suddenly it was impossible to move. He had his back to the light yet his dark eyes glowed, drawing her in. She wanted him. She recognised the feeling, but this was stronger, more overwhelming than anything she had ever known before. It would be so good to surrender, to give in, but she fought it, reminding herself of what she had to lose.

She tried to step away, only to find her retreat blocked by the solid planks of the box pew at her back.

'Please.' The word was little more than a croak. 'Please, stop it.'

'Stop what?' His breathing was not quite steady, but he kept his hands on her shoulders, held her gaze a prisoner with those dark, glinting eyes.

'S-stop flirting with me.'

'I am not flirting.'

His voice was low, deep, lulling her senses while his eyes were boring into her, dragging out her soul. In one last desperate bid to escape her own desire, she forced herself to twist away and turn her back on him.

'You *are*.' She fixed her hands on the edge of the pew, gripping the wood until her knuckles gleamed white. 'You must be. It is what rakes *do*. And you are undoubtedly a rake.'

'And you are a widow, Mrs Morgan. You are no innocent virgin. This is no flirtation, but neither am I forcing my attentions on you.'

She felt the weight of his hands again on her shoulders. He was standing close behind her, the heat of him radiating through the thin spencer and her muslin skirts. It was as much as she could do not to lean back against him and beg him to make love to her. His breath was warm on her cheek, his voice was low, seductive, and it wrapped itself around her like velvet. It would so easy to give in.

'You feel it, too, Molly. Admit it. You are trembling in your effort to resist.'

It was true. Her body was thrumming, taut as a bowstring. Desire tugged at her thighs and made her breasts ache. She remembered it well, that overwhelming sense of longing, but it faded as memories she had buried deep came back to haunt her. The agony of betrayal and the brutal, physical pain of being kicked and beaten until she could not even walk. She was seized by unreasoning fear.

'No, no! Let me go!'

Hearing the panic in her voice Russ released her and stepped away, frowning. Moments earlier she had been within an ace of falling into his arms, but now she was genuinely alarmed. She was scrubbing at her cheek with the back of her hand and he drew his handkerchief from his pocket.

'I beg your pardon,' he said quietly. 'Will you not tell me how I have upset you?'

She dashed another rogue tear from her cheek.

'I must go,' she muttered. 'I will finish this later.'

He turned to accompany her out of the church, half expecting her to wave him away, but she allowed him to walk with her to the lychgate, where they stopped and she held out the crumpled handkerchief.

'No, you keep it,' he said quietly. 'I give you my word I had not planned this, Molly. Truly I did not mean to frighten you. I would not have this affect our friendship.'

'Friends!' She gave a bitter laugh. 'We are not friends. We could never be friends!'

Russ watched her hurry away, head bowed against the downpour. He was startled to discover just how much her response had shaken him. He enjoyed spending time with Molly Morgan, they had grown very comfortable together and he had come to believe they were friends. But he could not deny the attraction, the sudden blaze of desire that had crackled between them as they stood together in the cool, silent church. Molly had felt it, too, he would stake his life on it, but she had shied away like a frightened animal and he had seen again that terror in her eyes.

Molly had disappeared from sight now, but still Russ stood sheltering at the lychgate. Part of him wanted to run after her and discover the cause of her fear, but something held him back. He did not want the responsibility. Women were trouble. His stepmother had taught him that at an early age. It was best not to get involved with the creatures. He had spent his adult life avoiding romantic attachments and he was not about to change that for a diminutive widow who strongly disapproved of him and his way of life.

'She is right,' he muttered, 'We cannot be friends and there's an end to it.'

And with that he settled his hat more firmly on his head and stepped out into the rain.

'Good heavens, we are invited to dine at Newlands this evening.'

'Surely not.'

Molly stared across the breakfast table at her brother, aware that her cheeks were heating up. Since her meeting with Russ yesterday, he had been constantly in her thoughts. She was distressed that such an enjoyable interlude had ended with her running away. Yet she had had no option. That moment in the church, the shocking attraction that had flowed between them, had threatened to overwhelm her. She had spent the time since then, including most of the night, berating herself for thinking she could flout the rules of propriety.

She should have made sure she never went out of doors without a maid in attendance.

'Yes, yes,' said Edwin, his eyes fixed upon the letter. 'I confess it is most unexpected. When I saw Gerald a few days ago he made no mention of it. However, we have no other engagements tonight so I shall write back and accept. I am sure we will both enjoy a little company this evening, will we not? That is...' He looked up at last. 'Molly, did you speak? Have you made some other arrangement?'

Much as she wanted to, Molly could think of no reason why they should not go. And deep down inside she knew she wanted to see Russ. Surely there could be no harm in it, as long as they were not alone together. Indeed, unless she was to become a recluse, there was no way she could avoid meeting the beau while he remained at Newlands.

She summoned a smile. 'No, Edwin, we are both perfectly free this evening, although I, too, am a little surprised that they should invite us again at such short notice.'

However, when Lady Currick called to deliver a receipt for a saddle of mutton for Molly's cook, the mystery was soon solved.

'The ladies are going away,' Lady Currick informed Molly and Edwin, as she enjoyed a glass of wine with them. 'The Claydons and Mr and Mrs Sykes are accompanying Miss Kilburn and her companion to visit friends in Scarborough, so there will be no more dinners at Newlands until she returns.'

'Miss Kilburn is going away—for how long?'

Molly saw the dull flush on her brother's cheeks as he blurted out his question and she made a mental note to observe him and Agnes closely that evening. Lady Currick made no mention of the departure of two of the gentlemen and Molly was not equal to the task of enquiring, but she did wonder if Sir Gerald would remain at the house with only Mr Russington for company.

The question was answered almost as soon as they arrived at Newlands that evening. Molly clung to her brother's arm as they were shown into the drawing room, but the warmth of Miss Kilburn's welcome and the fact that Russ made no attempt to approach her calmed her initial nerves. She must do this. She must meet the beau as an acquaintance, nothing more.

They were the only guests and it was soon clear

that Sir Gerald had not divulged the reason for the sudden departure of Aikers and Flemington.

'A prior engagement has called the gentlemen away and we, too, shall be departing soon,' remarked Mrs Sykes, sighing. 'I vow, Sir Gerald, I am surprised that you and Mr Russington will not come with us, rather than remain behind to rattle around in this house all on your own.'

'I expect we will spend most of our days out of doors,' returned Sir Gerald cheerfully. 'The park has been woefully neglected and overgrown, but there is plenty of sport to be had. The woodcock, for example, have been breeding very freely. I am planning a number of improvements to the estate, too, that need to be put into action.'

'I hope you aren't expecting Russington to advise you,' put in Lord Claydon, gently teasing.

'No, indeed,' replied Russ, smiling. 'I have excellent stewards on each of my properties, which leaves me with nothing to do but enjoy myself.'

There was general laughter at this and Molly wondered if she was the only one who heard the note of self-mockery in the beau's tone.

'I am sure it is not true,' remarked Edwin as the laughter died away.

'But it is, I assure you. My life is wholly given over to pleasure.'

'I pray you will not believe him, Edwin,' cried Sir Gerald, coming up. 'I rely upon his judgement in everything. Behind that languid and smiling exterior is a very sharp intellect.'

'I do not deny it,' drawled the beau. 'But that does not mean I waste my energies upon humdrum domestic matters. I have a very good man of business for that.'

'Aye, you do, and insist upon him giving you regular and detailed reports of all your lands and investments.' Sir Gerald clapped his friend on the shoulder and grinned at the assembled company. 'Russ would have everyone believe that he is a very frippery fellow, but you may take my word for it, it is all a hum.'

'Good heavens, Gerald, are you trying to put me to the blush?' Russ protested. He was smiling, but when he turned to look at Molly she saw that it did not reach his eyes. 'You will not deceive Mrs Morgan. She has had accurate reports of my reputation from the very best authority, is that not so, madam?'

Her chin went up. 'I believe one should judge a man on his actions rather than what is said of him.'

Edwin nodded his approval. 'Well said, my dear.'

He went off to talk to Agnes and Molly found herself momentarily alone. She tensed as Russ moved a little closer.

'Perhaps, ma'am, our host's *actions* in giving Aikers and Flemington their orders to quit have given you a better opinion of him than you have of me.'

'I do not think badly of you, Mr Russington.' After a glance to ensure no one could overhear them, Molly continued. 'We are agreed, sir, that you are a rake and I am a widow. *You* cannot help what you are and, as you pointed out yesterday, I am no innocent. I should have known better than to meet you without a chaperon.'

She gave a little nod and moved off. She was stronger now. Yesterday's weakness was gone and she would not submit to any man.

Russ made no attempt to speak to her again that evening and Molly did not know whether to be glad or sorry for it. Part of her was relieved that she was not having to fight down the undoubted attraction she felt for the man, but another part, an irresponsible, rebellious part, wanted to converse with him, to enjoy the verbal sparring that made her feel so very much alive. Thus, when she accompanied Edwin back to the vicarage late that night, she was aware of a feeling of discontent, as though some promised treat had not materialised. And as she blew out her bedside candle, she realised that with the ladies gone from Newlands, there would be even less opportunity to see Russ during the next few weeks.

'Oh, was ever life so trying!'

Molly was driving the gig and took advantage of the solitude to utter the words aloud. She was on her way home after her weekly visit to Prospect House and what she had learned there had left her seriously worried. One look at Fleur's radiant face was enough to tell Molly that her friend was in the first throes of a love affair. It had not taken Molly long to learn that Sir Gerald was an almost daily visitor to the farm and although he never came into the house itself, he and Fleur were in the habit of walking out each day. When Molly questioned Fleur about it, she merely laughed.

'You are making far too much of it.' Fleur's words were belied by the faint colour on her cheeks. 'Sir Gerald comes here to discuss farm management.

He is intent upon improving Newlands and comes to talk to Moses, and very often he asks me questions, too, about the kitchen gardens and the best way to set up the accounts.' Her clear, innocent laugh rang out. 'Who would have believed I should ever have been so knowledgeable about household and farm matters that a gentleman would want my advice?'

Molly could believe it, only too well. With his sister away, Sir Gerald was making the most of his time to flirt with Fleur, only she was far too innocent to see it, and to every attempt of Molly's to warn her off, Fleur would only blush, and laugh, and say she had no intention of letting Sir Gerald compromise her.

'But she does not *know*,' declared Molly to the empty lane, making the pony trotting between the shafts twitch its ears nervously. 'She does not realise how irresistible a man can be. How he can take you in with his soft words and allurements.'

Nancy might say that Fleur was old enough to look after herself, but Molly had seen the soft glow in her eyes when she spoke of Sir Gerald Kilburn. She was falling in love and that could spell disaster. Molly would do anything in her power to protect her friend.

* * *

Russ lowered the spyglass and exhaled a long, steady breath, well satisfied with his early-morning observations. The freshening breeze on his cheek reminded him that the seasons were changing and the summer birds would soon be leaving the moors. He would not have many more opportunities like this and he must make the most of it.

The distant thud of hooves made him turn. He saw a rider approaching... Molly Morgan! He shook his head, telling himself he was being fanciful, because with the morning sun behind the figure he could only make out an outline. He did not even know if she could ride. He lifted his hand to block out the sun and there she was, cantering towards him on a sturdy bay cob. As she drew nearer the horse slowed to a trot, and he lowered his hand, waiting for her to come up to him. Now she was closer he could see the way her mannish riding jacket was moulded to her petite figure, the tiny waist accentuated even more by the billowing lavender skirts. She wore a curly-brimmed beaver hat over her dark hair, but the veil was turned back, flowing behind her like a gossamer pennant. He was glad he could see her face, for the air had whipped a becoming colour into her cheeks and her eyes sparkled with the exercise.

'Good day to you, Mrs Morgan.'

'I was looking for you.' His brows and his spirits rose at her words and she flushed, shaking her head. '*Not* for the pleasure of your company, Mr Russington.'

'Well, that has put me in my place.' He reached out and rubbed a hand over the pony's velvet nose. 'How may I help you?'

'I remembered you had made a habit of these early-morning walks and thought it the best time to talk to you. Alone.'

He gave a little bow, saying politely, 'I am at your disposal, madam.'

She hesitated for a heartbeat before kicking her foot free of the stirrup and jumping nimbly to the ground. He knew a moment's regret that she had not asked him to lift her down.

She said, 'Will you walk with me?'

Intrigued, he fell into step beside her. 'What of your pony?'

'Christopher will be happy to follow. He knows I have treats for him in my pocket.'

'Christopher?'

'Edwin called him that when he bought him for

me. After the saint,' she added, a hint of laughter in her voice. 'because he is such a steady mount and will carry me anywhere.'

Russ glanced back at the cob, plodding along quietly behind them. 'By the look of him he is built more for endurance than speed.'

'He is,' she said, sighing. 'He cannot be persuaded to anything more than a gentle canter, but he has the most placid nature, nothing startles him.'

'I doubt if even cannon fire would move him,' he said frankly and was rewarded by hearing her low, full-throated laugh.

'I am sure you are right. His watchword is slow but steady! But I do not hunt and have few opportunities to ride, so there is no point in exchanging him for a faster mount that would only spend his time eating his head off in the stables. But I did not come here to talk about my horse.'

She fell silent. Glancing down at her, he saw the tiny crease in her brow and a downward tilt to her mouth. Her mood had grown serious and he was sorry for it, he liked her smile, the way she laughed. She did not do it often enough, he thought.

They had walked several more yards before the words came out in a rush.

'It is about Fleur. Mrs Dellafield. Sir Gerald has been showing her a great deal of attention.'

'Mrs Dellafield? I cannot recall meeting her.'

'She is housekeeper at Prospect House.'

'Ah. She was at the market, was she not? I have not seen her since. Unlike Kilburn's two departed guests, I have not been in the habit of visiting the house.'

'Well, your friend has,' she retorted. 'I understand he has become a regular caller there.'

'Has he?' Russ considered the matter. 'He has said nothing to me about it, but it is possible, I suppose. We do not spend the whole of every day in each other's pockets. It certainly explains his indignation when I told him of Aikers and Flemington's recent exploits.'

'And you said I was being cynical when I suggested he had an ulterior motive for sending them away.'

'I still think that. Kilburn is an honourable man. I have known him since we were at school together.'

'That is no recommendation!'

He exhaled in a long, exasperated hiss.

'Not all the tales you have heard of us are true, Mrs Morgan. Kilburn and I went to town together as young men. I admit we were rich, idle and ripe for a spree. We became part of a very fast set and we did kick up a dust in those early years. A couple of our number went beyond the bounds and were shockingly indiscreet about it, too. Kilburn and I condemned their actions and realised we had outgrown that particular group. We distanced ourselves, but it was too late, we were tainted by their scandals. Perhaps if we had withdrawn from town and lived as monks since those early years, or if we had married, we might have shaken off the reputation. But society has an insatiable appetite for gossip and eligible bachelors are always the subject of scandal and speculation.'

'But Prospect House cannot afford to be the subject of any such speculation. Your friend's attentions do Mrs Dellafield no good at all.'

'Hmm. Is she pretty?'

'Extremely pretty.'

'Then I cannot blame him for flirting with her.'

He heard her gasp of indignation, but she did not rip up at him. Instead she clasped her hands tightly together, as if suppressing her anger.

'He is inveigling himself into her affections,' she told him. 'He goes there supposedly because he wants to learn more about the farming methods.'

'It may well be true. He has certainly expressed that desire to me and it is common knowledge that Prospect Farm is one of the most productive in the area. Perhaps you are being too harsh upon Sir Gerald.'

'No.' She stopped and turned to look up at him. 'He could learn all he needs to know from Moses, who runs the farm, if that was his true intention.'

'And Mrs Dellafield could advise him to do so, if that was her wish.'

He spoke gently, but even so her eyes darkened with distress and a silent acknowledgement that he was right. She shook her head and began to walk again.

'She is besotted and cannot be made to see that he is trifling with her.'

Russ considered the matter. Gerald had certainly been rather preoccupied recently and the fact that he had said nothing about this liaison made him think it might be more serious than a mere flirtation.

He said abruptly. 'What do you know of Mrs Dellafield? What is her birth?'

'She is a gentleman's daughter and perfectly respectable, but like so many unfortunate women, she was obliged by circumstance to leave her home and seek refuge.'

'I take it she is not married?'

'No, but it is not unusual for housekeepers to use the appellation. She is an innocent, Mr Russington, and I will not allow her to be hurt.'

'I take it you have spoken to the lady about your concerns?'

She nodded, her hands twisting themselves even tighter. 'She does not see the danger.'

'Perhaps there isn't any danger.' He caught her swift, incredulous glance and smiled. 'Despite what you think, madam, Sir Gerald is a gentleman. He would never force himself upon any woman.'

'Perhaps that is so, but he is a very engaging, extremely attractive man and he could break her heart without realising what he has done. Can you not talk to him, dissuade him from his pursuit of Fleur?'

'My dear Molly, why should he listen to me? If the lady is willing—perhaps he is merely passing the time of day with a pretty woman. What does your brother say of the matter?'

'Edwin says I should not interfere.' She bit her lip. 'But *you* could speak to Sir Gerald. He respects your judgement. I have heard him say so.'

'And in this instance my judgement is that your brother is right. Let the affair—if it is an affair—run its course.' He looked up. 'We have almost reached the track that will take me back to Newlands. Unless you wish to come with me, and talk to Kilburn yourself, then we must part here.'

She was silent and he could almost feel her anxiety. The colour had quite gone from her cheeks, and as they stepped on to the track, she spoke again.

'What will it take for you to keep your friend away from mine?' Her voice was low, but the meaning was quite clear. His eyes narrowed.

'Is that an offer, Mrs Morgan? Knowing my reputation, you should be wary of asking such a question.'

'Fleur is a virgin, an innocent. She has a great deal to lose if your friend seduces her.'

'And you have not?'

She shrugged. 'One night with you would not harm me quite so much. I would survive.'

One night. She was offering herself to him for one night. For a heartbeat he allowed himself to imagine having her in his bed. Undressing her. Making love to her. The sudden jolt of desire scorched him, but it was quickly cooled and washed away by a wave of fury. How dare she think he could be bought in such a way? Even more galling was the fact that he *cared* about her opinion!

Blinded by rage, he grabbed her horse's bridle and brought the creature round on to the path.

He said, his words biting, 'Your less-than-flattering proposal does you no credit, Mrs Morgan. You had best leave before I show you just how badly a rake can behave.'

'I—I beg your pardon.' Her face was crimson. 'I did not mean to offend you. I thought—'

'I know exactly what you thought. That Gerald and I would take any woman for sport. I do not know what sort of life you have had, madam, what sort of men you have known, but I can tell you now that we are not all savages.'

Without waiting for her approval he put his hands around her waist and threw her up on to the pony's back. It was roughly done and for a moment he thought she might topple off again, so he kept his hands on her, holding her firmly in the saddle until she had found her stirrup.

'Thank you,' she said icily. 'I have control now.'

'Good.' He stepped away. 'Then I suggest you

go home, Mrs Morgan, and we will forget we ever had this conversation.'

He turned away and strode back towards Newlands. How dare she? How *dare* she think he would take her as payment of some debt? He had not yet met a woman who did not think she could use her body to get what she wanted. In his stepmother's case it was his family money and, not content with marrying his father, she had sought to gratify her lusts by seducing Russ, too. That had shown him just how grasping and avaricious women were. He had thought Molly Morgan was different, but no. She was the same as the rest.

But was she? The black rage abated slightly. She was by no means eager to throw herself into his arms. He thought back to that time in the church. She had panicked then at the mere idea that he might kiss her. And today, the thought of spending the night with him had been—he could not avoid the word—repugnant to her. His furious pace slowed. With the exception of her brother she did not appear to trust any of his sex. She was a widow—perhaps she had not enjoyed the marriage bed, but his instinct told him it was more than that. Someone, some *man*, had made her think they were all villains. Whoever it was had hurt her very badly.

He remembered holding Molly in the saddle, his hands almost spanning her tiny waist, and the thought of anyone hurting her made the bile rise in his gorge. Not that it was his problem. Molly Morgan was more than capable of looking after herself. And, it seemed, she had taken on the task of looking after the women of Prospect House, too.

'Well, I wish her well with that,' he muttered, lengthening his stride again. 'Let that occupy her time and keep her out of my way!'

Chapter Seven

Russ was still simmering with anger when he reached Newlands, and he made his way directly to his room to change. When he emerged some time later he learned that his host was still at breakfast, and he went downstairs to join him.

'So you *are* back!' Gerald was helping himself to more ham from a platter and waved his fork at Russ. 'I thought perhaps you had seen some particularly interesting species on the moors.'

'I did, but not the feathered kind.'

Russ dismissed his friend's enquiring look with a shake of his head and took his place at the table. A silent-footed servant appeared with a basket of warm bread rolls and he took two, suddenly realising how hungry he was. He wondered if Molly had yet broken her fast. She must have risen very early to ride out and find him. The decision could not have been the work of a moment. She must be very concerned for her friend.

He waited until the servants had left them alone and then said, at his most casual, 'Are you calling upon Mrs Dellafield today?'

'Ah.' Russ glanced up. Gerald was looking almost sheepish. 'How did you learn of it?'

'Did you think you could keep such a thing secret in a small town like this?' Russ countered.

'I have been meaning to tell you, when the time was right.' Gerald leaned forward, his eyes shining. 'She is an angel, Russ. Beautiful, innocent—'

'So I have been told.'

'No, no, it is true. She has confided in me. She was obliged to flee her home when her stepfather began to show an unnatural interest in her. Mrs Morgan is an old schoolfriend and took her in. Then, when Prospect House was set up, she became its housekeeper and has been there ever since, hiding from the world.' He sighed. 'Like Perrault's story of Sleeping Beauty in the wood.'

'It certainly sounds like a fairy tale.'

'I would have told you,' said Gerald, 'if circumstances had been different, I would have introduced you to her, but after Aikers and Flemington caused such a stir I did not want to suggest bringing another gentleman anywhere near the place.'

Russ reached for the coffee pot. 'How did it start?'

'You remember the day we were to ride to Knaresborough and my horse cast a shoe? It was such a fine day I decided to take a stroll on the far side of the valley—just exploring, you see—and found myself quite by chance beside the Prospect Farm orchards and that is where I first saw her. She looked such a picture that I could not help but stop and speak.' He laughed gently. 'She all but ran away from me, but I persuaded her to stay and talk. After that, well, I found myself riding that way quite often. I never go near the house but send a message, and if she is free, she comes out to meet me.' He frowned suddenly. 'It is no mere flirtation, Russ, if that is what you are thinking.'

'What else am I to think?'

Gerald smiled at that and Russ was startled to see the soft glow in his friend's eyes.

'She is like no other lady I have met before, but I assure you we just…talk. When she learned I really was interested in improving Newlands she was more than happy to discuss the running of the farm with me. She surprises me constantly. Her knowledge of the farm and its workings is almost as great as that man of theirs, Moses, who runs the place.'

'The devil she does!' Russ gave him a searching look. 'So you are not trifling with her.'

'Trifling! Good God, I should think not. But, it is a delicate situation. I need to be sure of my feelings and Fleur's before I introduce her to Agnes. I thought we were secure enough, for her friends at Prospect House would not say anything, I am sure. However, if tongues are beginning to wag—'

'They are not,' Russ cut in. 'I had it in confidence from a most discreet source. Nevertheless, I would urge caution, my friend. Many a man before you has been taken in by a pretty face.'

'If you think Fleur is trying to trap me into marriage then you are very far off,' retorted Gerald, bridling.

Russ put up his hands and quickly begged pardon.

'Very well,' said Gerald, only slightly mollified. 'And as it happens, I was planning to take the dogs out and go shooting today. My gamekeeper tells me there are woodcock in the West Park, if you wish to come.'

Russ agreed with alacrity and they both turned

their attentions to their breakfast, harmony restored. Gerald's affection for Fleur Dellafield was sincere. Molly Morgan should take some comfort from that. Not that she would learn of it from him, since he had promised himself that he would not go near the infernal woman again if he could help it.

True to his namesake, Christopher carried Molly safely back to the vicarage, although her eyes were so misted with tears and her thoughts so awry that she had no true memory of the journey. How could she have been so crass as to offer herself to him like that! It was a blunder of monumental proportions. Molly ran up to her room, dismissing the maid as soon as she had thrown off her muddy habit and saying that she would lie down for a while.

She curled up on the bed, appalled at her behaviour. It had been building, this feeling that she must do something, ever since the baptism of Marjorie's baby. The sight of the child in its mother's arms had brought on such a wave of longing and regret that Molly had hardly been able to stand through the service. It brought back how much her own seduction had cost her and Molly was determined Fleur should not make the same mistakes. But to think that she might buy off Beau Russington with her favours was unforgivable. For all his reputation, she knew in her heart he was nothing like the men who had destroyed her life.

How would she be able to look him in the face when they next met? And they must meet, because Edwin and Agnes had become such friends that it was impossible that they would not be thrown into each other's company. At least with the ladies being absent Edwin would not expect her to visit Newlands and if she was to see Russ in the town then they might ignore one another. That was the best she could hope for.

By afternoon the rain had set in, steady and relentless. The grey skies reflected Molly's low spirits and she moved from room to room, unable to settle to any task. Edwin was dining out and for want of any other occupation she ordered her own dinner to be served at five. The solitary meal did nothing to soothe Molly's nerves. She left the table more restless than ever and went upstairs to fetch her cloak. Her maid glanced out of the window.

'You ain't never going out in this, ma'am.'

'It is no more than a drizzle. I shall not melt.'

'No, but you will get soaked through,' Cissy retorted in a tone of long suffering. 'I suppose I had best get my cloak.'

'No, there is no need for you to get wet, too,' said Molly quickly. 'I am not going far, only to the church. My brother has mislaid his book of sermons, and I thought I might look for it. There will be no one abroad at this time and in this weather.'

'Not if they can help it,' muttered Cissy. 'Very well, ma'am. I'll build up the fire in your room for when you return. And put a hot brick in the oven, for you are bound to be chilled to the bone when you comes back and will catch your death if we don't take care.'

With these dismal words ringing in her ears Molly ran lightly down the stairs, flicking her hood into place as she stepped out of the house. The rain had turned the roads to mud and she kept her head down, trying to find the cleanest path, but by the time she reached the church her boots and her skirts were liberally splashed with dirt and her cloak felt heavy and cloying on her shoulders. If she did catch her death, as Cissy put it, then she would be well served, she thought miserably, her eyes dwelling on the table where she and Russ had left the plants they had collected. They had been so at ease together, collecting the ivy and green boughs for the church. Even now she could remember him standing close, enveloping her with his presence. Molly had not realised how much she had come to enjoy Russ's company until that moment when she had pushed him away and killed their burgeoning friendship.

'But if I had not… If he had kissed me…'

She dared not finish the sentence, dared not let her thoughts linger on what might have been. She knew now they could never be friends, but, oh, how she missed him. And they might at least have been acquaintances, able to exchange civil pleasantries, if only she had not tried to enlist his help in keeping Fleur safe from Sir Gerald.

She pulled her cloak a little tighter, but her shudder had little to do with the weather. It was shame and remorse, brought on by the memory of the disdain she had seen in his eyes. If only she could have that time over again! She should have asked him, begged him to help her. She might have appealed to his better nature, his honour as a gentleman. He might well have refused to help her, but at least he would not hold her in such contempt.

Molly sighed, her eyes wandering listlessly around the church. She had forgotten why she had come. Ah, yes, Edwin's little book of sermons.

She made a half-hearted search, but it was now too dark to see very well and she knew she should go home. She carefully shut the door behind her, pulled her hood a little further over her head and hurried back to the road. She kept her eyes on the ground, trying to miss the worst of the puddles. A damp chill was settling on the back of her neck where the rain was seeping through her cloak and she thought she might have to admit to Cissy that it had been foolhardy to come out in such weather.

Something made her look up and she stopped. Russ, hatless and with his hair plastered to his head, was standing in the rain, blocking her way. She knew from the look in his eyes that this was no chance meeting, he was not going to let her pass. She swung about and began to hurry away, but the next moment he was beside her, gripping her arm.

'We must talk.'

'In this weather? Do not be absurd.'

'You are already wet through. Another few moments won't hurt.'

They had reached the junction with Hobbs Lane and he turned into it, taking Molly with him.

'If you want me to apologise,' she began, 'for what I said this morning, then I do. Wholeheartedly. I should never have said such a thing. Now I pray you will let me go.'

'Not yet. I want to talk to you.'

The high hedgerows and overhanging trees offered some shelter from the misty drizzle, but they increased the gloom and the sense of danger. Molly's heart was thundering, making it hard to breathe.

'There is nothing to talk about,' she told him, struggling against his iron hold. 'We cannot meet without upsetting one another.'

'Tell me,' he said. 'Tell me what happened to make you hate men so much.'

She tried to prise his fingers from her arm. 'Please. Please let me go.'

'No. I want to understand why you are like this. Your commitment to Prospect House, your abhorrence of men. Something occurred in your past and I want to know.' His grip tightened. 'Since this morning I have been imagining the worst.'

Molly stopped struggling. He would not be satisfied until she told him something.

'I fell in love,' she said simply. 'It is a familiar story, shockingly commonplace, in fact. I was just seventeen. He was a handsome Irish soldier, here with his regiment for the summer. He was very charming, told me he loved me and promised we would be married. I was quite prepared to follow the drum, but the militia left. He went with them and I—' She turned her head, gazing up the lane and blinking rapidly. 'I was left behind. I was too proud to make a fuss, to tell my family until he was gone and it was too late.'

The memory was still painful, but at that moment she would not have resisted if Russ had put his arms about her. She would have taken comfort from his sympathy, his strength. Instead, with a sigh that might have been compassion, he released her and the thought that he pitied her was like salt in an open wound. She dragged together her few final shreds of pride to keep her head up and her voice level. 'I was ruined. As many another foolish girl has been before. Now you know the truth.'

'A broken heart? Abandoned by your lover?' He shook his head. 'There is more you aren't telling me.'

'Is that not enough?'

'No!' He raked one hand through his hair. 'A failed love affair is not enough to give you this... this *aversion* to men.'

'I do not have an aversion,' she protested. 'I am

perfectly friendly with many of my neighbours in Compton Parva, and I love Edwin, very much.'

'These are men who pose no threat to you!' His eyes narrowed. 'Was your marriage unhappy?'

'That is none of your business. I shall not listen to you!'

When she turned to walk away he stepped in front of her, so close she found herself staring at the solid wall of his chest.

'Do not try to fob me off, Molly.'

She gave a little cry of frustration and beat her fists against him.

'You have no right to pester me like this.'

'I am determined to know,' he said, covering her hands and holding them still. 'If you will not tell me, I shall ask your brother.'

'He knows nothing about it!'

Her words had shocked him. His head went back, as if she had struck him.

'No one knows,' she whispered. 'It is in the past. Finished.'

'It is not finished,' he said slowly. 'It is eating away at you and it will ruin your life if you do not stop it. You are a young woman, Molly Morgan. Young enough to marry again, to fall in love again.'

'Never! I am done with all men.'

'I do not believe that.' His fingers tightened. 'Can you deny you feel something when I touch you? You are trembling now.'

'That is because I am angry.'

'Are you sure about that?' he said gently, 'You have a passionate nature, Molly. You can love again, if only you will let yourself. I know it.'

'Of course, you do.' Her rising panic manifested itself in scorn. 'You think yourself irresistible to any female!'

'No, no, I do not mean me. I mean a good man. A man of the cloth, perhaps. Someone who thinks as you do. But you will need to stop running.'

He put his fingers under her chin and eased her head up, holding her eyes with his own. They were full of gentleness and understanding. Molly's tongue flickered nervously over her lips. It would be so easy to throw herself against him, to take comfort and strength from him, just for a while. She knew it was wrong, it could not be, but even as she told herself she must not give in, the look in his dark eyes changed. She could not move, could not breathe. Her body was no longer her own. The hood slipped back as she tilted her face up, eyes half-closed, inviting a kiss that did not come. His mouth was tantalisingly close and she pushed up on to her toes to reach him.

At first touch, his lips were soft and cool against hers. There was a heartbeat's hesitation before he began to kiss her and then she was lost. She forgot about the rain on her face, the soft whisper of it in the hedgerow. She was aware only of Russ's mouth on hers, his arms around her, binding her to him. She whimpered, a soft sound in her throat, and he deepened the kiss, his tongue flickering, teasing, exploring and, tentatively, she responded. She had never been kissed like this before, so tenderly, so thoroughly. Desire blossomed in every inch of her body and her heart, silent for so many years, began to sing.

Molly gave a little sigh of regret when at last the kiss ended. Russ kept his arms about her and she rested her head against his shoulder, gazing up in wonder at his face. He was looking down at her, a tiny crease in his brow, as if he was seeing her for the first time. Then he seemed to recollect himself and he gently released her.

'You see, I was right. There is passion in you, Molly Morgan.'

Molly stared at him. The light was fading and although she knew he was smiling she could not make out his features in the gloom. It was as if she was waking slowly from a dream. The feeling of well-being was slipping away and a chill was seeping through her damp clothes. She put a hand to her lips. They felt bruised, swollen and she had a sudden urge to weep, although she was not sure why.

Russ swallowed a sigh as he regarded the silent, dejected little figure in front of him. He hated seeing her thus, he wanted to drag her back into his arms and kiss away her unhappiness. His body was aroused and aching to do that and more. He wanted to set her up in luxury, shower her with gifts and spend the long nights in her arms, awaking the passion he had just glimpsed within her. But that was impossible. He reached out to pull her hood back over her head. 'I am the very last man who can give you lasting happiness. But, do you know? I envy him, whoever he may be.'

Still she said nothing and just gazed at him with stormy, troubled eyes. Then, without a word, she picked up her skirts, turned and fled.

Neither Russ nor Sir Gerald were present in church the following Sunday, for which Molly was very thankful. She had no idea how she was to face Russ after that kiss. Her insides twisted into knots every time she thought of it, which was almost constantly. The thick shell she had painstakingly built around herself was shattered, the desire she felt for Russ was as strong as anything she had ever felt for her first love. Stronger. She wanted him with an aching intensity that left her feeling weak, while the desolation that accompanied it tore at her. He could never be hers, he had told her so himself. He would not even beguile her with soft words and empty promises. The sight of Fleur, radiant and clearly very much in love, no longer filled Molly with the desire to save her friend—instead, she envied her. Molly sat through the service with her head bowed, not hearing the sermon but praying intently that this madness would soon pass.

Although Molly did not see Russ or Sir Gerald for the next few days, it was impossible not to hear about them. Lady Currick invited Molly and a number of other ladies to take tea with her, ostensibly to discuss charitable works in the parish, but once these matters had been dealt with the conversation turned to the latest gossip from Newlands.

'I have heard the two gentlemen are living there

like savages now the ladies have departed,' said one of the matrons, her eyes wide and twinkling in her round face. 'The servants have all been turned off. Heaven knows what they are up to!'

'Nothing to excite your imagination,' replied Lady Currick dampeningly. 'Sir Gerald discovered the housekeeper is suffering very badly from rheumatism and he has sent her off to Harrogate for two weeks to take the waters. She is accompanied by her niece, who happens to be first housemaid.'

'Well, I have never heard the like!' declared the matron. 'Two weeks, for a servant.'

'Quite.' Lady Currick paused while the tea cups were refreshed. 'Sir Gerald knew it would be highly improper for the other female servants to be above stairs with no one to manage them, so he gave them all leave to go home until the housekeeper returns. Paid them, too! Well, of course, that set up a protest from the rest of the house staff, and the result was that Sir Gerald said they might *all* have a holiday, if they so wished. Of course, some of them had nowhere to go and preferred to remain, but the result is that there are barely half a dozen servants at Newlands now, all male, and they are doing everything that is required for their masters.'

There was a general cry of disbelief and Lady

Currick could not suppress a little smile of superiority.

She said, 'I know it is true, because Currick went shooting with the gentlemen yesterday and stayed to dine at Newlands. That was when Sir Gerald was obliged to explain everything, because his valet was serving dinner for them. However, Currick had no fault to find with the dinner, nor the house, so it is to be supposed the gentlemen will go on quite comfortably until their servants return.'

Mrs Thomas, wife of the prosperous local mill owner, gave a loud tut of disapproval. 'Paying for the housekeeper to go to Harrogate for treatment is one thing. She is, after all, a very necessary member of the household, but to be giving the servants their wages and sending them off to do what they will—I am shocked, Lady Currick. Shocked. Such behaviour could lead to a general discontent amongst our servants. It sets a very bad example to the town.'

'It shows a generosity I had not expected of Sir Gerald,' put in Molly, feeling obliged to defend the gentleman.

'Well, I only hope he does not live to regret it,' muttered Mrs Thomas in ominous tones. 'And heaven knows what state the house will be in by the time the servants return!'

* * *

It was clear to Molly that the ladies of Compton Parva considered any past scandals attaching to Sir Gerald paled into insignificance against this latest outrage and she lost no time in relating the news to Edwin at dinner that evening. She was a little disappointed, but not surprised, to discover that he already knew of it.

'So Kilburn has done it, has he?' Edwin grinned. 'He asked me what I thought of the scheme when I rode over there on Monday last. I believe he and Russ were quite looking forward to living informally for a while, although I am sure they will be very glad to have their comforts restored after a fortnight.'

'I feel sorry for the staff who are left,' said Molly. 'They will all be working twice as hard.'

'I did mention that to Sir Gerald, but he said he would give them extra wages, so he did not think they would object overmuch. Trouble is,' mused Edwin, helping himself to more rice and mutton from the dishes on the table, 'this sort of thing can have unforeseen consequences. Servants with too much time to spare can get up to mischief. They may not even return at all. But it is something for Compton Parva to talk about, what?'

'With the harvest to be gathered in they should have more than enough to occupy them. They should not be gossiping at all.'

'People must have some entertainment and talking about others provides endless amusement. You are too severe upon our neighbours, Molly.'

'Am I?' She fixed an anxious gaze upon her brother. 'Do you think they consider me too serious and disapproving? Do *you* think it?'

Edwin put down his fork. 'I think you have grown old before your time,' he said gently. 'You are only four-and-twenty, my dear. I worry sometimes that I have allowed you to take on too much here.'

'But I enjoy helping you, Edwin.'

'I know and I very much appreciate it.' He hesitated, as if choosing his next words with care. 'But what if I should marry?'

Molly laughed. 'My dear Edwin, if that should happen, then naturally I should move out. We agreed as much when I first came to live with you and it is even more necessary now. I would not expect your wife to share a house with such a managing female as I have become!'

Edwin laughed, too, plainly relieved, but his words only deepened Molly's unease. Her brother often talked of Agnes Kilburn and it was clear his attachment to her was serious. If they should marry, the links with Newlands would be strengthened. Unless Molly moved away from the area altogether, there would be no avoiding Sir Gerald and his friends.

There would be no avoiding Russ.

Compton Parva was taking advantage of a spell of hot, dry weather to bring in the harvest. Molly drove over to Prospect House on Tuesday to help pack up the surplus produce from the farm, ready for market day. She was glad of the activity, for it helped to keep her mind from dwelling on Russ. She desperately wanted to see him again, but she must keep her distance from a man who had the power to make her lose all sense of judgement. A man who, by a touch, could reduce her to a quivering mass of need and longing.

The house was unusually quiet when she arrived. She was met by Marjorie, who took her into the morning room where her baby was sleeping peacefully in a crib.

'Everyone else is out of doors,' she told Molly. 'I have been sorting out things we might sell at market tomorrow.'

She indicated the table, which was covered with embroidered goods, including fine handkerchiefs and exquisite children's nightgowns. Molly spent an hour with her, admiring the baby and helping her to choose and price the various items to be sold, before making her way to the dairy, where Nancy was hard at work with the butter churn.

'In good time,' Nancy greeted her. 'All the others have gone to help in the fields, so I am left alone to deal with everything here.'

'I thought that might be the case,' said Molly, stripping off her gloves. 'What can I do?'

'If you could cut and wrap the butter I have already prepared, that would help, my love. Thank you.'

'I thought Fleur might be helping you,' remarked Molly, slipping into the clean linen apron Nancy handed to her.

'She is with Moses and the others at the farm. I said with her fair complexion she would be better staying out of the sun, but she insisted.'

There was something in Nancy's tone that made Molly look at her.

'And do you think Sir Gerald will pass this way?'

'Undoubtedly.' Nancy gave the handle a couple more turns before opening the barrel and giving a satisfied nod. 'They manage to see one another nearly every day. I wish you would speak to her, Molly. I have tried, but she is in such a daze of happiness she will not listen to me. She has thrown her hat over the windmill and will return by Weeping Cross.'

Molly nodded, saying nothing. She was beginning to think the old saying applied to more than just Fleur.

'Molly—have you been here all day?' Fleur embraced her warmly, then broke away, smiling. 'Now I feel guilty for not coming back earlier, but there was so much to do at the farm.'

'There always is, at harvest time.' Molly took her arm. 'Come along into the morning room. I am about to prepare tea and I am sure you are ready for a little refreshment.'

'I am indeed,' agreed Fleur, laughing. 'Only give me a moment to take off my bonnet and wash my face and hands and I shall be with you.'

Fleur ran upstairs and Molly busied herself with making tea until she returned. She was still trying to decide how to introduce the topic of Sir Gerald without sounding as if she was lecturing when

Fleur came into the morning room and asked if Nancy was joining them.

'No,' replied Molly, distracted. 'She is too busy in the kitchen today.'

'Just as well, since she is at outs with me over Sir Gerald. Has she told you?'

Molly said cautiously, 'She says you see him regularly.'

'I do.' There was no doubting the happiness shining from Fleur's eyes. 'You will not believe how much we have to discuss.' She laughed. 'We talk about farming and husbandry and crop yields. Can you believe it?'

'Yes, I can, if he wishes to ingratiate himself with you.'

Fleur blushed and shook her head. 'It is not like that, Molly. He will not come to the house because he says he is fearful for my reputation. We meet out of doors. Moses or one of the girls is always nearby. You look sceptical, my love, but he is most truly a gentleman. H-he has done nothing more scandalous than to kiss my hand! He says the farms at Newlands are in a pitiable state and he is determined to improve them. He has even sent his steward across to discuss our farming methods with Moses.'

'That I can understand, since we have been at pains to make Prospect Farm a success. But, Fleur, do you honestly believe he is only interested in the farm?'

'No, of course not. He has said he would like to bring his sister across to meet me, when she returns to Newlands. But you need not lecture me, Molly. I know full well I must not read too much into that.' Fleur sighed. 'I believe we are friends, you see. I know it cannot be anything more, but when Gerald eventually leaves Newlands, I shall have such happy memories.'

'And will that be enough?' asked Molly, aware of the ache she felt inside whenever she thought of Russ and that was after so very few encounters.

Fleur's smile slipped a little. 'It will have to be.'

Chapter Eight

Molly returned from Prospect House just as the sun was setting and was surprised to find Edwin waiting for her in the hall.

'Molly, love, you are later than I expected. Is all well at Prospect House? Marjorie, and her baby?'

'Yes, yes, everything is well, but there was so much to do—butter and cheese to be packed, eggs to be collected. Oh, a hundred little things. And with Marjorie looking after her new baby, they were glad of another pair of hands. However, Marjorie has been able to return to her sewing and is once more overseeing the other girls. They have produced some delightful work, including several pairs of gloves and embroidered slippers to sell to-morrow.' Weary as she was, she summoned up a laugh. 'I might even buy a pair for you, Edwin.'

His responding smile was distracted.

'Molly, my dear, do you remember I was talking of the unforeseen consequences of Sir Gerald's sending his staff away to enjoy themselves?'

'Of course. Edwin, what is it?'

Her immediate concern was dispelled when she saw how his eyes were dancing. 'I think you had best come into the drawing room, my dear.'

Russ had been surprised when Gerald informed him that he had paid most of his staff to go away for a while, but he had no objection to living frugally for a few weeks. Indeed, it suited his mood very well and since Gerald refused to quit Newlands, a period of self-denial where he might feel sorry for himself was just what he wanted.

'It will not be so bad,' Gerald had told him. 'Remember when we first arrived in London and had only one manservant between us? The stables are still fully staffed, so what with riding, hunting and shooting, we shall be out of doors every day. And for the rest, your man and mine are both capable of turning out a good meal. Besides, there are some servants left below stairs. No, my friend, we shall go on very well.'

And so it seemed. They sat very comfortably in the kitchen in the evenings, drinking wine while the two valets cooked, and when they met the squire out shooting and invited him to take pot luck with them, they sat down to succulent beef-steaks with oyster sauce. Even Sir William had confessed it was very pleasant to be able to relax in one's stockinged feet occasionally.

The good weather held into their second week, allowing Russ and Gerald to ride out regularly, but no matter how hard he rode or how tired he might be, Russ was aware of a simmering disquiet and a wish to see Molly Morgan. She was on his mind constantly, and when, late one afternoon, he and Gerald returned from a long day's riding and they glimpsed a figure moving past the drawing-room window, his pulse leapt.

'Now, who the devil can that be?' muttered Gerald.

With no women servants in the house it must be a visitor and Russ thought, *hoped*, it might be Molly. He quickened his stride, preceding Gerald indoors and making his way directly to the drawing room. He threw open the door, but it was not Molly standing before the fire in the sprigged muslin gown. This visitor was much younger than Molly, and instead of a mass of unruly dark locks, she had honey-gold curls that cascaded down from

a topknot and framed a lively countenance enhanced by a pair of mischievous brown eyes.

'So you are back at last,' she said in her pretty,
musical voice. 'I thought you would *never* come!'

Russ heard the door close behind him and found
Gerald standing at his side, an enquiring lift to his
brows.

'Gerald' he said, fighting to keep his voice level,
'let me introduce you to Miss Serena Russington.
My half-sister.'

She clutched her hands before her and fixed those
large, imploring eyes upon her host. 'I hope you
do not mind my calling unannounced, Sir Gerald,
but I had no choice. I am quite, quite desperate!'

'Are you, by Jove?' Gerald looked at Russ. 'Perhaps I should leave you two alone.'

'No, no need for that,' said Russ, keeping his
eyes on Serena. 'Perhaps, my girl, you will tell us
just why you are here and where is your chaperon?
And your carriage? I did not see one in the stables.'

'I am alone and I took the mail to Compton
Magna and then a very kind farmer took me up
and dropped me at your gates.' She drew a breath.
'I have run away.'

For the first time Russ became aware of the two
bandboxes beside the sofa.

'The devil you have!' Before he could say more, Gerald announced that such a situation required some refreshment and he lounged out of the room. Russ looked at his half-sister with brooding suspicion. 'Do you mean to tell me you have travelled the length of England to reach me?'

'No, no, of course not.' She sank down into a chair. 'I left the Tonbridge seminary two months ago, because they said I was unteachable.' She threw him a look of mild reproach. 'You are joint trustee for my affairs, Russ, so Henry must have written and told you of it all.'

'Perhaps his letter went astray,' he suggested, cravenly putting the blame for his ignorance upon his brother.

'Fustian. You ignore him, as I do, as much as I can,' she replied frankly. 'Well, Henry collected me from Tonbridge and took me directly to Mrs Wetherby's academy, which is near Harrogate. And I have *tried* to be good and to settle in, Russ, but it is impossible. They are so very severe.'

'Possibly that is why my brother chose it.'

'That and the fact that it is so far north he knew it would be impossible for me to get home. It is like a convent, Russ. Everyone is so serious and the teachers are so strict with me, I am not enjoying it one little bit. They will not allow us to go out of the building unattended.'

'Clearly you have managed it, however.'

Her eyes twinkled. 'I knotted the bedsheets and climbed out the window at midnight! I had to get away, Russ. I am nearly seventeen and far too old for school now. I promise you, I was at my wits' end to know what to do. Then I saw the report in the society pages of the local paper, saying that Sir Gerald had purchased Newlands and was in residence there with a party of friends, including— now, how had they worded it?—*several prominent bachelors*! Well, knowing you are Sir Gerald's best friend *and* the most prominent bachelor in London, I guessed you would be here, so I caught the night mail, determined to throw myself on your mercy.' She smiled, but then gave a sigh. 'I did write to Henry and suggest I might live at home with him and Dorothea until I am presented, but his reply said that was not possible. It is Dorothea's doing, of course. She does not want me to live with the family.'

Russ thought this very likely. The last time he had seen his two nieces, they were promising to take after their mother—short, plump and affected.

There was no doubt they would be very much cast into the shade by Serena with her glowing vivacity.

'What do you expect me to do about it?' he asked at last.

'Since you are also my guardian, you can write to the school and tell them I am not coming back. Then, I thought, perhaps, you might talk to Henry, explain how desperately unhappy I was. Perhaps he could find some lady for me to live with until my come out. I shall be very good, I promise you, if only I am not confined in a school with lots of silly, giggling girls.'

He laughed at that. 'I wish I might believe you, Serena.'

Gerald returned, carrying a tray full of decanters and glasses and, with his half-sister's permission, Russ explained the situation to him.

'I will write to Henry about it, I give you my word, Serena,' he concluded. 'But for now I see no option other than you to return to the school.'

She turned her soulful gaze upon Gerald as he handed her a very small glass of ratafia.

'You would not force me to go back to such a place, would you, Sir Gerald?'

'Well—' he glanced at Russ '—it might be necessary for you to return. Just for a short time, until other arrangements can be made.'

'May I not stay here?'

'Impossible,' said Russ immediately. 'It would be most improper. There are no other females in the house.'

'But you are my brother.'

'Half-brother,' he corrected her. 'And *my* reputation would do nothing to improve the situation!'

The dark eyes widened. 'Then what shall do? I made sure you would not turn me away, and it is almost night.' She heaved a sigh. 'P-perhaps you will escort me to the local inn.'

'Can't do that,' said Gerald, shaking his head. 'Tomorrow is market day. All the local hostelries will be as full as they can hold. And not with the sort of people one would want mixing with one's sister.'

'That's true.' Russ pushed his fingers through his hair. 'I will have to take you back to Compton Magna. We should be able to find accommodation for you at the White Hart, and I will pay for a chambermaid to sleep in your room tonight.'

'But that is a good ten miles away,' cried Serena. 'You would not abandon me there, would you?'

'Of course not. I shall remain there, too.'

Serena gave a small sniff and he ground his teeth.

'What else do you expect me to do with you? I am aware it is not ideal, but it is the best I can think of, so late in the day.'

Sir Gerald cleared his throat. 'I think I know someone who might help.' He glanced at Russ. 'I am sure the vicar and his sister would take Miss Russington in for the night.'

Serena wrinkled her nose. 'That sounds very dull, but I suppose for one night it would do no harm.'

Russ wanted to say no. He did not want to go cap in hand to Molly and ask for her help.

'Frayne would never turn away anyone in need,' Gerald went on. 'But if you *are* going, Russ, I should send for the gig now. Any later and they will be sitting down to dinner.'

Whatever Molly had been expecting, it was not this. Russ was in the drawing room, standing before the empty fireplace, and hanging on his arm was the most ravishing young lady she had ever seen. A searing pain, almost physical, ran through Molly, but before she could fully recognise it, her emotions were thrown into further turmoil when Edwin introduced the beauty as Russ's half-sister.

'Miss Russington arrived at Newlands, fully expecting Agnes to be there to receive her,' he explained.

Molly regarded the visitors in uncomprehending silence for some time after Edwin had finished. Russ cleared his throat.

'I understand what an imposition it is, Mrs Morgan, and if there was any other solution, I assure you I would not ask this of you.'

Molly's confusion was lifting. She knew full well that if there had been any choice, Russ would not have come here, but she could not deny that his sister's plight tugged at her heart. Whatever her differences with Beau Russington, his sister was not responsible and must be put at ease. She summoned all her inner strength to focus on her role as the vicar's sister.

'Oh, dear, how very unfortunate for you.' She smiled warmly at Serena. 'I assure you it is no trouble at all to have you stay here. If Edwin has not given instructions for the guest room to be prepared, then I shall do that immediately. And perhaps you would like to come up to my room? You may take off your pelisse and bonnet and we may both tidy ourselves before dinner.' She directed her polite society smile towards Russ. 'I hope you mean to stay and dine with us, too, Mr Russington?'

'If I may, yes. Thank you.'

Was it a trick of the candlelight, or did some of the darkness leave his eyes?

'Capital!' Edwin cast his beaming smile over them all and rubbed his hands together. 'Very well then, Molly, if you would like to take our guest upstairs, I will find a bottle of claret for Russ and I to enjoy while we wait for you!'

Serena was chattering away quite happily by the time they reached Molly's bedchamber. She had decided they must be on first-name terms and she lost no time telling Molly about her flight from the school. Molly did not comment, but she could quite understand that a strict regime would be very galling to such a lively girl on the verge of womanhood.

'It is very good of you to take me in,' said Serena, throwing her powder-blue pelisse and matching bonnet carelessly over a chair. 'Russ was quite at a loss to know what to do with me.'

'I am sure he was,' Molly murmured. 'But you

say he plans to drive you back to Harrogate in the morning. Will you not be tempted to run away again?'

'Oh, I am sure I shall, but he has promised me he will write to Henry—Lord Hambridge, our older brother,' she explained, seeing Molly's puzzled frown. 'It is Henry and his wife, Dorothea, who have had the ordering of my education. Russ has never bothered himself with me, but he is also my guardian, and I think it is time he stirred himself to do something, do not you?'

'Are you an orphan, then?' asked Molly, ignoring the question.

'Not exactly. Mama left when I was eight years old.'

'Oh, you poor child!'

Serena gave a little shrug. 'I barely knew her, so it made little difference. She only married Papa for his money. He quite doted on her, I believe, and was forever buying her presents. When Papa died, poor Henry found his inheritance sadly depleted. Mama ran off and married a rich Italian count almost as soon as she was widowed, so it is very likely that they were already lovers, do you not think?'

Molly was shocked at this matter-of-fact recital

of Serena's history, but her murmurs of sympathy were waved aside.

'I am not supposed to know any of this, but between the servants' gossip, what Henry could be persuaded to tell me and the reports in the scandal sheets, I was able to discover almost everything.' She accepted Molly's invitation to sit down at the dressing table and brush her curls, but the revelations were clearly uppermost in her mind for she said as she stared at her reflection, 'Mama was very beautiful and I am said to be her image. I suppose that is why Russ was so reluctant to allow me to stay at Newlands tonight. He told me it was because his reputation is so bad, but I think he is afraid for *my* reputation. He thinks people will say I am too much like my mother.'

Molly was silent, imagining the hurt the children must have felt, to be abandoned whilst still grieving for their father. Serena reached out and caught her hands.

'Now I have made you unhappy,' she said. 'Please do not be sad for me, Molly. I do not feel it now, I assure you. And I am very glad that Russ brought me here, because I think we are going to be very good friends!'

Privately Molly thought that one would always

feel such a loss, but she merely smiled and said that as soon as she had changed her gown they would go down and join the gentlemen.

'May I help you?' offered Serena. 'It will save you waiting for your maid and I am in the habit of helping the other girls at the academy to dress.' Her eyes twinkled. 'It is one of the better rules of the establishment, that no matter how wealthy the family, ladies should always know how to help themselves!'

Molly accepted this gesture of friendship. She was herself naturally reserved and since moving to Compton Parva had made no close friends, so it felt a little odd to have a young and lively companion in her room. Odd but not unpleasant, she thought, smiling to herself.

'Now, what are you going to wear?' Serena threw open the doors of the linen press.

Molly stepped up beside her and looked at gowns neatly piled on the shelves. For the first time she noticed how dreary they looked, dominated by shades of black, grey and lavender.

'My dear Molly, I thought you had been a widow for years.'

'Six years, to be precise.'

'And you are still wearing these dull colours?'

Serena regarded her in wide-eyed awe. 'You must have loved your husband very much.'

'I have some colours,' said Molly, ignoring her remark. 'Look on the top shelf. There is my yellow dimity and a sage-green muslin.'

Serena's snort in response was derisory. 'The dimity is too faded to be of any use and even the muslin is almost grey—I have no doubt you look positively haggard in it! Do you have nothing else?'

'No. That is, there are a few gowns in the bottom drawer of the chest, but I have not worn them since...' Her voice faded.

Since my wedding.

Serena was already opening the drawer and pulling out gowns that had not seen the light of day since Molly had put them in there when she moved in, five years ago. Three colourful silk gowns purchased as bride clothes and rarely worn. Molly watched Serena spreading the gowns over the bed and she waited for the painful memories to flood in, but there was nothing more than a little sadness, which was soon dispelled by Serena's unflagging cheerfulness. Serena lifted an apricot silk and declared that was what Molly should wear to dinner.

'It is not in the latest style, but no one will care for that,' said Serena, shaking out the gown and holding it up against Molly. 'It compliments your colouring perfectly.'

Molly laughed, suddenly feeling much more frivolous and carefree. 'Very well, just for you I shall wear it! And perhaps my coral beads instead of the pearls.'

'Perfect,' Serena declared. 'After all, this is an informal dinner for friends and there are only the four of us. Now, if you will tell me where you keep the coral beads, I shall fetch them for you.'

Molly was throwing the apricot gown over her head as she answered, 'In the box that sits in the top drawer.'

Too late did she remember what else was in that drawer. She flew across, just as Serena was lifting out a man's handkerchief, laundered and pressed with the embroidered monogram clearly displayed.

'Yes, the box is there, in the corner,' she said, whipping the handkerchief from Serena's hand. 'Do not bother about this. It…it is an old kerchief of my brother's that I keep forgetting to give back to him.' With a laugh she buried it deep beneath the combs, pouches and other mementos and shut the drawer. Nothing more was said and Molly could only hope Serena had not recognised that it was Russ's initials embroidered on the linen square and not Edwin's.

Having assured Edwin that there was no need to send a note to Newlands, that Gerald would not be expecting him to return until after dinner, Russ settled down with his host to await the ladies. The wine was very good and the vicar cheerful company, but he could not be at ease until he saw Molly again. True, she had issued the invitation for him to stay for dinner, but after their last meeting was she really prepared to sit down at table with him? After what had been said—after what he had said to her—how could they converse naturally? He shifted in his chair. Confound it, there was something about the woman that brought out the worst in him!

'I am sure they will not be much longer,' said Edwin, mistaking his sudden frown for impatience. 'I have no doubt that they are chattering away and have forgotten the time. But I am glad of it,' he continued, refilling their glasses. 'Molly takes life far too seriously. She was such a lively child. Fearless, headstrong, even, but she married very young, you see.'

He broke off, his cheerful countenance momentarily shadowed, but his smile returned as the door opened and the ladies came in, arm in arm.

Molly was laughing at something Serena had said and Russ felt the breath catch in his chest. He thought she had never looked better, the creamy tones of her skin enhanced by the warm colour of her silk gown, and for an instant he caught a flash of the spirited, carefree girl she must have once been. Then it was gone. Molly was still smiling, but she had withdrawn a little and he was sorry for it.

During dinner Russ put himself out to please, exerting all his charm as he attempted to draw Molly into the conversation. Serena's natural vivacity was an advantage, for there were no awkward silences to be filled and he thought, by the time the ladies withdrew, that Molly was looking a little more at ease. She even met his eyes for one brief, shyly smiling moment.

The ladies were waiting for them when they returned to the drawing room but Russ noticed immediately that Serena was looking tired. Hardly surprising, he thought wryly, if she had been awake since midnight. He politely declined Edwin's invitation to remain until the tea tray was brought in.

'My sister needs her sleep,' he said, rising. 'I shall return in the morning to take her back to Harrogate.'

'Will we travel in your curricle, brother?'

He shook his head. 'Much as I am sure you would like to cut a dash, Serena, the weather does not look promising and I have no intention of being crushed under the hood with you and your bandboxes! Kilburn has already offered to lend us his *berline*.'

He had expected Serena to pout at the use of this rather staid vehicle, but she gave him a beaming smile.

'That is very good, because it means there will be room for Molly to come with us.'

Molly's exclamation and her look of shock convinced Russ that she had not been a party to this idea.

'You must not be selfish, Serena. We have already imposed enough upon Mrs Morgan. We cannot expect her to give up the whole of tomorrow for you.'

His sister gave a loud and heartfelt sigh, worthy of Mrs Siddons.

'Just the thought of going back to that place fills me with dread.' She turned her soulful gaze upon Molly. 'Oh, pray, ma'am, do say you will come along to support me in my interview with Mrs Wetherby. She is sure to be very angry with me and my nerves will be in shreds before we have gone half the distance if I do not have you to sustain me.'

Russ's lips twitched at this masterly performance, but he said gravely. 'And is my presence not sustaining enough, Serena?'

'But you are not a woman,' she replied, with unarguable logic. 'Molly is the nearest thing I have for a friend in the whole world, and besides that, she is eminently respectable, which is sure to impress Mrs Wetherby much more than if I turn up with only my rakish brother for escort.'

Russ was at a loss how to answer this. Edwin had broken into a fit of coughing, no doubt to cover his laughter, but Molly was looking distressed and he could not bear that.

'I am not interested in impressing Mrs Wetherby,' he retorted. 'I have no doubt Henry and I pay the woman an extortionate sum for your place at her academy, so she will do as she is bid!'

'Yes, I am sure she will, while you are present,

but once you are gone I shall be at her mercy and subject to a thousand petty tyrannies.'

Russ was unimpressed, but Edwin was clearly moved as Serena began to hunt for her handkerchief.

'Perhaps there is some truth in that, Russington,' he said. 'Take Molly with you. She is accustomed to dealing with such matters in the parish and she may well be able to smooth things over with this Mrs Wetherby. Well, my love, what do you say? *Have* you any engagements tomorrow that cannot be rearranged?'

'It is too much of an imposition,' Russ objected. 'Mrs Morgan is not even related to Serena.'

'With Mama living in Italy my only other female relative is Henry's wife, Dorothea, and she is hundreds of miles to the south.' Serena gave a little sniff. 'Not that she has ever liked me. I am quite, quite friendless.'

Molly watched, listened, knew it was a performance, of sorts, but still she did not hesitate.

She said, 'That is not true, Serena. Of course, I will accompany you, if you think it might help.'

Serena's woeful looks vanished immediately, replaced by a beaming smile. She flew across the room to embrace Molly, words of gratitude tumbling from her lips. It was some moments before she could be persuaded to sit down, but then Molly was able to observe the gentlemen's reactions. Edwin nodded at her, sure she was doing the right thing, but Russ was staring at her with dark, troubled eyes.

'No, we cannot ask that of you, ma'am.'

'I do not see why not,' argued Serena. 'Molly has offered to come with me and, as Mr Frayne says, she has some experience in these matters, which you most certainly do not, brother.'

'I am perfectly capable of dealing with an elderly schoolmistress,' he retorted, bridling.

'I am sure you are, sir.'

Molly knew her cynical agreement would not help matters, but the words were out before she could stop them. There was more than a suggestion of clenched teeth as Russ went on.

'And it would hardly be fitting for Mrs Morgan to travel back alone with me in a closed carriage.'

'No, indeed, Mr Russington.' She met his angry glare with a glittering smile. 'You would be obliged to ride on the box!'

'Oh, I am sure Russ would have no objection to

doing that,' remarked Edwin, blissfully unaware of the tension behind this interchange.

'Then it is settled,' declared Serena, getting up. She walked across to kiss her brother's cheek. 'Thank you, dear Russ, I promise you I shall be ready to travel at whatever hour you choose in the morning and so will Molly!'

Molly stretched her lips into a smile but said nothing, wondering how she would survive a whole day in the beau's company.

Sir Gerald's elegant *berline* came to a halt before the vicarage, the horses snorting and tossing their heads as if impatient to be moving again.

'Good heavens, what an impressive equipage,' declared Serena, peering out of the morning-room window. 'We shall be travelling in style today!'

'Then let us not keep the horses standing longer than necessary,' replied Molly, shepherding her charge to the door.

Russ was already coming up the path to meet them as they stepped out of the house. He handed Serena into the carriage, then held his hand out to Molly.

'It is very good of you to give up your day for

my sister.' He lowered his voice, 'I am very grateful, when you have every reason to hate me.'

'I do not hate you,' she replied, not meeting his eyes.

He turned so that his back was to the carriage, his words for Molly alone.

'What, not even for that kiss?'

Even without looking at him, she knew he was smiling. She could imagine the teasing glint in his eyes and she felt the familiar fluttering inside. She said quietly, 'I believe I have given you even more reason to hate me, for what I said to you.'

'Then let us forget the past, if we may. I would like to think we could still be friends. Do you think that is possible?'

The weight on her spirits lifted, just a little. 'Perhaps.'

'Good. I am glad.' He stepped aside, allowing her to enter the carriage before jumping in.

They were away, the glossy black horses proving they were more than just a good-looking team as they bowled out of the town and away towards Harrogate. Molly had chosen to sit beside Serena, but now she wondered if that was wise, because she was facing Russ and her wayward eyes wanted to rest upon him, to take in the elegance of his blue coat and white waistcoat, the intricately tied cravat with a diamond winking from its folds, and if she allowed her gaze to drop then she could not avoid seeing his powerful thighs encased in tight-fitting pantaloons.

One glance had been enough to take everything in and it was imprinted in her mind, from the thick, glossy black curls on his head to the highly polished Hessians on his feet, he was every inch the fashionable gentleman. There was nothing for it but to keep silent and feign an interest in what was passing outside the window, although they had not yet left Compton Parva and she was familiar with every building.

Serena knew no such reserve. She declared that her brother was looking as fine as fivepence.

'And what do you think of Molly's walking dress?' she went on. 'I helped her decide upon it this morning because we need her to look as dull and respectable as possible, and I vow she looks so severe I am quite afraid of her.'

'I do not believe you are afraid of anyone,' Molly retorted.

'You are right.' Russ grinned. 'My sister may be a minx, but I have never doubted her spirit. And Serena is quite wrong about your gown, it does not look dull at all. That shade of charcoal grey suits you. I have never seen you look better.'

The unexpected remark drove the heat into Molly's cheeks, but Serena appeared delighted with it.

'Good heavens, do not listen to him, Molly. He will turn your head with his compliments.'

Molly laughed. 'I cut my eye teeth long ago and I am no longer susceptible to compliments from rakes such as your brother.' She clapped her hands to her mouth. 'Oh, dear, I beg your pardon. I should not have called you that.'

'Not in front of my little sister, perhaps, but friends should be able to say what they wish to one another, should they not?'

His smile reassured Molly, but she upbraided herself for speaking so freely and she lapsed into silence, resolving to guard her tongue in future when dealing with Beau Russington.

They rattled on, making good time, but Molly noticed that Serena grew quieter as they approached Harrogate.

'I recognise this part of the road.' Serena peered anxiously out of the window. 'We will soon be at the school.'

Russ reached across and touched her hand. 'Don't sound so worried, brat, I will not let her eat you.'

'No, of course, she won't, not with my handsome big brother to protect me,' replied Serena, clearly trying to throw off her nerves. 'And looking every inch a London gentleman.'

'I want to make a favourable impression upon Mrs Wetherby. That is very important, if we are to persuade the woman to take you back.'

His words crystallised the thoughts that had been whirling around in Molly's head for the past half hour. She would be making the return journey alone with Russ. True, it had been agreed that he would ride up top with the coachman, but would he? Would she be strong enough to insist upon it?

You must be strong, Molly. A lot more than your reputation will be at risk if you spend two hours alone in a closed carriage with him.

'We must do our best to persuade Mrs Wetherby to give you a second chance, Serena,' said Russ. 'I have no doubt Mrs Morgan will agree with me on that point.'

Thus addressed, Molly had no option but to look at him, but that was a mistake because he was smiling at her and all her resolutions melted away before the warm look in his eyes. Suddenly there was nothing she wanted more than to be alone with him. Serena's voice broke into her thoughts.

'She would have to be made of stone not to be impressed by you, Russ. Is that not so, Molly?' Serena giggled. 'But then, I have always thought of Mrs Wetherby as a gorgon.'

'A gorgon turns other people to stone,' said Molly, pushing her own concerns to one side. 'I hope very much that isn't the case today!'

The carriage was slowing to negotiate the narrow gateway to Mrs Wetherby's Academy for Young Ladies. Russ sat forward and studied the house with narrowed eyes.

'Well, we are here, Serena. We had best get this over.'

'I have no doubt she will scold me royally.'

'Then you must prepare yourself to be suitably chastened.' Almost before the carriage had stopped he jumped out and let down the steps. 'Come along, ladies.'

They were admitted by a maidservant and shown into a small waiting room while Mrs Wetherby was apprised of their arrival. Russ stood with his hands behind his back, looking out of the window and the two ladies perched on the edge of a very hard and underpadded sofa. The silence stretched on for several minutes, marked by the steady tick, tick of the longcase clock in the corner, before footsteps could be heard and the maid returned to announce that Mrs Wetherby would see them in her office. As they followed the maid out of the room Serena slipped her hand into Molly's.

'I am very glad you are here to help me face the gorgon,' she whispered.

Chapter Nine

'Well,' said Serena, settling herself comfortably on her seat. 'That was not at all what I expected, although I cannot say I am sorry.'

They were all three of them in the *berline* again and on their way back to Compton Parva. Russ leaned back against the squabs, his anger draining away. He had not expected to lose his temper. He had politely explained everything to Mrs Wetherby, who had given instructions for Serena's bandboxes to be returned to her room. She had then invited them all to sit down in her office to discuss the matter and Russ had thought the situation was well in hand. Serena had been suitably, nay, admirably repentant and had kept silent with her eyes lowered while the schoolmistress rang a peal over her.

It was not unexpected and Russ listened, if not

with pleasure, then at least with equanimity to the woman's homily. After all, Serena had acted outrageously in running away from the school. He accepted the schoolmistress's recriminations and held his irritation in check, even when she turned her wrath upon him, condemning his morals and his lifestyle before reproaching both him and Lord Hambridge for allowing their young sister to become wild beyond control. Mrs Wetherby had been angry, impolite and even offensive, but still he had said nothing.

Serena was regarding him now with something bordering on awe.

'You demolished her in a most masterly fashion, brother. I thought she was going to burst into tears when you said she lacked both the good manners and the intelligence to teach young ladies of refinement. I wish you had not sent me off at that point to pack my things and order my trunks to be taken back to the carriage, for I should dearly love to have heard what else you said to the gorgon.'

'It was wrong of me to have said half so much,' he said curtly, 'but when she turned upon Molly in that fashion I could not remain silent.'

It was the sight of Molly, white-faced and trembling, that had broken the hold on his temper. She had merely suggested to Mrs Wetherby in her quiet, diffident way, that perhaps the school's excessive restrictions might be expected to rouse rebellion in a lively sixteen-year-old and that had drawn the woman's ire. She had launched a blistering attack upon Molly, culminating in thinly veiled aspersions upon the widow's status and respectability.

'No, I could see that put you in a rage,' said Serena, cheerfully. 'But I am very glad that it did, for you left her in no doubt that I shall not be returning to her horrid school.'

He scowled at her. '*You* may be glad, brat, but it has left me in the devil of a fix. I shall have to hire some respectable female to keep you company until I can take you to Henry and Dorothea.'

'Who will immediately look for another horrid school for me!'

'You cannot know that. They might keep you with them until your come-out in the spring.'

'Ha, Dorothea will not allow that. She has never liked me.'

'Nonsense.' Russ uttered the denial without much conviction.

'And although she has agreed to take me to London for my come-out,' Serena went on, eyes sparkling and her cheeks flaming with indignation, 'I have no doubt she will want to marry me off as soon as maybe, to the first man who comes along!'

'Now, on that point you are very far out, my girl, because Henry and I would not agree to it.'

'If I might make a suggestion?' Molly's quiet voice interrupted their heated altercation. Russ and Serena both turned to look at her. 'Edwin thought that something like this might arise. That is, that Mrs Wetherby might refuse to take Serena back into the school. He mentioned it to me last night and suggested that, perhaps, Serena might stay with us at the vicarage until Miss Kilburn returns to Newlands at the end of next week. That would give you time to write to your brother, Mr Russington, and make more permanent arrangements.'

'Oh, yes.' Serena clapped her hands. 'That would be an excellent solution.'

'No, it would not. We could not impose upon Mrs Morgan and her brother in that way.'

'I should be delighted to have Serena's company.'

'But you are very busy with your committees and your...charities.'

Molly's chin went up. 'I take it you are referring to Prospect House.'

'Of course.'

'Prospect House?' Serena's interest was caught. 'Oh, what is that?'

'A scheme of Mrs Morgan's. A home for females who have…er…fallen on hard times.'

'It is a refuge,' explained Molly, 'And although it was my idea, it could not succeed without the approval of the townspeople. There is also Prospect Farm, which the women run to support themselves.' She looked back at Russ. 'I went there yesterday and can easily miss my visit next week.'

'No, no, why should you do that?' cried Serena, looking from one to the other. 'It sounds fascinating. I could come with you. I should like to help.'

Russ was frowning, but Molly was thankful he did not speak. She knew Serena well enough by now to guess that a direct order for her to stay away would only pique the girl's interest in Prospect House. She must reply cheerfully and make little of it.

'No, no, that will not be necessary,' she said. 'There will be a few household tasks that require my attention, but I thought I might take a little holiday from parish matters while you are with me.'

'Oh, yes, indeed, what a capital idea. We could go riding and Russ can escort us.'

'Before you make plans that involve us all, Serena, please bear in mind that your presence here is unexpected and dashed inconvenient.'

Serena did not appear at all cast down by her brother's curt reprimand.

'I do bear it in mind and if you and Sir Gerald have already made arrangements, then I do not expect you to change them for me. Although it does make me even more grateful to Molly and Mr Frayne, who are putting themselves to such inconvenience for a total stranger.'

'If you are trying to make me feel guilty, Serena, you won't do it,' Russ growled. 'My withers are not wrung in the slightest.'

Serena pouted and Molly said quickly, 'I am sure there will be plenty of opportunity for you to ride once Miss Kilburn returns to Newlands.' She added, with a laugh, 'And your brother will tell you that my pony is such a slug, you would be forever waiting for us to catch up.'

'Ah, well.' Serena sighed, then she tucked her arm in Molly's, saying cheerfully, 'I am sure you and I will find a host of other things to do. And I shall make an especial effort to behave!'

Russ gave a crack of laughter. 'Then heaven help you, Mrs Morgan!'

* * *

Although Molly said nothing to either Russ or Edwin, she was anxious about how she was going to keep such a lively young lady entertained for a week. However, she need not have worried. Serena threw herself into life at the vicarage with cheerful energy. She was as happy sorting the linen cupboard as she was accompanying Molly to the shops in Compton Parva or gathering fruit from the kitchen garden. She even volunteered to help Molly with the Sunday school, as she informed her brother after the morning service.

'...so you may be easy, Russ. Molly is keeping me very busy and out of mischief.'

'I am glad to hear it.'

'And you must not be cross with Molly, brother, but I now know much more about Prospect House.' She waved a hand towards the line of veiled figures making their way out of the church. 'We met them on their way in, so Molly had no choice but to introduce me. They are all very agreeable and I mean to visit, although Molly explained about why they are living there and I quite see why they say it will not do for them to call upon *me*. But, Russ, Nancy—she is their cook, you know, even though she is a *lady* and the most delightful creature!—Nancy tells me that one of their number, Marjorie, is at home with her new baby, whom I long to see. And even more than that, they have a puppy, whom they are training to guard them all! And Molly has agreed to take me with her when she goes there on Tuesday.'

Molly added quickly, 'Only if your brother does not object.'

He shrugged. 'It was inevitable that Serena would hear more about the refuge from someone. Perhaps it is best that she has learned of it from you.'

'Then I may go, Russ?'

'Yes, as long as Mrs Morgan thinks you can be of use to her.'

Molly was relieved that he was not angry, but the glinting smile in his eyes brought the colour rising to her cheeks. She was annoyed at her own weakness and murmured an excuse to move away towards the little party preparing to walk back to Prospect House.

Nancy greeted her in typically blunt fashion. 'Do you think it was wise to take in Beau Russington's sister, Molly?'

'It was Edwin's suggestion.' Molly bit her lip. 'Besides, where else could she go?'

'Her brother might have hired a companion for her. Or there are several mothers in Compton Parva with daughters of that age who might have obliged him.'

'But all that takes time, and as for other families, Serena knows none of them.' Molly smiled. 'Truly, I am enjoying her company.'

'She is very engaging, I grant you, but it is bound to bring you into company with her rakish brother, which cannot be what you want. Or is it?'

Under Nancy's scrutiny Molly felt her colour rising even more. She said slowly, 'I do not believe he is as black as he is painted.'

'Oh, good heavens. Do not tell me you are developing a tendress for the man!'

'Of course not.' She tried to laugh it off. 'I merely wish to be just.'

'Is that why you have stopped lecturing Fleur about her friendship with Sir Gerald?'

Molly followed Nancy's eyes to where the couple were standing a little way apart, deep in conversation. She sighed.

'Fleur says she knows nothing can come of it.'

'Perhaps not.'

Nancy's thoughtful gaze moved to Russ. Serena was still chattering to him, but his eyes were fixed on Molly, who held her breath. She was waiting for the inevitable comment, but Nancy surprised her.

'It is time I gathered up my flock and took them back to the house. Shall we see you as usual next week, Molly? Good. Until Tuesday, then.'

With that Nancy was gone, sweeping Fleur up as she passed. With something between a sigh and a smile Molly turned away. She beckoned to Serena, who parted from her brother and ran over to join her.

'The local children will be arriving soon for their Sunday lessons,' Molly told her. 'We must prepare the little room set aside for them. Mrs Birch, who usually runs the class, is gone to stay with her daughter, so your help is much appreciated today.'

'Well, I do hope I am being useful,' said Serena seriously. 'I had no idea there was so much to be done in a parish, what with organising relief for the poor, raising funds for the widows and orphans and paying charity visits. We have not had a spare moment!'

Molly smiled. She was deliberately working Serena hard, not only to keep her from boredom, but also to show her a little of the world outside her normal sphere. She would not allow Serena to go into houses where there was sickness, but they had taken baskets of food to several needy families and even called upon a newly bereaved widow with a parcel of mourning clothes, including two gowns that Serena had persuaded Molly to give away.

'You wear far too much black and can well afford to part with some of them,' Serena had told her. 'All those dark gowns make you look so *dull*, Molly, and I know full well that you are not in the least dull!'

Molly laughed at that. 'It is impossible to be so in your company!'

It was true. Molly was enjoying herself much more than she would have guessed. Russ called almost every day to enquire after his sister and sometimes stayed to take tea with them. On these occasions Molly's attempts to keep in the background were thwarted by Serena, who included her in every conversation. Russ was unfailingly polite, but Molly felt tongue-tied and shy in his company, knowing how drab and colourless she must seem compared to Serena's vivacity and youth.

That thought returned to Molly when she and Serena were in Hebden's the following day. Serena was making polite conversation with Lady Currick, to whom she had been introduced at All

Souls on Sunday, and Molly moved across to take a closer look at the roll of deep red lustring lying at one end of the counter.

'Is it not beautiful?' commented Miss Hebden, coming over. 'I took delivery of it only this morning. Just look at the way it shines when you move it. 'Tis just the colour I imagine the finest rubies would be.'

'And it would look very well on Molly,' put in Serena. 'Do you not agree, Lady Currick? What a fine gown it would make for her!'

'It would indeed.' Lady Currick moved closer. 'And I have seen the perfect design for it in my latest ladies' magazine. An evening gown. Nothing too fancy, but suitable for dining and dancing. As soon as I get home I shall look it out for you, Molly.'

'And if you want the lustring, Mrs Morgan, you shall have it on account,' said Miss Hebden eagerly. 'I can have a length packed up and sent over to you in a trice.'

Serena clutched her arm. 'Oh, yes, do have it, Molly. I should so love to see you dressed in such a colour.'

'As would all her friends,' Lady Currick agreed.

Molly looked at the smiling faces around her and gave a nervous little laugh.

'I feel you are all conspiring in this.' She looked back at the material. 'It *is* lovely...'

'Then if Lady Currick will send me the illustration I will work out how much material you will need and send it all over by the end of the day, complete with ribbons, buttons and thread.' Miss Hebden beamed at her. 'How would that be, Mrs Morgan?'

'Perfect!' said Lady Currick. 'And you can take everything to that clever little seamstress at Prospect House to have it made up for you.'

'No, no, I must not. I need to think about this.'

'You do not,' Serena told her. 'Your friends have thought about it for you. All you have to do is to agree!'

Molly was still unsure the following day when she and Serena set out for Prospect House, the precious parcel resting at their feet.

'It is such an imposition,' she declared, neatly turning the gig on to the drive. 'Everyone here is so busy that I do not like to ask them for such a favour.'

'Well, you have already told me you will pay for

the sewing, so it is not as if you want the gown made up for free,' Serena reasoned. 'And you do not need to ask, for I shall do it for you!'

Any plans Molly had for working that morning were thwarted as soon as Serena explained about the material. Fleur and Nancy immediately called for Marjorie to join them in the morning room, where Molly laughingly submitted to being measured, pinned and prodded while the ladies discussed how quickly the gown could be made up.

'My brother and Sir Gerald are coming to the vicarage for dinner on Thursday night,' Serena told them. 'It would be above anything great if Molly could wear her new gown.'

Molly's protests against such haste were silenced by Fleur.

'Of course, we shall do it,' she said. 'Both housemaids can sew a fine seam now. I shall help, too, and Marjorie shall direct us all.'

'And you are not to be worrying about the baby,' added Marjorie, anticipating Molly's next argument. 'Once I have fed her, Nancy and Daisy can watch her for me.'

'But it is market day tomorrow.' Molly made one final bid to dissuade them. 'Who will take the goods to market if you are all working on my gown?'

Nancy put her hands on her hips and looked at her. 'Heavens, Molly Morgan, do you think we are capable of doing only one thing at a time? We shall manage, especially with you and Miss Serena here to help us today. Come along, ladies, let us get to work!'

'Well, are you glad we persuaded you?'

Serena gave Molly's skirts a final twitch and turned her to face the looking glass. The ruby-red silk glowed in the candlelight and hung in fine folds from the high waist with just enough fullness in the skirts for them to swing out slightly over her hips. Short, puffed sleeves were finished with Vandyke cuffs, which were mirrored by the decoration around the waistline and the hem.

Molly's fingers traced the swirling embroidered pattern on the bodice, then her hand moved up to her bare neck. The square bodice was cut very low, just as it had been in the illustration.

'Perhaps I should add a muslin fichu,' she murmured.

'There is not the least need,' declared Serena, with all the conviction of one who knew about these things. 'The neckline shows off your fine skin, Molly, and once you have added your pearls you will look very elegant indeed. Are you sure you will not wear the cap, too?'

Molly glanced at the matching hat they had made for her, decorated with two curling feathers. She smiled. Did they think she was going to be attending grand balls and assemblies?

'Not tonight.'

'You are quite right,' agreed Serena. 'It would be de trop for a small dinner. Come along then, shall we go down?'

Russ did not need to look out of the window to follow the route his friend's carriage was taking that evening. He had come this way every day since Serena had been a guest at the vicarage and it was not only out of duty. He had wanted to see Molly. He was well aware she did her best to avoid him, but it did not matter that she kept in the background, not speaking unless it was necessary, he was aware of her with every fibre of his being. Not that anything could come of it. She had made it quite clear that she was afraid of him and he knew in his heart that he was not the man for her. She needed—deserved—someone who would live up to her high moral standards. Someone she could trust.

The carriage drew up at the gate and he followed Gerald to the door, reflecting that after tomorrow he would have no excuse to call again. Agnes would soon be back at Newlands and Serena would come there to stay, until he and his brother decided just what they were to do with her.

'Ah, gentlemen, come in, come in.'

Edwin Frayne came forward to greet them as they walked into the drawing room. Pleasantries were exchanged, but Russ's eyes went round the room, looking in vain for Molly.

'The girls are not yet come down,' said Edwin, ushering them towards the fire. 'They have been closeted together these two hours, prettying themselves for you! But that need not stop us enjoying a glass of wine together. Sit down, sirs, and I will serve you.'

The three gentlemen were well enough acquainted to talk freely on sporting matters until the sound of female voices from the hall heralded the arrival of the ladies. They all rose as the door opened. Serena and Molly came in together, but Russ lost sight of his sister, for it was Molly who held his attention.

He had never seen her look better. Her face was alight with laughter and the creamy whiteness of her skin was enhanced not only by her dark hair, but also by the deep red of her gown. The silk skirts whispered and flowed as she moved, the soft folds catching the candlelight and glowing jewel bright. Her hair was simply dressed with a few dusky curls framing her face and the rest piled high on her head, except for one glossy ringlet that rested on her shoulder. He imagined drawing her close and pulling out the pins to let those luxuriant dark locks tumble down her back. But it was not the red silk he wanted beneath his hands, it was her smooth naked skin.

'Well, brother, do you like Molly's new gown?'

Serena's voice brought the pleasant daydream crashing down. Not by the flicker of an eyelid would he allow his thoughts to show, but a polite smile was beyond him. All he could manage was a short reply, his voice devoid of emotion.

Molly had felt his eyes upon her when she came in, and she hoped he might say how well the colour suited her or approve the new way of dressing her hair.

'Mrs Morgan looks very well.'

'Very well? She looks perfectly splendid!' Sir Gerald came up to take her hand. 'Do come and sit down, ma'am. I was saying to your brother how kind it is of you to take pity upon us. I had not realised how dependent I had become upon luxury until I gave the staff their holiday.'

She responded, grateful for his jovial chatter, and accepted a glass of wine from Edwin, but she resolutely kept her eyes away from Russ.

'It could be worse,' she told herself, keeping her smile in place and pretending to listen to the conversation flowing around her. 'He might have offered you insincere compliments and paid you the sort of attentions you most abhor.'

But for all that she could not deny the stab of disappointment at his lack of interest.

Edwin was refilling the gentlemen's glasses and he said to Sir Gerald, 'Have you heard from Miss Kilburn?'

'Aye. I had a letter from her only today to say she is looking forward to returning to Newlands on Friday, which means that you, Serena, can come to us the following day. Mr and Mrs Sykes are returning, too, and Agnes tells me they have concocted some plan between them to hold a ball at

Newlands, so it is to be hoped all our staff do return to us!'

'A ball!' cried Serena, 'Oh, that will be beyond anything.'

Russ put up a hand to quell his sister's raptures. 'It will not be for several weeks, Serena, you may no longer be with us.'

'Oh, you would not be so cruel as to send me away beforehand!'

'Since I have not heard back from Henry nothing is yet settled.' His expression softened a little. 'And I suppose you would very likely run back here if I did send you away.'

'I should indeed! And, Sir Gerald, you will invite Molly and Edwin to the ball, won't you?'

'Of course, they are top of the list,' he replied. 'But we hope they will come to Newlands before that. Agnes expressly mentions you both in her letter and hopes you will be able to join us for dinner next week, on a day to suit you—no need to commit yourself now, Frayne, I know how busy you are with your parish matters. You may send back your reply with our coachman on Saturday, when he comes to collect Serena.'

'Oh, there is no need for that,' replied Edwin. 'We shall be only too pleased to deliver Miss Russington to you and we may confirm the engagement with Miss Kilburn in person.'

Russ laughed. 'I have no doubt you will be glad to see the back of my bothersome sister, eh, Frayne?'

'No, no, I wasn't…' Edwin trailed off, a telltale flush on his cheeks.

'Do not allow my *tiresome* brother to tease you, Mr Frayne,' Serena retorted. Putting her nose in the air, she pointedly turned away from Russ. 'And will all your servants be returned by then, Sir Gerald?'

'I sincerely hope so,' he declared. 'The housekeeper arrived back from Harrogate today and the rest should be here by the morning. Pleasant as it has been for Russ and me to have the place to ourselves, we shall be glad to have a full complement of staff again. And, of course, Miss Russington, I shall set them to work immediately to prepare a room for you.'

Serena thanked him prettily, adding, 'Although I shall be exceedingly sorry to leave Molly and Mr Frayne.'

'But it will be a relief to your brother,' remarked Molly, rising as the servant came in to announce dinner. 'Mr Russington will no longer be obliged to call here.'

* * *

There was no mistaking the sting in the words, but Russ had no opportunity to respond. Molly had taken Gerald's arm to go into dinner and he followed with Serena and Edwin, wondering what he might do to make amends. He had not intended to wound Molly, but his reaction to seeing her tonight had shocked him. When she had entered the room tonight, her eyes sparkling and a laugh trembling on her lips, his heart had soared, but then Serena had asked his opinion of the red gown and his only thought had been how quickly he could remove it. He had felt like a callow youth. Out of his depth, out of control.

For years now Russ had considered himself immune to female charms. There were few women for whom he had ever felt affection and he had been able to leave them with no more than a momentary pang of regret. He was damned if he knew what it was about little Molly Morgan, with her serious demeanour and her high morals, that had found the chink in his armour.

The answer came as he watched her presiding over her brother's dinner table. He liked her. He admired the quiet way she went about her duties as her brother's helper, her fierce dedication to protecting the women at Prospect House. Her honesty. He liked the little things about her, too. The way she pondered a serious question before answering, the way her face lit up when she laughed. In his opinion she should laugh a great deal more, which brought him full circle. He had hurt her tonight and he must make amends, if he could, before he left the vicarage that evening.

Russ curbed his impatience as Edwin refreshed the brandy glasses, but thankfully neither the vicar nor Sir Gerald were in roistering mood and it was less than an hour after dinner that they joined the ladies. Kilburn immediately crossed the room to where Serena was sitting at the piano and Russ watched them for a moment, aware of his duty as guardian, but Gerald was behaving very much as he did with his own sister.

Serena and Gerald were happily engaged at the pianoforte and the others settled down to listen to them. Molly moved to a seat beside the table in the corner, ostensibly to take advantage of the candle-light for her sewing, but Russ had seen her do this before, effacing herself in company, avoiding attention. Avoiding him.

With the fire blazing and curtains pulled against

the autumn night it was cosily warm in the little drawing room and soon Edwin was dozing in his chair. Russ went across to Molly. She looked a little wary at his approach, but her first words were not unfriendly. She glanced towards the pianoforte.

'Your sister and Sir Gerald perform well together.'

'Yes. I am pleased to see Serena has learned something at the various establishments she has attended.'

'She is a very accomplished young woman,' Molly replied. 'She also has the knack of putting strangers at their ease. I have noticed it during the past week, when she has come about the town with me.'

He nodded. 'She may be a minx, but she is an engaging one. As her guardians, Henry and I will need all our wits to keep her out of scrapes. Until she has a husband to take over that role.'

'There will be no shortage of admirers for such a lively young heiress.'

She glanced across the room again and he said, anticipating her question, 'Serena is too young to be forming an attachment for a few years yet.'

'She is sixteen,' said Molly. 'She is not too young to fall in love.'

Russ knew she was talking of her own experience. He wanted to ask her if she still loved the villain who had stolen her dreams, but he was afraid to know the answer. She bent her head once more over her sewing.

'And what of Sir Gerald?' she murmured. 'Has he any thoughts of settling down?'

'Good heavens, no. He is far too old for Serena. They get on very well, I think, because he treats her very much as he does his own sister.'

Russ paused. Gerald's ease of manner made him think of his own fractured family. The comparison did not please him.

He said suddenly, 'Henry and I have seen very little of Serena. It would have been better, perhaps, if we had spent more time together. Henry was one-and-twenty, and already married, by the time our mother died. Father married again within a twelvemonth and barely a year after that Serena was born.' His jaw tightened. 'I remember all too clearly Father bringing home his new bride. He was besotted and only too happy to indulge his new wife. They pursued a life of pleasure, splitting their time between London and visits to friends.'

'And did you go with them?'

'No. I was at school and saw them but rarely.

Henry set up his own establishment, and when Serena was born she was left to the care of servants.'

'That must have been a lonely time for you and your sister,' murmured Molly.

'Yes.'

It was the first time Russ had admitted it. Molly was still setting her stitches, not looking at him, and sitting here beside her, within the cosy glow of the candles, he felt more at ease than he had done for years.

'I never thought about it at the time, but Henry had a hopeful family, Father had his new wife, I was not necessary to anyone's happiness. Serena, I thought of not at all. My godmother died and left me her fortune, which meant I did not need to consider any career, other than a life of idleness and dissipation.

'My father died suddenly when I was twenty, by which time my habits were fixed. I was living in town, with sufficient fortune to enjoy myself.' He fell silent, looking back over the years, before continuing quietly, 'That was when my stepmother approached me. Having run through my father's fortune, she hoped to seduce me into sharing mine with her. When I rejected her advances, she ran off with her Italian lover.'

* * *

Molly's sewing lay unheeded on her lap as she listened to Russ calmly relating his history, but this last revelation was too much, even though she had heard something of it from Serena.

'That is very sad,' she said quietly. 'How could any mother abandon her children?'

He shrugged. 'Her Italian count is very rich. Women will do anything for money.'

'Not all women, Russ.'

The words were out before she could stop them. He fixed his dark eyes on her, and she returned his look steadily, her heart going out to the wild and lonely young man he had been. She should not have spoken and should not have used his name, but it had been instinctive. Even now she wanted to reach out to him, to take his face in her hands and kiss away the years of hurt and pain.

The sudden crashing of chords and Serena's trilling laugh shattered the moment. Molly carefully fixed the needle into the material and folded up her sewing. What a conceited fool she was to think she might give comfort to Beau Russington, who had his pick of the most beautiful women in the land. He might talk to her as a friend, but he did not want her in his bed, his reaction earlier this evening had shown that all too clearly.

'I should ring for the tea tray.' She went to rise.

'Not yet.' He put out his hand to stop her. 'Gerald and Serena have embarked upon another duet. Why not let them finish that first?'

She sank back on her chair. His touch had sent a shower of burning arrows through her skin and she rubbed her arm as the lively strains of an English folk song filled the room. She searched around for something cheerful to say.

'Despite everything, your sister is a most delightful young lady. She has enchanted everyone in Compton Parva.'

'I am glad to hear you say that.' Russ shifted in his seat to watch the singers. 'She was barely eight years old when her mother left England, but Eleanor had no more time for her daughter than for her stepsons. Perhaps that was for the best. She would not have been an influence for good.' He turned back to Molly. 'I have to confess I can take no credit for the way she has turned out. I did not wish to involve myself in my half-sister's education, I left all that to Henry. She lived at Hambridge Hall with Henry and Dorothea in the short periods when she was not at school and he occasionally invited me to join them. A belated attempt to instil some family feeling into us, I suppose, but for the most part we went our own ways. However, I need to bestir myself a little now. My brother has a daughter, you see, who is to be presented in the spring. The last time I saw my niece she was not at all promising, so I suspect Dorothea is reluctant to have Serena live with them until her daughter is safely married off. I confess I am at a loss to know what to do with the chit!'

'She is a young woman,' Molly reminded him gently.

He sighed. 'Aye, you are right. It is clear that she has outgrown school. She needs a chaperon or a companion who can match her spirit and energy. Someone who can guide her and keep her safe without stifling her natural liveliness, but they must be of good birth and impeccable character.'

Neither of them had noticed that the music had ended and Serena was approaching with Sir Gerald.

'Are you talking about me, Russ?' she cried, dropping a hand on her brother's shoulder.

'Aye, I am wondering what the devil I am to do with you.'

'Perhaps you should take a wife,' Serena murmured, wickedly. 'Then I could live with you.'

Gerald laughed. 'I wish I might see Beau Russington leg-shackled to a woman of impeccable character!'

Molly saw Russ's brows rise, and he replied with a touch of hauteur, 'My dear Kilburn, I could not settle for anything less.'

Feeling slightly sick, she flew off to ring for the tea tray. She did not want to hear any more.

A woman of impeccable character.

The words had taunted Molly throughout her sleepless night. She had as good as told Russ that she had had a lover before her marriage.

Yet he left Serena in your care.

Only because there was no one else.

She had tossed and turned, thumping her pillow, throwing off the covers, trying to find some rest and solace in the darkness, but her mind would not be quiet. By the time the sun came up she was resigned to the fact that Russ would never consider her for his wife. But she had never expected that he would, and until recently she had never even thought of marrying again. She had been quite content with her life in Compton Parva.

Hadn't she?

Molly stopped brushing her hair and stared at her reflection. Russ had stirred up feelings and regrets she had thought long dead and she was not sure if she was most pleased or sorry for it.

Chapter Ten

'Steady, boy. Easy, Flash.'

Russ eased his horse back from the headlong gallop that had seen them flying across the moor. He cursed himself for being so foolhardy. That last stumble might have seen him take a tumble or, worse, Flash might have broken a leg. And however careless of his own life Russ might be, he should not risk his faithful mount.

He came to a halt on the highest point of the promontory that forced the road in the valley bottom into a curving arc around it. The sun was still shining over the high ground, but below the land was already in shadow and a few lights twinkled in distant Compton Parva, nestled at the western end of the valley. He would wager that at least one of those lights came from the lamp outside the vicarage, shining out to welcome all souls, however damaged.

A movement caught his eye—a solitary vehicle had come into view from the east. He could see it was a gig making its way at a smart pace towards the town. The driver was a woman and although Russ could not be sure at this distance, he thought it might well be Molly on her way back from Prospect House.

Molly. Why was it that at their every meeting, he acted like a crass fool? Last night he had been brusque to the point of rudeness when Serena had asked his opinion of Molly's new gown. Then, just when he thought he had mended those fences, Serena, the minx, had said he should marry. That had caught him off guard, because at that very moment he had been thinking that Molly might well make the perfect wife. As if that was not enough, Gerald, damn him, had chosen that moment to tease him and he had answered angrily and without thinking. He wished now he had cut out his tongue before speaking. It was only after the words had left his mouth that he recalled what Molly had told him about being seduced by a rascally soldier. He had never thought any the worse of her for that, but he was sure she would consider herself disgraced.

He closed his eyes and shook his head in disbelief that he, the celebrated Beau Russington, famed for his polished address, should behave like a doltish schoolboy over a woman. The fact was that he had never *cared* about a woman before. He had thought them all self-seeking fortune hunters, like his stepmother. Selfish beings, selling their favours to the highest bidder. It had been made abundantly plain to him from an early age that no matter how badly he behaved, any one of the beauties that graced the town could be his for a sum. But the price for the virginal debutantes who filled the London salons was marriage and that was a price he was not prepared to pay.

Until now. He rubbed a hand across his face. Molly Morgan had already suffered in her young life and she deserved a better husband than a jaded rake with a dubious past. Opening his eyes, Russ glanced down, expecting to see that the gig had rounded the bend by now, but the road to the west was deserted. He followed it back until he saw the vehicle had stopped just short of the bend. He pulled out his spyglass and through the deepening gloom he could see that the vehicle was resting at an ugly angle. His heart jolted in alarm until he saw that Molly was on her feet and standing beside it. Without hesitating he touched his heels to his horse's flanks.

'Come up, Flash. It would appear the lady is in distress.'

The lurching jolt as the wheel cracked and splintered sent Molly tumbling out of the gig. She was winded, but not hurt, and scrambled to her feet. The mare was standing between the shafts, trembling violently, but she, too, appeared unhurt. The gig's wheel, however, was smashed beyond repair. There was no possibility of moving on.

Molly tried to unfasten the harness, but found her fingers would not work properly. She was shaking and decided she would need to sit down and recover a little before she tried to do anything. A convenient milestone provided a seat, which was much more welcome than its message, that she was still three miles from Compton Parva.

She glanced up and down the road, but it was deserted and likely to remain so, since it was growing dark and there was no moon tonight to aid travellers. If only she had not hit that stone. If only she had not stayed so late at Prospect House. Her meeting with Fleur had lasted longer than usual, then she had spent a good half hour talking to Daisy about her good fortune.

And it *was* good fortune, she thought now, to be offered the post as Sir Gerald's housekeeper. Fleur had explained about Miss Kilburn visiting Prospect House and telling her how the old house-keeper had returned from Harrogate with her rheu-matism no better for taking the waters, and how Agnes and her brother had agreed that she should be given a pension and allowed to retire to a tied house on the estate.

'And then, dear Molly, Agnes offered Daisy the post of housekeeper, with a place for Billy in the stables. Is that not wonderful news?' Fleur had ended, a soft glow of happiness shining in her eyes, 'Agnes did not say so, but I think Sir Gerald must be behind this, do not you? I cannot recall having told anyone else that we have been training Daisy for just such a position.'

As the main patron of Prospect House, Molly had felt it incumbent upon her to talk to Daisy and assure herself that she was willing to take the position. Ten minutes in Daisy's company was long enough to convince her. There could be no doubting it, nor Billy's joy at being employed as a stablehand. Molly began to wonder if she had misjudged Sir Gerald. Perhaps his attachment to Fleur was more serious than she had first thought. She wanted to believe it, for Fleur's sake, but could he be trusted, any more than his friend? Russ had flirted with her, even kissed her, but last night he had left her in no doubt that she could never meet his exacting standards.

And yet he had confided in her, told her how shamefully his stepmother had behaved. Molly felt a tiny flicker of hope, although she was afraid to acknowledge it. Did that not argue a level of intimacy that went beyond friendship? She was still pondering the matter when she heard someone trotting along the road. Even in the semigloom she knew it was Russ, even before he spoke. It was as if she had once more conjured him by the sheer power of thought.

'Mrs Morgan, are you hurt?'

'A little bruised, perhaps, but nothing serious.' She came forward, waving one hand towards the gig. 'I am going to walk back to town, but first I n-need to unharness T-Tabby.'

She could not keep the quiver from her voice. Russ jumped down and quickly led her back to the milestone.

'Sit down again and I will do it.'

She resumed her seat and looked down at her hands. They were still shaking and for the first time she noticed the mud and grass stains on her pelisse. No doubt her hair was an unsightly tangle, too. She wondered idly when she had become so concerned about such things. She glanced up at Russ, knowing he was the reason. Becoming acquainted with Beau Russington had made her much more conscious of her appearance. Much more dissatisfied with it, if she was to be honest.

Molly watched him as he ran his hands gently over the mare, murmuring softly to reassure her while he checked for injury. There was little hope that such a connoisseur of women would spare her more than a glance when he could have his pick of the most beautiful women in society. And no hope at all that he might form any serious attachment. Although he might find it diverting to indulge her in a little flirtation, a few stolen kisses.

If they were alone and she was sufficiently encouraging he might go further. He might lie with her on some grassy bank and make love to her. He had kissed her once. He might be tempted to do so again. *She* might tempt him to do so. A pleasurable shiver ran through Molly at such an outrageous thought, rapidly succeeded by panic as cruel memories intruded. She looked up and down the deserted road and glanced uneasily behind her at the dense woodland. Oh, why had she not brought her maid or a groom? She had thought herself quite safe, driving in the gig.

'There now, all done, we can get on.'

Russ gently led the mare from the shafts. A low whistle brought his own horse closer and Russ caught up the reins. He waited for a moment, observing the two animals, then gave a satisfied nod.

'These two will walk together, I think, and without the carriage, we will be able to take the pack-horse trail across the hill, that will save a good mile.' He turned towards Molly. 'If you will take my arm, I shall escort you home.'

Molly was surprised how shaky her legs were as she stood up. Dropping the reins, Russ reached out to grab her as she stumbled. She was already feeling foolish for her wicked thoughts and now she was mortified to display such weakness. She glanced up to see that he was smiling down at her and her cheeks grew painfully hot.

'My dear Molly, you cannot walk all the way back to Compton Parva.'

All her good sense had disappeared. She was quite unequal to protesting at his form of address and could only watch in silence as he pulled the big hunter closer and jumped nimbly into the saddle.

'Come along.' He held out his hand. 'Put your foot on my boot and I will pull you up.'

Worse and worse. She wanted to weep with vexation and her own feebleness. Instead she silently followed his instructions and moments later she was sitting across the saddle in front of him, almost cradled in his arms.

'You are perfectly safe,' he told her, his breath fluttering through her untidy curls and playing havoc with her already-disordered nerves. 'I shall not let you fall.'

She kept her eyes lowered. She had no fear of slipping off the horse, but sitting across a gentleman's lap, and in particular *this* gentleman's lap, was not making it easy to relax. Then, when they began to move, she had no choice but to lean against Russ and allow her body to move with the big horse's gait. She settled herself more comfortably and it was impossible not to rest her cheek against his shoulder. She closed her eyes, breathing in the smell of him, the wool of his coat, the well-laundered linen of his shirt and neckcloth, the spicy scent of citrus and musk that mingled with the fresh sweat on his skin. It was very male. Frightening and exciting. Intoxicating.

Two miles. Russ gazed up at the darkening sky, where the first stars were making their appearance. It was not long enough, even at this slow pace. He wanted to ride for ever through this twilight world with Molly in his arms, feeling her soft body resting against him, trusting him to protect her. That last thought made him feel like a giant, the hero from some Greek myth or perhaps a chivalrous knight from the pages of a medieval romance.

He smiled but without humour. There was nothing noble about his life. He had followed a selfish, hedonistic existence, careless of anyone or anything. Even now, when he should have been thinking only of escorting Molly to the safety of her home, he felt the temptation growing, the desire to make love to her, to awaken the passion he knew lay just beneath the surface. But it must not be. She was a respectable pillar of this community and a liaison with him would destroy everything she had worked for.

He fought against the attraction, forcing aside his desires while he silently raged against the injustice of it all. However, he could not suppress a low growl of frustration and she stirred, one dainty hand coming up to rest against his chest.

'Did you speak, sir?'

'We shall not be back before dark,' he replied, prevaricating.

'It is of little consequence. In a situation such as this I think my reputation will survive.'

'It is not your reputation that concerns me.'

'N-no?' Her hand moved up, the fingers clutching at the lapel of his coat. 'Then what, sir?'

He knew he should keep his eyes on the road. He knew that to look down at her would be his undoing, but he could not resist. She was gazing up at him, the starlight reflecting in her eyes. The breath caught in his throat.

'I am afraid,' he muttered, bringing his horse to a stand, 'I am very much afraid I will not be able to help myself.' She was leaning back against his arm and he tensed the muscles, pulling her closer. 'I might… I might do this.'

She gazed up at him, unprotesting, as he lowered his head. Her lips parted beneath his and at the same time her hand on his lapel tugged him closer. He was lost. Her body melted against him as he took her firmly in his arms and deepened the kiss. She responded and, when her tongue tangled with his, little arrows of desire fired his blood. Time had stopped, nothing mattered but Molly, her delicious softness in his arms, the taste of her on his lips. He slid one hand to her breast and she whimpered with pleasure. It was only when Flash shifted restlessly that he came to his senses. He broke off the kiss, dragging in a long, shuddering breath.

Molly eased herself upright as the horse began to walk on again. She was dazed, her body still trembling with the powerful shock of that kiss. She had not wanted it to end and she knew Russ felt the same, because she was practically sitting on his lap and, even through the layers of material between them, his arousal was evident. A shiver of exhilaration ran through her. Did he want more than that one stolen kiss? Was he about to offer her carte blanche? The excitement pooled deep inside and a delicious lightness began to curl up through her. She wanted him. She could not deny it. She wanted to throw caution to the winds and ride away with him into an unknown future.

The last time she had felt anything like this she had been a girl of seventeen, in the heady throes of first love. The feelings and sensations might be familiar, but now they were so much hotter and stronger than anything she had experienced before. How could this be? Had she not learned anything in the past seven years? He would not offer her marriage. She was a lost soul as far as he was concerned, certainly not the woman of impeccable character he demanded for his bride. But all her arguments were fruitless. All she knew was that she wanted him. Desperately. She put a hand up to her mouth, stunned at her own wantonness.

'I beg your pardon,' he said, misreading her distress.

She shook her head, swallowed and tried to make light of it.

'I cannot say you did not warn me,' she said. 'Let us call it your reward for rescuing me.'

'No hysterics, no outrage?' He gave a shaky laugh. 'Ah, darling Molly, you are very calm when you must be aware how much I would like to carry you off this minute!'

Darling Molly!

The hand that had been covering her mouth dropped to her breast, as if to stop her pounding heart from breaking through. Her whole being ached for him and she was ready to agree to anything, *anything* he might suggest.

'I cannot do it,' he said. 'You bravely told me

about your past, so I know what a struggle it has been for you to build your reputation here. I cannot destroy all those years of work for a few hours' pleasure.'

Is that how he thought of her, a quick, brief coupling before he moved on? Molly was not at all sure what she had been hoping for, but his words fell on her like cold water, shocking her back to the reality of the situation. For a brief, heady period she had allowed her body to rule her head. She could not deny the deep pleasure of his kiss, but she knew—*she knew*—it would only lead to disappointment. She had not only her own experience to draw on, but also that of the girls and women living at Prospect House.

Those who had given into men's blandishments lost their maidenhood, their good name and almost all chance of living a respectable life. A hasty marriage had saved her from ruin once and she had been about to sacrifice everything and give in to her desires. She should be thankful that Russ refused to take advantage of her. She *was* thankful. But it did not stop her feeling angry, an anger made all the hotter by the bitter and irrational disappointment that she was not desirable enough to tempt him. She drew on every ounce of pride to formulate an answer.

'I am very glad we have clarified that point, sir,' she said with icy politeness. 'We may now be easy when we meet and know exactly where we stand with one another. We are almost at the vicarage. If you let me down here, there will be no need for anyone to know you brought me home.'

'Molly, are you angry with me? Surely you did not *want* me to—'

'Too late, someone is already coming out to meet us... It is Edwin. He must have been looking out for me.'

She waved to her brother, holding on to her brittle cheerfulness as he ran up to them.

'Molly, thank God you are back. I was about to come looking for you! Tell me at once what has happened. An accident?'

'Yes, yes, but nothing serious. Do help me down, Edwin, then we need not trouble Mr Russington to dismount.'

'Of course, but what happened?' Edwin demanded as he reached up for her.

'The gig wheel smashed on a stone,' Russ explained briefly. 'Your sister was thrown out. Thankfully she suffered no hurt. I brought her home and the horse. The gig is a couple of miles out of town, but it is slewed on to the grass verge and not blocking the highway. It should be safe enough until morning.'

'Thank goodness it was not more serious,' said Edwin, putting an arm around Molly. 'Although even in this light I can see you are distressed, my love. Let us get you inside. And, Russ, you must come in, too. Come and take a glass of wine with me, sir.'

'Thank you, but no. Allow me to take your carriage horse to the stable, but then I must get back.'

To Molly's relief, Edwin did not press him to stay, but he reiterated his thanks as Russ trotted away to the yard.

'Well, well, Molly. This is the second time Russington has come to your rescue. Who would have thought a notorious rake could behave so chivalrously?'

'Who indeed?' said Molly and promptly burst into tears.

Edwin ushered Molly indoors, clearly worried by her lachrymose behaviour, but she did not realise just how alarmed he was until the following day, when she received two sets of callers. Agnes

Kilburn and Serena were shown into the morning room, where Molly had been sitting for an hour with her embroidery lying untouched on her lap. Serena bounced in, explaining that Edwin had called at Newlands that morning.

'He told us all about your accident yesterday. He *said* he had come to thank Russ for bringing you home,' she chattered on, untying the strings of her bonnet and casting it aside. 'But he would have done that last night, would he not? *I* think his real reason for calling was to see Agnes. He is so smitten that he cannot keep away!'

Molly invited a blushing Agnes to come and sit beside her and admonished Serena with a look.

'There really was no need for you to make a special journey to see me,' she said. 'It was the veriest spill and I was not at all hurt, I assure you.'

'But Edwin told us you had spent the evening crying, which he says you never do,' argued Serena. 'I thought my brother might be the cause. Was he uncivil to you?'

'No, of course not.' Molly tried to sound indignant, but Serena was not deceived.

'You are blushing, Molly Morgan! Did he flirt with you—did he try to kiss you?'

'That is enough, Serena!' Agnes chided her. 'Horrid girl, I shall take you back to Newlands this minute if you do not behave yourself.'

'But I want to *know*,' protested Serena, not a whit abashed.

'There is nothing to know,' replied Molly. 'Mr Russington came upon me standing beside the broken gig and—and brought me home.'

'But Edwin says he carried you before him on his horse. In his arms!'

'I was too shaken to walk, so he took me up.' Molly put up her hand. 'And no, Serena, he did not try to flirt with me.' She added, trying not to sigh, 'Far from it.'

Agnes gave her a searching look, but at that moment the door opened and more visitors walked in. Molly jumped up to greet them.

'Why, Fleur, Nancy, I had no idea you intended to come to town today.'

'How could we stay away?' cried Fleur, flying across the room to take Molly's outstretched hands. 'As soon as we heard of your mishap we had to come and see you.'

There was a pause while greetings were exchanged and Molly was persuaded to sit back down on the sofa between Agnes and Fleur. It was some moments before she could ask how they had learned the news.

'From Sir Gerald, of course,' said Nancy. 'He told Fleur Edwin was most anxious about you.'

'All this fuss over a little tumble,' exclaimed Molly. 'I assure you all I am perfectly well.'

'No, she is not,' put in Serena. 'She is in love with my brother.'

This declaration brought an indignant protest from Molly and a reprimand from Agnes, but Nancy laughed.

'So we have another pair of lovers. Oh, pray do not look at me like that, Fleur. You and Sir Gerald have been smelling of April and May for weeks now and Molly herself told me that Edwin will use any excuse to visit Newlands. Anyone would think it was spring in Compton Parva, rather than autumn.'

'Nancy, you are jumping to conclusions,' muttered Fleur, her cheeks crimson. 'What will Miss Kilburn think…?'

'Miss Kilburn has already guessed it,' replied Agnes, smiling. 'Why else would Gerald be so eager for me to make your acquaintance? But as for Mr Frayne's attentions to me—' it was her turn to blush '—nothing has been said, there is no understanding between us.'

'Only that you cannot keep your eyes from one another when you are in the same room,' remarked Serena gleefully.

Despite her blushes, Agnes drew herself up and said with gentle dignity, 'We did not come here to talk about me. It is Molly who concerns us.'

'And I assure you there is no need,' Molly replied, her own colour much heightened. 'The idea that I am…am in love with Mr Russington is laughable. He…he would never give a thought to me.'

Fleur tutted softly. 'You do not know that.'

'Yes, I do.' Molly forgot to play her part and this time the sigh escaped her. 'He told me so himself.' She realised her words had caused a flutter of indignation in her audience and added hurriedly, 'Pray do not think I mind, he was merely trying to reassure me that I was perfectly safe, travelling alone with him.'

'Then it shows he was concerned for you,' said Fleur.

'It shows a sad lack of tact,' countered Nancy. 'One would expect a hardened flirt to have more address.'

'He clearly does not think me worth the effort.'

'And he never will while you are wearing those old gowns.' Nancy eyed Molly's sober grey silk with disfavour. 'You should have more bright co-lours, like the red lustring.'

Fleur took her hands. 'It really is time for you to leave off your mourning, Molly,' she said gently. 'You are still a young woman and may yet find another husband.'

Molly shuddered and crossed her arms. 'I do not *want* another husband.'

'A lover, then,' said Nancy.

Agnes gave a little cry of alarm. 'I am not sure we should be discussing this here.'

'If you are afraid for my sensibilities, pray do not be,' put in Serena cheerfully. 'After all, it is my brother who is responsible for all this, so I think I must have some part in it. And if you were to ask me,' she went on, 'I do not think he is indifferent to Molly. He told me he likes her very well.'

Molly blinked rapidly. 'There is a great differ-ence between like and love.'

'I hope you are not going to go into a decline,' said Fleur, giving her a searching look.

'No, of course, she is not,' Nancy retorted. 'She is going to show she does not give the snap of her fingers for any man.'

That made Molly smile. 'I thought I had been doing that for the past six years.'

'No, you have been hiding behind your widow's weeds,' Nancy told her. 'It is time now to throw them off.'

'No, no, I cannot. I would not feel right. I am the vicar's sister. I have my place to maintain.' Molly's voice died away as she wondered how soon she would have to relinquish that position to his wife.

'A change of clothes will not make you any less capable, my love,' said Fleur, squeezing her arm. 'I remember when we were at school together you loved bright colours and you looked so well in them.'

'And she will do so again,' said Nancy. 'Now, do not argue, Molly. We are your friends, and we are determined on this change for you.'

'Yes, and our ball takes place in three weeks, which will be the perfect time to show off the transformation,' said Agnes, her eyes dancing.

'Perfect!' Serena clapped her hands. 'We shall turn you from a dull little caterpillar into a gorgeous butterfly. And we shall show my foolish brother just what he is missing!'

'You are a fool, Russington. You are torturing yourself unnecessarily. Go back to London and forget Molly Morgan.'

It was not the first time Russ had looked into

the mirror and offered himself advice, but he had never yet taken it. He pushed the diamond pin firmly into the folds of his cravat and stood back to admire the effect. He looked every inch the fashionable gentleman, perhaps a little too fashionable for a country ball. The snowy linen was almost startling in the candlelight and showed how tanned his face had become during his stay at Newlands. Hardly surprising, since he and Gerald spent most of their days out of doors. His black curls had been brushed until they glowed, the coat of blue superfine fitted without a crease over his shoulders and, combined with the immaculate white waistcoat, pale breeches and brilliant black leather dancing pumps, it was an ensemble that drew admiring glances in the smartest London salons. It certainly impressed the good people of Compton Parva, but then, thought Russ, a faint, self-deprecating smile curling his lip, they would expect nothing less of Beau Russington, the darling of fashionable society.

He turned away from the mirror, his ears picking up the sounds from below of the orchestra tuning up. The dancing would begin soon. He would have to hurry if he was not to be late. Not that it would matter very much, a smiling apology and a few words would smooth things over with Agnes, he was sure. His mind returned to Molly. It was strange how all his charm and polished address disappeared when he was in her company. She was not impressed by him and he did not wish her to be. He just wished she liked him a little more.

Like. He considered the word as he ran lightly down the stairs. She was attracted to him, but he was a rake and she strongly disapproved of rakes, even when they rescued maidens in distress. Admittedly he should not have kissed her, but she had taken that very well, and it was only when they reached the vicarage that she had become agitated, even angry with him, and since then she had shown very clearly that she wanted nothing more to do with him.

In the three weeks since he had carried her home on horseback she had studiously avoided his company, crying off from a dinner party and darting away if she spotted him in the town. If any other woman had shown such an aversion to his company, he would have laughed and put her out of his mind, but he could not do that with Molly. She filled his thoughts during the day and kept him awake at night. Confound it, he should be grateful to her for her efforts. It was best that they did not meet, but knowing she would be at the ball to-night filled him with a mix of apprehension and anticipation, the like of which he had not known since his boyhood.

The reception rooms were already crowded with chattering guests when he entered. His hostess was standing a little way from the door with Serena and Edwin Frayne and, judging by the way Agnes was blushing and the vicar's beaming smile, it was clear that Miss Kilburn's recent absence had in no way lessened the attraction between them. Across the room, Gerald caught his eye and winked. Russ walked over to join him.

'I think my sister has made a conquest,' he murmured, sweeping a glass of wine from a passing waiter and handing it to Russ. 'I confess after the tragic loss of her fiancé, I thought she would end up an old maid, but I am very hopeful now. Frayne would be just the man for her.' He laughed suddenly. 'Who would have thought it? Perhaps there is something in the air of Compton Parva that makes love blossom.'

There was a glint in his friend's eyes that made Russ think he was about to refer to Molly, so he said quickly, 'I believe your sister invited Mrs Dellafield. Is she here?'

'Molly convinced Agnes that there was no hope of the invitation being accepted, so she decided not to embarrass the lady by sending one.' Gerald's reply was offhand, and his eyes were constantly moving about the room. 'Ah, more guests are arriving. I had best go and meet them. And talking of Mrs Morgan, I'd be obliged if you would take a glass of wine to her and make sure she is enjoying herself.'

Russ shot his friend a suspicious look, but Gerald met it with a bland smile before walking off. Surely Gerald did not suspect Russ was developing a tendress for the widow? He had been at pains not to give himself away, but then so, too, was Gerald very reticent when it came to talking about Fleur Dellafield. Russ hoped that meant his friend's interest was waning. He recalled Molly's foolhardy attempt to protect her friend and he could not be sure she would not try something even more rash. Russ looked around the room. Despite her diminutive figure Molly Morgan should be easy to spot, there were very few ladies wearing blacks or greys tonight. Unless, of course, she was wearing that dark red gown.

Then he saw her and he was transfixed.

* * *

Molly was enjoying herself and could only be grateful to her friends for their persistence. As she listened politely to Sir William expounding on the virtues of the new closed stove he had purchased for Currick Hall, she reflected upon everyone's kindness to her. She had met with nothing but praise at her appearance this evening. Even one of her elderly neighbours had indulged her in a little flirtation, but in such a gentle, kindly way that she had not felt at all alarmed by it. In fact, it had, along with a second glass of champagne, given a much-needed boost to her confidence.

She had not wanted to be *transformed*, as Serena put it. Indeed, she had argued against it, but her friends had convinced her that a change of style was the best way to answer Russ's snub and show him she cared not a jot for his opinion. So she had allowed Nancy to cut her hair to make the most of her natural curls and Serena, Agnes and Fleur had spent happy hours in her bedchamber, removing all but a few of her mourning clothes. She had not allowed them to throw out anything, but the alacrity with which Cissy packed the garments into a trunk for storage in the attics told Molly that her friends were not alone in their opinion that it was time for a change.

News of her transformation had quickly reached all her neighbours, and shortly after her friends' visit, various packages had begun to arrive. A parcel of coloured ostrich feathers and assorted ribbons that Miss Hebden said had been lying unsold at the back of her store, Mrs Thomas sent over a length of emerald-green velvet and Agnes brought her a bolt of blue satin that she declared she would never use.

Marjorie had immediately fashioned the velvet into an elegant pelisse and matching bonnet and the sapphire-blue satin had been made up into the beautiful evening gown that Molly was now wearing. It was trimmed at the bodice, sleeves and hem with silver net that shimmered in the candlelight whenever she moved and a chaplet of silver foil was wound twice around her hair and glinted between her dark, glossy curls.

Molly glanced down at the blue satin slippers that peeped out from beneath her gown. Lady Currick had brought them to the vicarage earlier that day and when Molly had demurred she had pressed them upon her, saying earnestly, 'Do please take them, Mrs Morgan. I bought them thinking they would do for Nell, but she will not be wearing such strong colours at her come-out, and she has such dainty feet. You are the only lady I know who could wear them!'

Everyone had been so kind, so generous, and to think she had been tempted to throw it all away, to sacrifice her good name and give up her place in this town, just because a man had kissed her.

'I really do think the committee should consider a Rumford stove for Prospect House,' Sir William declared. 'What say you, Mrs Morgan, will you support me if I suggest it?'

His lady tapped his arm with her fan. 'My dear man, we are at a ball! This is not the place to discuss such matters. Tell Molly instead how fine she is looking.'

Sir William looked so taken aback that Molly felt the laughter bubbling up.

'No, no, I assure you I want no compliments, ma'am, and Sir William knows I am always delighted to talk about Prospect House.'

Someone had come up beside her and she looked up, still laughing. It was Russ, looking so handsome that her heart leapt. There was no time to pretend indifference, the laughter slid into what she hoped was a polite smile, but she could not drag her gaze from his face. He was holding out a glass to her.

'Our host thought you might like some champagne.'

'Why, thank you.'

She took a sip from the glass and peeped up at him. There was no doubting the admiration in his eyes and she felt a little kick of satisfaction. She wanted him to experience a moment's regret for what he had rejected. He looked as if he would speak, but Lady Currick came in first.

'Well, Mr Russington, what do you think of our little friend? Is she not looking very well tonight?'

'Never better,' he replied. 'I hope you will be dancing this evening, Mrs Morgan.'

He had not taken his eyes off Molly, but for once she did not blush and look away. She gave him an arch smile.

'I might be persuaded to do so.'

Sir William gave a crack of laughter. 'There you are, Russington. Go to it and *persuade* the lady.'

Molly waited while Russ made her a little bow. 'They are striking up for the first dance now, madam, if you would do me the honour?'

'Ah, how unfortunate, Mr Russington,' she said gently. 'You see, I am already engaged.'

Only by the slightest change in his countenance did he show his surprise, but she was looking out for it.

'Ah, I see. Perhaps later, then?'

'Perhaps.' She glanced past him at Mr Sykes, who had come up to them.

'Well, Mrs Morgan, shall we take our places?'

With a wide smile Molly handed Russ her champagne glass and went off with her partner.

Molly felt the exhilaration fizzing through her blood. Perhaps it was naughty of her to tease Russ, but such an opportunity might not arise again. It was very likely that he would now shrug those broad shoulders and forget all about her. If he did, then she had lost nothing, but it had soothed her pride to be able to refuse him. She was engaged for the next three dances, the final one with Sir Gerald and as he led her off the floor he asked her if she was enjoying herself.

'Oh, immensely,' she told him. 'I am very grateful to your sister. She secured partners for me even before I came into the room tonight. Everyone has been so kind, including yourself, Sir Gerald.'

'It is no hardship to be kind to a pretty woman, ma'am, and you are looking particularly well this evening.' He glanced across the room. 'And if I am not mistaken Russ is waiting to pounce on us. Agnes told me you were punishing him for some slight.'

'She did?' Molly blushed. 'It was not so very serious. I assure you.'

'I am glad to hear it. She said I was not to let him near you until after supper, but he is my friend and I cannot help feeling sorry for the fellow.' He looked down at Molly, placing his free hand over her fingers as they lay on his arm. 'So, ma'am, shall I tell him you are engaged to me, or do you think he has waited long enough?'

Could she do this? Molly had been laughing and joking all evening, even flirting in a gentle, harmless way, but could she do the same with a man whose very nearness turned her into a trembling mass of longing? She put up her chin. That was all in the past. She had far too much to lose to let herself be seduced by any man, but a little flirtation in the safety of the ballroom, what harm could that do?

'Oh, I think I should take pity on Mr Russington, sir, do not you?'

Chapter Eleven

Russ kept smiling as Gerald brought Molly over to him. His jaw tightened as he watched them talking together, Gerald leaning in a little closer and giving her hand a comforting pat. Something very like jealousy ripped through him. He was too experienced to let it show, however. He greeted their arrival with all his usual urbanity and this time Molly accepted his invitation to dance.

'Here she is, then,' declared Gerald, 'but 'tis with reluctance that I relinquish my fair partner to you, Russ. Look after her!'

He lounged away and Russ led Molly off to take their places in the next set.

'I feared I should not be able to dance with you tonight, madam.'

'Then you should have come in earlier.' She added, 'There are any number of ladies without partners tonight, so I hope you have not been standing at the side, watching me.'

'By no means. I have danced with Agnes and Mrs Sykes. And Lady Currick's daughter, Helen.'

'How delightful for them and it is especially useful for Nell,' she told him. 'She needs a little practice at dealing with roués before her come-out.'

She met his frowning glance with a look of pure innocence. Nettled, he changed the subject.

'I have the strangest feeling you have been avoiding me, Mrs Morgan.'

'Now, why should I do that, Mr Russington?'

'Something to do with our last meeting perhaps.'

She laughed. 'That would be a sad recompense for your rescuing me that night.'

'But you have already rewarded me for that service,' he reminded her. She blushed adorably at that and he glanced about to make sure they could not be overheard before he continued. 'At the time you appeared angry that I did not want more than that one kiss.'

Her eyes widened. 'You said you did not wish to ruin me. Why should I be angry about that?'

They were silent as they performed their part in the dance, stepping up and away, gracefully circling as they progressed through the set.

'Perhaps you *wanted* me to ruin you,' he murmured, when at last they came back together.

To his surprise, she did not react angrily to his suggestion. Perfectly calm, she appeared to consider it while they waited for their next turn.

'I should be very foolish to want that, Mr Russington.' They were moving again and as she put her hand into his, she added softly, 'So much better to meet you on occasions like this, when I can enjoy your considerable charms without the least danger of yielding to them.'

By heaven, she had learned the art of dalliance very quickly! Russ was glad when the dance parted them again, relieved to have some time to think about this new Molly Morgan. It was not only her clothes that had changed, but her whole demeanour. He had seen signs of it occasionally in the past, when she had been at her most relaxed, but this evening was different. She was positively goading him.

And he was enjoying it.

Russ had to stifle a laugh. She had acknowledged the attraction between them, agreed nothing could come of it, but instead of keeping her distance she was determined to meet him head on. A dangerous policy, but he was more than willing to oblige her. After all, as she said, they were safe enough in company.

* * *

No danger?

Molly might be able to deceive everyone else this evening, but she could not lie to herself. Every smile, every word she shared with Russ was intoxicating, but all the time she had to keep reminding herself that it was not real. The banter, the coy looks, the teasing smiles were all part of a game and she was playing it with a master. He knew to a nicety how to engage with her, when to challenge, when to tease or praise her and Molly was pleased to discover that she could hold her own with him.

She allowed Russ to take her into supper, but insisted they sit with their hosts. Edwin was already at the table, deep in conversation with Agnes, and since Gerald soon went off to talk to his guests, any hope Molly had entertained of being spared the full force of Russ's attraction was dashed.

He was the perfect companion, moving the candles so they did not glare in her eyes, selecting the choicest morsels for her plate and bringing the tray of sweetmeats within her reach. She was outwardly calm, but it was an effort with Russ sitting beside her, his sleeve brushing her arm, his thigh only inches away. When he beckoned a waiter to bring them more wine she covered her glass, knowing that she must keep her wits about her.

'Lemonade, then,' Russ suggested, nodding to the waiter to attend to it. 'The evening is young yet, and you will need some refreshment.' He leaned closer. 'I am set upon a second dance with you tonight.'

Her hand hovered over the sweetmeat dish. 'You may well be disappointed.'

'Oh?' She observed with satisfaction the way his hand tightened around his wine glass. 'Are all the remaining dances taken?'

She picked out a small sugar bonbon. 'And if I told you they were?'

'I should be obliged to dispose of one of your partners.'

The quiet menace in his voice startled Molly and she dropped the sweetmeat.

'It…it is as well then that that is not the case.'

His hold on the wine glass eased.

'It is very well,' he said, smiling at her. He picked up the bonbon and popped it into her mouth. 'Very well indeed.'

Molly was aware that anyone watching them at supper could have been in no doubt that Russ was flirting with her and now they were standing up

together for a boisterous country dance which demanded she hold his hands as they skipped and
twirled about the room. After a good supper and a
generous supply of wine, everyone was much more
relaxed and the ballroom was full of laughter and
chatter that all but drowned out the music. It was
very hot, too, even though the long windows had
been thrown wide. By the time the music ended,
Molly knew that this second dance with Russ was
a mistake. She had enjoyed it too much, the control she had kept over herself all evening had vanished and her wayward body wanted him as much
as ever.

She was fully aware of the danger when she allowed him to escort her out on to the terrace and
she offered no resistance as he gently pulled her
into the deep shadows and kissed her. On the con-
trary, she clung to him, pressing her body against
his as she returned the kiss with a passion she had
not known she possessed. It frightened her, a little,
but by the time they broke apart she had made her
decision. She put a hand up to his face.

'Russ, I want you to take me to your bed.'

Russ closed his eyes. How many times had he
dreamed she would say those words to him? If she

had done so when they first met he would have complied willingly, but not now. Now he cared too much for her. It would not just be her reputation that would be destroyed if he went further. She was not some rich society widow who could retire to her country estates for a few months until the scandal had died down. If Molly lost her good name, she would lose her standing in Compton Parva. She would no longer be able to help her brother or to promote the charitable causes so close to her heart, including Prospect House.

'Molly, do not tempt me.' His arms tightened around her. 'You are a widow and I have awakened feelings that you thought long dead. You need a husband, Molly, a good man who will love you as you deserve.'

She drew in a long breath. 'My body is crying out for *you*, Russ.' She pushed herself away, trying to read his face in the shadows. 'Do you deny that you want me?'

'No, of course, I do not deny it.' He looked up at the sky and sighed. 'I have no constancy, Molly. I have had many mistresses, but my interest rarely lasts more than a month. Such fleeting lust would destroy you. You deserve a steady, faithful husband, not someone like me. You know what I am.'

'Yes.' She buried her face in his shoulder. 'You are a rake. You have a reputation as a lover and… and I am ready to endure—'

'What is this?' He took her arms and held her away from him, frowning. 'Endure? Molly, I am talking of pleasure, not pain.'

She averted her face and said quietly, 'I believe men experience these things differently.'

'You are wrong. The women I have taken to bed enjoyed it every bit as much as I.'

'Perhaps I am made differently.'

He said savagely, 'I do not believe that.' He put one hand beneath her chin, compelling her to look up at him. 'If you have not enjoyed lovemaking, then the man was at fault, Molly, not you.'

He felt a wave of anger growing against whoever it was who had hurt her so badly.

She sighed. 'I thought you wanted me.'

'I do.' Russ closed his eyes. She must never know how much he wanted her! He said gently, 'I do, Molly, but I would not take another man's prize.'

'Prize!' With a cry she tore herself away from him. 'I am no *prize*,' she said bitterly. 'I am just a…a *thing*, to be used and—and broken for a man's pleasure.'

His anger boiled over into a red rage that manifested in a growl.

'Aye, you told me! You were seduced by some blackguard who took your innocence and abandoned you—'

She had her back to him, but he saw her hand come up as if to silence him.

'I was not talking of that,' she whispered, dragging out her handkerchief to wipe her eyes. 'It was far, far worse than that.'

Russ stopped himself from reaching out for her. He should say something soothing, let it pass. Tomorrow he could leave Compton Parva and go back to London, to his old, carefree life and she would remain only a faint, pleasant memory. But looking at the small, dejected figure in front of him, he knew it was already too late. He put his hands on her shoulders and guided her towards the far end of the terrace, away from the open windows.

'Tell me,' he said, sitting down on a stone bench and pulling her down beside him. 'Tell me what happened.'

For a while there was only the muted sounds from the ballroom and the occasional call of a night bird to break the silence. Then he heard her sigh.

'Niall was a rogue,' she said slowly, dragging her

handkerchief between her fingers. 'A handsome, Irish rogue with a smooth tongue and a roving eye. I was seventeen and so in love that I desperately wanted to please him. I will not lie, I wanted it, too. I wanted to give myself to him, wholly. But when it happened it was rushed and painful and… disappointing. It was only the once, then he was gone, my Irish soldier. He left before he even knew he had got me with child.

'My parents were horrified when they discovered my situation. They found me a husband, or more accurately, they *bought* me a husband. Morgan was a yeoman farmer, not a gentleman, but then, I suppose they were thankful to find anyone to marry me. I insisted Morgan should be told about the baby. He swore it would make no difference to the way he felt about me. That he loved me. Love!' She shuddered. 'I experienced no love at his hands. He t-took me for his pleasure. It was brutish and punishing. To him I was an undeserving slattern who should be grateful that he had married me and saved my good name. It was worse when he had been drinking, because if he could not… If he could not p-perform, he would beat me. I always tried to stay on my feet, because—' her hands crept over her stomach and her voice was barely a thread '—it was a kick that killed the baby. My baby.'

Silently Russ took her in his arms, and she turned her face into his shoulder, weeping. There was nothing he could say to make it better, so he rested his cheek against her head and held her. At last the tears subsided. When she struggled to sit up he released her, but she did not object when he kept one arm about her shoulders. She wiped her eyes and began to speak again.

'Morgan never knew what he had done. He died in a drunken brawl the night after that last beating. I was very near my time and everyone thought it was the shock of Morgan's death that made the baby come early, but I knew the truth. I could not bear to go back to my parents, they had already made it clear they considered that losing the baby was a…a judgement upon me for my sins. As soon as I was well enough I sold the farm and came north to live with Edwin. I used Morgan's money to set up Prospect House and tried to forget my old life. The bruises have healed, but I have never been able to throw off the repulsion of being married to such a man.'

She fell silent and he gave voice to the question that had been nagging at him.

'And yet you offered yourself to me, to save your friend?'

She gave a little shrug. 'Having endured a man's attentions in bed before, I thought I could do so again, if I must.' She hung her head. 'I thought I *could* do so, if it was with you.'

With a sigh he pulled her into his arms. 'How could you even think of making such a sacrifice?'

She turned her face into his chest, muffling her response. 'I have made a mull of everything. I am such a fool.'

'Yes, you are fool,' he agreed, resting his cheek against her hair again. Even in the chill of an autumn evening she smelled of summer flowers. 'But a very adorable one.'

'It is kind of you to say so,' she said. 'And very generous, but I think I should go now.'

She pushed herself out of his arms, but he held on to her hand. 'Are you engaged for any other dances this evening?'

'No, but—'

'Then come with me. By my reckoning we have at least two hours.'

'For what?'

He smiled. 'Come with me.'

He led her down the steps and around the house

to a side door. It opened on to one of the servants' halls and, as he had hoped, it was deserted. They climbed the stairs, guided by the lighted lanterns that hung at intervals from the bare walls. He uttered up a silent prayer when they reached his bedchamber without seeing anyone. Once they were inside he turned the key in the lock. Molly's fingers tightened nervously around his.

'My man is the soul of discretion,' he explained, 'but I do not want anyone to disturb us.'

He took a taper to the small fire burning in the hearth. Soon the room was bathed in the soft, golden glow of candles. He turned. Molly had not moved from where he had left her, by the door. He shrugged himself out of his evening coat and threw it over a chair, then he held out his hands to her.

'Will you trust me not to hurt you?'

Slowly she walked towards him and gave him her hands. He drew her into his arms and kissed her gently. She was tense, nervous and he made no move to deepen the kiss until she relaxed against him. He would not rush her, she was as nervous as a colt, but slowly she began to respond. Her arms slipped around his neck and her tongue tangled with his, stirring his blood. Without breaking the kiss he lifted her and carried her across to the bed.

She drew away from him in alarm as he laid her on the covers and he murmured again, 'Trust me.'

Even in the shadows of the bed's canopy he could see her eyes were wide and anxious. He waited, making no move to join her until she reached for him. Russ measured his length against hers, cupping her face and gently kissing her lips before placing soft, butterfly kisses across her cheek and over her jaw. Her head went back, inviting him to trail his lips along the length of her throat. He paused to give particular attention to the little dip between the collarbones and she sighed. His hand cupped her breast and she pushed against his fingers. Even through the silk and silver net, he could feel the nub harden as he caressed her. With practised ease he slipped his hand inside the bodice. She flinched and he paused, raising his head to gaze down at her.

'You only have to tell me and I will stop,' he whispered. 'I will do nothing against your will. You have my word.'

The look in her eyes and her tremulous smile made his soul soar and he bent his head to kiss her again, long and deeply, while his fingers caressed the cushioned roundness of her breast. Then he shifted his position, eased the breast from its silky wrapping and took the hardened peak in his mouth while his fingers moved across to work their magic on its twin. She began to stir restlessly, her hands moving over his shoulders, plucking at his shirt. He raised his head and shifted until he was kneeling beside her. His breath caught at the sight of her breasts, unconfined and wantonly displayed, but he must not be distracted from his purpose. Gently he gathered her skirts, uncovering the dainty ankles and silk stockings, fastened at the knee with lacy garters. He shifted again, positioning himself between her legs and bending to kiss her mouth once more.

This time when he raised his head she reached for him, gripping his shirt to pull him back for more, but he resisted. Gently easing her hands away, he slid down the bed and began to kiss her leg, just above the knee. She tensed, but made no protest, so he continued to caress her, his lips moving upwards across the soft inner thigh.

Molly closed her eyes and gave herself up to the sensations that were flooding through her. Her very bones felt like liquid, soft and pliant. Russ's gentle hands had taken control of her body, easing her apart so that his mouth, his tongue could smooth over the tender skin of her thigh, moving ever closer towards her aching core. She whimpered, but she did not pull away, instead she was arching, inviting him.

He shifted again, his hands slid beneath her hips and held her firm while his mouth finally reached the hinge of her thighs and his tongue licked and flickered with unerring precision. She felt the pressure building, rippling through her, and she tried to move away from the sweet, delicious torture but she was his prisoner. A very willing prisoner, was her last coherent thought as her body convulsed in white-hot spasms of unbearable ecstasy. She was flying, higher, higher, until her world splintered and she cried out in sheer joy as her body shuddered and she felt herself falling, tumbling from heaven into oblivion.

Russ was cradling her in his arms as consciousness returned. She raised a hand to touch his cheek.

'Thank you,' she whispered.

'It is for you, Molly. To show you how wonderful it can be.'

Her scent was on his lips as he kissed her. His hand slipped once more to her breast and she felt her body waking again beneath his touch. She gave herself up to the pleasure of it as he used his hands and his mouth to bring her again and again to the edge of climax and beyond. Until she collapsed against him, sated and exhausted.

She allowed herself a few moments' recovery, then her hand slid over his chest and down towards the buttoned flap of his breeches. His body reacted to her touch, but he caught her fingers.

'There is no need,' he murmured, his breath warm against her cheek. 'Tonight is about your pleasure, Molly.'

'And it would please me to satisfy you,' she replied, moving closer and unfastening the flap. He was already hard and aroused as her fingers pushed aside the cloth to release his erection. He had been denying himself while he attended to her needs, but now she returned the favour eagerly, revelling in her power over him as she kissed, caressed and stroked him until he caught her hands, pushing down as he reached his own satisfying release.

They lay together, wrapped in each other's arms, their bodies resting from the onslaught, but at last Russ stirred.

'I would like to keep you with me all night, but we must return. There is such a crush in the ballroom that I doubt our absence has been noted, but just in case, we must get you into the ladies' retiring room, and I will return via the terrace.' He sat up. 'We must protect your reputation.'

He helped her from the bed, and straightened his clothes while she shook out her skirts.

'Ah, yes, my reputation.'

He watched as she went across to the looking glass, checking that her bodice was once more decorously arranged and tidying her curls.

'I have no wish to ruin you, Molly.'

'I am aware of that.'

When she turned back to him it seemed the most natural thing in the world to open his arms to her and equally natural for her to walk into them. She rested her head on his shoulder and he heard her sigh.

'I am most truly grateful to you for this, Russ. It has been wonderful. A revelation. But you may be easy. I shall not pursue you to do this again.'

Her words, so matter-of-fact, so understanding, hit him like a body blow. He had known from the start it must only be for one night but now he discovered that he did not want to let her go. He wanted her in his bed, to make love to her night after night. To consummate their union. But Molly Morgan would never consent to be his mistress and he would never ask it of her. The only solution would be marriage.

No! Russ shied away from the thought in panic. He was a confirmed bachelor. What he had seen of marriage had given him an aversion to that state. His stepmother and his sister-in-law were both grasping, selfish women, hell-bent on sucking a man dry of his fortune and his energies. He knew Molly was nothing like that, but her goodness frightened him even more. He had never loved anyone in his life and he doubted if he could remain faithful.

He said now, 'You need a good man for your husband, Molly. A man who will treat you as you deserve, one who loves you. What you do not need is a hardened libertine who will be bored with you within a month.'

She moved out of his arms and looked at him, perplexed.

'I never expected you to love me Russ,' she said. 'Neither did I expect you to marry me.'

'How could I?' He barely heard her, for he was desperately trying to convince himself as much as Molly that marriage was out of the question. 'I am not made for domestic felicity, Molly, nor do I want a clinging wife. And you, with your provincial morals and good deeds, would be the very worst partner for me. It would destroy you, my dear, and I do not want to do that.'

Molly listened with increasing dismay. Did he not believe her? Perhaps he thought she was trying to shame him into making her an offer, but nothing could be further from the truth. What they had just shared had been quite, quite wonderful and she was angry that he should now sully it with this unwarranted attack. Her head came up.

'You have made yourself very clear, sir. Now, let me be equally so. I never came here looking for a husband and I agree that your rakehell ways would never be acceptable to someone with my... my *provincial morals*. I am only sorry that you believe I would even contemplate such a union.' She gave her skirts one final shake and walked towards the door. 'My only concern now is to return to the ballroom without causing a scandal!'

Molly gained the safety of the retiring room without being seen by any of Newlands's servants or guests. She could only hope that the attendant there would put her flushed cheeks and tousled appearance down to the lively dancing. She stayed there as long as she dared before making her way into the ballroom. Another country dance was in progress and the room buzzed with happy chatter, voices raised to make themselves heard above the music. Molly looked around. Serena was dancing, but Edwin was standing with Agnes and Sir Gerald at the side of the room. Molly made her way over to them, more than a little afraid they would ask her to explain her absence. Edwin saw her approaching and held his hand out to her.

'Molly, do come and join us. I looked for you earlier, for I wanted you to be the first to know, but somehow things got a little out of hand.' He flushed and looked a little conscious. 'Almost everyone here seems to know it now—have you heard? Agnes has agreed to be my wife!'

Molly did not need to feign her delight. She kissed Agnes and then Edwin before turning to Sir Gerald to express the hope that he was happy at the news.

'Overjoyed, ma'am,' he replied, his open, cheerful countenance suffused in a beaming smile. 'Agnes mentioned it to me shortly after supper and from that moment word spread like wildfire. By the time the musicians struck up for the *boulanger*, everyone seemed to know of it!'

'And to approve, thankfully,' added Edwin.

'Lady Currick is already talking of a party, to celebrate our betrothal.'

'At the King's Head,' put in Agnes, 'so that everyone in the town may come and celebrate it.' She touched Molly's arm. 'I know this is very sudden, Molly. Are you sure you do not object?'

'Not at all,' she said, smiling. 'You are made for one another and you, Agnes, will be the perfect vicar's wife, I am sure.'

'I am so glad you approve,' said Agnes, slipping her arm through Molly's. 'And you will live with us,' she continued. 'Edwin and I are agreed that you should continue to make your home at the vicarage.'

'That is very kind, but I intend to set up my own establishment.' Molly added, with perfect sincerity, 'I have been feeling restless for some time now, so perhaps I shall begin by going away for a short holiday.'

Somewhere far away, where she might reflect on all that had happened and dispel the nagging ache that had settled itself around her heart.

'Yes, but not until after the wedding,' said Edwin quickly. 'You will be needed to help with all the arrangements.'

Gerald laughed. 'I said as much to Russ just now.

He was all for leaving Newlands in the next few days, but I told him I expect him to support me, especially at the betrothal party which Lady Currick hopes to arrange for a week tomorrow. There is no way I shall allow him to abandon me before that!'

There was no escaping talk of the forthcoming nuptials for the rest of the evening or the following week. Molly could only be glad no one had noticed that she and Russ had been absent from the ballroom for more than an hour. Her head told her that she must now put that whole incident behind her, but her heart refused to obey. She wanted Russ more than ever and it was impossible to avoid him in the town, or at Newlands, where Edwin and Molly dined three times in almost as many days. It was a struggle to keep her eyes from following Russ as he moved across a room, or to converse with him calmly, when her whole body cried out for his touch. Her only consolation was his announcement that he had urgent business in London and must leave Compton Parva as soon as the betrothal party was over.

Word of the engagement had even reached Prospect House, as Molly discovered when she met

Fleur and Nancy after the Sunday service at All Souls.

'And what a good thing it is we persuaded Gerald not to invite me,' said Fleur, glancing around to make sure there was no one near enough to overhear. 'I understand a report on the ball and the announcement was sent to the *Herald* and they will doubtless send it on to the London papers. Miss Hebden told me the *Herald* always gives a full list of guests at any such occasion. Just imagine how it would have been if I had gone and if Papa had read of it.'

'If, if,' exclaimed Nancy impatiently. 'You didn't go and there's an end to it. Instead of worrying about what might have been, you should be telling Molly your own news.'

'Sir Gerald has proposed?' Molly asked quickly.

'Shh.' Fleur was blushing furiously. 'Yes, he has. He had spoken of it a week ago, but I told him I could not accept his offer without his sister's blessing. Then Agnes announced her engagement and he was emboldened to discuss it with her yesterday, and he rode over directly to tell me that she has no objections, so now we are to be married. But it is still a secret, Molly. Apart from Nancy, you are the only one who knows of it at present, and I would be obliged if you did not make it generally known, if you please, but—oh, Molly, was ever anything so wonderful?'

No, thought Molly, stifling a sharp stab of self-pity. She did not begrudge her brother and her friends their happiness, but it threw into sharp relief her own predicament and the growing realisation that she had lost her heart to a rake.

Molly did not see Sir Gerald again until market day, when she returned to the vicarage just as he was leaving. She greeted him with a smile and asked him if he had come upon his sister's business, or his own.

'So Fleur has told you,' he declared, relief in his voice. 'I hope we have your blessing?'

'Of course. Does this mean we will be arranging a double wedding?'

His face clouded. 'I should like that, but Fleur lives in fear of her father. She knows he is still searching and is afraid if the *banns* are read for three weeks he will find her before we can be married. That is one of the reasons we are not making any announcement, in case the scandal sheets should get wind of it. I have been discussing the matter with Edwin and we are agreed that a licence would be the very thing. He has told me he is meeting with the bishop at Nidderton very soon and has promised to discuss it with him then.'

'I suppose you have told Mr Russington?' said Molly, trying to sound casual.

He paused. 'As a matter of fact I haven't. Russ has been more than a little discouraging about the whole affair. When he learned I was serious, he even suggested Fleur might only be interested in my money! That quite upset me, I can tell you, and we haven't mentioned the matter since. But to be truthful, the fewer people who know of it the better. You know what servants are like and in a small place like Compton Parva once word gets out…'

'Yes, I do know.' So Russ *had* tried to dissuade his friend from pursuing Fleur. Molly felt more than a little guilty for asking him to do so. She tried not to think of the inducement she had offered him, nor his indignant refusal. She said now, 'But he is your close friend, Sir Gerald. You should tell him.'

'I will, of course, but he has been so out of temper this past week he has bitten my head off for the slightest thing! No, once Edwin has spoken to the bishop, then I shall ask Russ to be my grooms-man and also to go with me to make the application.' A rueful twinkle came into his eyes. 'Given his reputation and my own, I think perhaps I am wise to have your brother speak to the bishop for me, don't you think?'

'I do, but Edwin told me that his business will keep him away for a week, at least,' said Molly. 'How will you bear the wait?'

Gerald caught her hands. 'Bless you for your concern, Molly. Your brother has promised to write as soon as it is agreed, then we may be easy. Not that there will be an unseemly rush to the altar,' he added, looking as stern as was possible for such an easy-going gentleman. 'I will have no hint of scandal attached to Fleur. I am in no way ashamed of my future bride and mean to reinstate her into her proper place in society. I swear to you, Molly, that Fleur's well-being is and always will be paramount to me.'

With that he went off, leaving Molly convinced that her friend could not be anything but happy with such a caring husband.

No one observing Russ's calm and smiling demeanour on Friday evening would have known that he would rather have been anywhere than at the King's Head. He stood with the Newlands party and watched as Agnes and Edwin received the congratulations of each new arrival.

'This is such a happy time,' declared Serena, who was standing beside him. She gave a little laugh and took his arm. 'I do hope there will be another announcement shortly, Russ.'

Russ glanced down sharply. 'What makes you say that?'

Her limpid look was innocence itself. 'Just the way two people have been behaving recently.'

She certainly could not mean Molly and himself, for they had barely spoken two words together all evening. He allowed his eyes to shift to where Molly was standing beside her brother. She was wearing another new creation, this time of plum-red satin over a white petticoat.

'Molly looks very well tonight, do you not think?' murmured Serena, following his gaze. 'She has changed a great deal since I first met her. Very much like a butterfly, in all her new finery.'

Russ did not reply. The vicar and his fiancée were taking to the floor for the first dance and he wondered if he might ask Molly to stand up with him, but before he could move, Gerald had stepped up and Molly was taking his hand and smiling up at him, her cheeks gently flushed. Not for the first time in recent weeks Russ felt a stab of jealousy towards his oldest friend.

Serena squeezed his arm. 'Since quite the prettiest lady in the room is engaged, you had best stand up with me,' she told him.

Hiding his frustration beneath a smile, Russ led his sister out to join one of the sets. The dance seemed interminably long and when it ended he spotted Molly crossing the room to talk to Sir William and Lady Currick, who had just arrived with their daughter.

When Serena begged him to take her over to speak to Nell Currick, he was only too pleased to oblige, but as they came up, Sir William carried Molly off to join the next set. Robbed of a second chance to dance with Molly, Russ excused himself quickly before Serena could suggest he stand up with Nell or her mother. He moved away to the side of the room, where he stood, watching the dancing and trying hard not to scowl. Hell and damnation, he was behaving like a mooncalf, something he had vowed he would never do over any woman. Molly, meanwhile, appeared to be enjoying herself immensely. Serena was right. Dressed in her bright new gowns she was indeed the prettiest woman in the room. Damn her.

* * *

Molly wished she might stop smiling but she knew Russ was watching her and she was determined not to give him any clue that she was unhappy. When her dance with Sir William ended, she thought Russ might ask her to dance with him, but instead she saw him leading out Agnes Kilburn. Molly would have liked to sit out the next dance, but pride would not allow her to refuse when Mr Sykes asked her to stand up with him.

There was a break in the dancing after that and Molly accompanied Mr and Mrs Sykes to the refreshment room. She was helping herself to a glass of lemonade when she heard the familiar deep voice at her shoulder.

'You are quite the belle of the ball this evening, Mrs Morgan.'

She turned to Russ and made a little curtsy.

'La, thank you, sir. I shall take that as a compliment.'

'You have certainly been too busy to dance with me, have you not?'

His eyes were glinting and the slight upward curve to his lips caused her insides to flutter. The temptation was to smile back at him, maybe even hint that she was not engaged for any more dances, but Molly was not ready to make her peace with him yet. She must show him that she was immune to his charms.

'It is gratifying to be in such demand as a dance partner,' she said airily. 'I do not know when I have enjoyed dancing more.'

'And will you honour me with your hand for one of the next dances, madam?'

She widened her eyes. 'Oh, heavens, I cannot make any promises, Mr Russington. I do not know yet who may ask me to stand up with them.'

'Would you not prefer to dance with me?'

He moved closer, unnerving her, and she said sharply, 'I have no preferences, Mr Russington.'

'No? Surely all this new finery is aimed at finding a husband.'

He was rattled. Molly knew she should be pleased, it gave her the upper hand, but instead she felt only a sick kind of misery that they had lost the easy-going camaraderie she had come to enjoy.

'I have no wish for a husband,' she told him, her voice low and angry. 'And if I did, it would be a man of integrity, a man I could trust and who would make me comfortable. Certainly not a *rake*.'

She closed her lips firmly before any more rash

words could escape. She had spoken to wound him and his silence and the muscle working in his cheek showed she might just have done it. At the very least she had made him angry.

'This is plain-speaking indeed, madam.'

'I find it best to speak honestly, sir, so there can be no misunderstanding. But our situation makes it necessary for us to be civil to one another, Mr Russington.' She kept her smile in place as she met his eyes with a defiant look. 'I hope we can continue to do that.'

'Do you?

'But of course.' She gave a tinkling laugh, light and brittle as glass. 'I would not have our friends and family think there is anything amiss between us.'

He smiled then, a cold, courteous smile that did not reach his eyes.

'Nor I, madam. I think our family and friends can rest assured there is *nothing* between us.'

With a stiff little bow he walked away and not a moment too soon, for Molly felt her resolve crumbling and she turned away, blinking back tears. Serena and the others should be proud of her. She had shown the great Beau Russington that she did not care the snap of her fingers for him. Now all she wanted to do was to crawl away into a dark corner and cry.

After that things went from bad to worse. She was standing with Mr and Mrs Thomas when she saw Russ approaching her and in a fit of pique worthy of a schoolgirl, she put her nose in the air and turned her back upon him.

Foolish woman. Cutting off your nose to spite your face!

Ashamed of her own behaviour, she excused herself from dancing with anyone else and made her way towards the door, eager to be alone.

'Molly, are you quite well?'

Serena was at her side and looking anxiously at her.

'I need a little air, that is all.'

'You cannot go out alone,' said Serena, taking her arm.

'I am not going very far,' said Molly, desperate for solitude. 'And no one will see me if I remain on the balcony.

'But you might be taken ill. I shall come with you.'

Unequal to the fight, Molly allowed Serena to accompany her out of the assembly rooms. The outer doors led on to the balcony and from there a flight of stairs ran down to the yard so that patrons might enter and leave the rooms without passing through the inn itself. Molly stepped out into the cool air, thankful for the shadows thrown up from the lanterns that illuminated the yard below them.

Serena wrinkled her nose. 'Are you sure you want to stay out here? All I can smell is the stables.'

'But it is cooler.'

'True. Are you not enjoying yourself, Molly?'

'I think I am a little tired,' she replied. 'I am not accustomed to dancing so much.'

Serena chuckled. 'Our plan to transform you has worked beautifully. And Russ has been watching you all evening.'

'I do not want him to watch me,' Molly retorted, feeling that tears were very close. 'I merely want him to go away.'

Serena turned towards her and took her hands. 'Is that truly what you want, Molly? I thought you loved my brother.'

Swallowing hard, Molly averted her gaze, staring down into the yard. 'Of...of course not. He is not at all the sort of man to suit me.'

With my provincial morals and good deeds.

'Well, that is a shame,' sighed Serena, 'because I think you are just the sort of woman Russ needs.'

If only that were true, thought Molly sadly.

Below her, a dusty travelling chaise clattered over the cobbles and the yard burst into life. Ostlers ran to the horses and the landlord came bustling out to open the carriage door, bowing low as an elderly man climbed out. There was something vaguely familiar about the portly, bewigged figure and instead of turning away to answer Serena she moved a little closer to the rail. The old man's strident voice carried clearly up to her.

'My name is Dellafield. I sent ahead to bespeak a room for the night.'

'Dellafield,' said Serena, beside her. 'Isn't that the name of the housekeeper at—'

Molly grabbed her wrist and pulled her back into the shadows.

'Serena,' she hissed, 'promise me you will not say a word about this.'

'If you wish, but—'

'Promise!'

'Yes, yes, of course.'

Molly nodded, her mind racing. 'Let us go back inside. And, Serena, remember, I rely upon you not to say a word to anyone!'

* * *

They returned to the ballroom to find the music had stopped and Sir William Currick was standing on a chair, congratulating Miss Kilburn and Mr Frayne upon their engagement. All eyes were on the speaker and Molly made her way through the crowd until she was beside Sir Gerald. She plucked at his sleeve and drew him to the side of the room, where she quickly explained what she had overheard.

'So Fleur's father has found her,' he exclaimed.

'Not necessarily,' Molly said slowly. 'It's more likely he saw my name or Edwin's on the list of guests at your ball. The Dellafields were our neighbours in Hertfordshire, and Fleur and I were at school together. Having tried all other avenues, perhaps he hopes Fleur and I may have kept in touch.'

'Even if you do not tell him it is only a matter of time before he learns about Prospect House.' Gerald was thinking quickly, one fist thudding into his palm. 'I must delay no longer—once Fleur is my wife, I shall be able to protect her. Come, Molly, let us find your brother. Fleur and I will go with him to see the bishop tomorrow.'

But Edwin had by this time replaced Sir William on the chair and was making a speech of thanks.

They were obliged to wait until he had finished before they could pull him to one side and explain what had happened.

'I shall send word to Prospect House this very night,' said Gerald, 'and we will accompany you to Nidderton in the morning. Once we have the licence we can be married there and then Fleur will be safe.'

Edwin put out his hands. 'I wish that were possible, Gerald, but my meeting is tomorrow morning. If I am not to be late, then I must be leaving Compton Parva before dawn and on horseback. I delayed my departure so I might attend this party with Agnes, you see.'

'Then we will follow on in the carriage at daybreak,' Gerald stated. 'You will come with us, will you not, Molly? I will not have any hint of impropriety attending Fleur. Not only do we have to drive in a closed carriage all the way to Nidderton, but we will be obliged to spend at least one night there before I can make her my wife.' He took her hands. 'Pray say you will do it, Molly. You are Fleur's oldest friend. I know she will want you with her.'

'Yes, I will come,' she replied. 'To tell the truth I shall be glad to be out of town when Fleur's father comes calling!'

* * *

Across the room, Russ watched as Gerald kissed Molly's hands, one after the other, saw her obvious pleasure at the gesture. A man of integrity. A man she could trust. Damnation, had she set her cap at him? Had Gerald been dangling after her all along and using Fleur Dellafield as a smokescreen? He turned away, feeling as if he had been punched in the gut. He could no longer think clearly and the sooner this damned evening was over the better.

Edwin touched Molly's arm. 'My dear, I have sent for the carriage. I think it is time I was leaving. I have a very early start in the morning.'

'Of course. I will collect my wrap and come with you.'

'No, no, there is no need for that. Lady Currick or one of the other ladies will see you home. There will be at least two more dances. I pray you will stay and enjoy yourself.'

'I have had all the enjoyment I shall get this evening,' she said, trying and failing to make light of it.

Thankfully her brother was too preoccupied to notice. He glanced back across the room. 'I think Gerald, too, would like to be going home and preparing for the morrow, but he knows it's best to stay. He does not want to rouse any suspicions.' He touched her arm. 'I persuaded him he must tell Agnes about this before he leaves in the morning, but he is adamant that no one else should know of his plans at the present time, Molly, so we must be careful.'

Molly wondered if Russ would disapprove of what amounted to an elopement. Would he disapprove of her for helping them? Her eyes grew hot and she blinked rapidly. Not that it would make any difference now, since their friendship was quite at an end.

They had reached the yard when the landlord came running out of the taproom.

'Mr Frayne, there is a gentleman arrived, sir, and he was asking about yourself and Mrs Morgan. I think he wishes to call upon you tomorrow—since you are here, would you like to see him now, before you leave?'

Edwin helped Molly into the carriage before answering the landlord.

'I think not. My sister is far too fatigued for that. But we don't wish to offend the fellow, so you had best not mention that we were here tonight. He can call at the vicarage tomorrow—but tell him not to call too early, mind you!' He jumped in after

Molly and muttered as the door closed upon them, 'Hopefully by the time he comes, we will both be away from home.'

Russ strode out across the moors, hoping the fresh early-morning air would clear his head. He had risen before dawn and slipped out of the house as soon as there was light to see his way. He had spent a restless night, the images of Gerald and Molly haunting his dreams. Molly dancing with Gerald, laughing with him. Talking with him. Allowing him to kiss her hands.

Surely there was nothing in it, yet Gerald had been oddly distracted on the journey back from the King's Head and, unusually, he had not shared his thoughts with Russ. They had not clashed over a woman since their schooldays and Russ hoped that his suspicions were unfounded, but there was no doubt that Molly had been very friendly towards Gerald last night. Whereas towards him— his thoughts veered off. He had only himself to blame if she was angry with him. He had taken her to his room, pleasured her—yes, *pleasured* her, he reminded himself—but then he had explained why it could go no further. Why he was not the man for her.

He whipped his stick across the dying heather. Confound it, he had spoken no more than the truth. He was trying to save her from the hurt and disappointment of losing her heart to a rake.

He stopped. Had she lost her heart already? Was she—*could* she be in love with him?

The idea was enticing. He wanted it to be true and he could almost believe it was. Molly was no flirt, but she had kissed him, trusted him. He began to walk again, more slowly this time. Above him the clear grey sky was slowly changing to blue as the first bars of sunlight appeared on the horizon, and the golden rays seemed to pierce his soul. He had already acknowledged that Molly was not greedy and grasping like his stepmother. Now he was forced to recognise his own feelings. He loved her. Deeply. But was it possible he could be a faithful husband?

No. A ridiculous fancy. Most likely due to lack of food—after all, he had been walking for more than an hour and had eaten nothing since last night. He turned to make his way back to Newlands, but the idea of marriage had taken hold and he could not shake it off. It might already be too late. Perhaps Gerald had stolen the march on him and was going to offer for Molly today. After all, it was no secret that Edwin was going away, so she would be alone. Russ recalled now when he had pressed Gerald to tell him what was the matter, all his friend would do was laugh and say he would explain everything once tomorrow was over. The leaden weight was now dragging at his heart. Did Molly think Gerald a man of integrity, a man who would make her comfortable?

'But she does not love him!'

The words burst from him. He would stake his life that they were true, yet he feared she might accept an offer from Gerald. After all, Russ had awakened the passion in Molly, had told her she would find happiness with another man. Why should that man not be Kilburn? Suddenly the thought of losing Molly hit Russ like a physical blow. He veered away from the house and almost ran to the stables. He must go and see her, tell her what a crass fool he had been and put his future, his happiness, in her hands.

He was surprised to find the stable yard already bustling with activity. The Kilburns' barouche was being wheeled out of the carriage house and while Russ waited for his horse to be saddled he asked the head groom who had ordered the carriage.

'Miss Kilburn, sir. She and the other ladies are

driving into Compton Parva this morning.' The fellow allowed a grin to split his weather-beaten features. 'I believe they're going shopping again, sir.'

Russ realised he had been holding his breath. So Gerald had not ordered the barouche and a quick glance in the stables showed that his friend's grey hack was still in its stall. He scrambled up on to his horse and gathered up the reins. He had the chance to get to Molly first and put right the damage he had done.

Once they had clattered out of the yard, Russ gave Flash his head and galloped through the park to the gates, but he steadied the big horse once they reached the road. Impatient as he was to see Molly he did not wish to arrive looking flustered.

The morning sun was warm on his back as he trotted into the town and, as he knocked on the vicarage door, his spirits were high.

They sank moments later with the news that Mrs Morgan had gone out. The manservant was very polite, but refused to divulge his mistress's direction. Even when Russ asked him directly if she had gone to Prospect House, the fellow remained tight-lipped.

'And when do you expect her back?'

'I'm afraid I cannot say, sir.'

'Come, man, surely you know when your mistress will return.'

The man coloured, but stood his ground. 'My mistress has given me no instructions to divulge such information, sir.'

Russ wondered if she had seen his approach and had given orders to deny her. As the door closed he stepped back and looked up at the first-floor windows, but they were blank. Not even the twitch of a curtain to suggest anyone was watching him. Yet the feeling persisted that the manservant was hiding something and he wondered whether Gerald would be admitted if, or when, he called. Russ decided he would not leave town just yet. There was a small coffee house just across the road from the vicarage and he strolled over. There were not many customers and he positioned himself at a table near the window, from where he had a good view of the vicarage door. If nothing else, it would give him an opportunity to break his fast.

Two hours later the only caller at the vicarage had been an elderly gentleman, who had also been turned away, and Russ left the coffee shop, cursing himself for being so foolishly jealous of his best friend. He walked back to the King's Head, where he had left his horse, but as he passed the door and headed for the yard a tap boy came running out to beg him to step inside and join Miss Kilburn and her party, who were taking coffee in a private parlour. Russ guessed the ladies had finished their shopping trip. He would be expected to escort them back to Newlands and in truth he did not object, so he turned back and entered the inn. Hopefully conversing with Agnes, Serena and Mrs Sykes might take his mind off Molly.

The ladies greeted him cheerfully and bade him sit at the table with them. While they waited for fresh coffee to be brought in, Russ evaded questions about what had brought him to the town so early.

'When you did not join us for breakfast we assumed you were out with Gerald,' remarked Serena, as the servants withdrew again.

'Oh?' Russ looked up. 'Where has he gone?'

'He left word that he is visiting friends,' explained Agnes, pouring coffee for everyone.

'Strange that he should say nothing about this last night,' remarked Russ.

Agnes waved a dismissive hand. 'Perhaps he

only had word from them when we returned from the King's Head.'

'Russ, you will never guess what we heard when we arrived in Compton Parva this morning,' declared Serena, her eyes wide. 'Miss Hebden told us that Molly was seen getting into a carriage early this morning. The whole town is buzzing with it.'

'Then the whole town should be ashamed of themselves,' retorted Agnes, directing a frown at Serena. 'Most likely Molly was going to Prospect House.'

'Then why did she not take the gig?' argued Serena. She turned to Russ, her eyes wide. 'But what if she has run off with someone? Did you know that Gerald left at dawn and in a closed carriage? What if they were running off together?'

'Serena!' Agnes was laughing and shaking her head, declaring that she was talking nonsense.

'So Gerald is not at Newlands?' Russ tried to subdue his growing suspicion.

'No,' said Agnes, avoiding his eye. 'He left word that we were not to expect him to return before tomorrow evening at the earliest. Oh, dear, this coffee pot is empty. Ring the bell, Serena, if you please, and we will order more.'

Russ schooled his countenance to indifference

and kept silent while they waited for the servant to refresh the coffee pot. He would not believe there was any intrigue between Gerald and Molly. It was one thing to think Gerald might go to the vicarage and propose, but he was quite sure Molly would never agree to an elopement. Besides, she was of age and had no need to run away. No, it was a ridiculous idea and once the servant had withdrawn Russ asked cheerfully what other news the ladies had gleaned in the town that morning.

'Why, nothing,' replied Agnes, smiling at him. 'Do you think we are such sad creatures that we only live for gossip?'

'Well, there was the altercation Serena and I overheard between the landlord and one of his guests as we came in today,' declared Mrs Sykes. 'The gentleman was complaining that the landlord had misled him and he was asking all and sundry about Mrs D—'

'Oh, la, but that is nothing to do with us,' exclaimed Serena, rudely talking over the older lady. 'We should be more concerned about Gerald. Russ, I think he has *eloped* with Molly.'

He said sharply, 'Do not be so foolish, Serena. I beg you will not utter such damaging nonsense again.'

'Oh, I shall not say it to anyone else,' Serena replied sunnily.

'You will not say anything more at all!' he growled.

'Only I could not but notice that Gerald and Molly were on such good terms last night,' she continued, quite ignoring her brother. 'But I suppose that is not surprising, for Molly was looking exceptionally well, did you not think, Russ? She is quite transformed these past few weeks. Or had you not noticed?'

'Pray do not tease your brother, Serena,' Agnes begged, her cup clattering in its saucer.

'And why not? It is clear that he loves Molly Morgan.'

'Mercy me!' Mrs Sykes began to fan herself rapidly.

Russ barked, 'Serena, that is enough!'

But his minx of a sister merely turned her frank gaze upon him and demanded that he deny it, if it was not true.

'And Molly is quite as much in love with you,' she continued, reaching for another piece of cake.

He ground his teeth. 'If…*if* that were so, she would hardly be running off with Kilburn.'

Serena studied the cake for a moment before taking a tiny bite. 'Well, after the way you behaved last night I think she might well run off with *anyone*, just to teach you a lesson. And I cannot but think it a mistake. They will both be very miserable, don't you agree?'

A stillness had fallen over the room. Russ clenched his fists, trying to steady his breathing and to think calmly.

'No,' he said at last. 'Molly is not the sort to elope with anyone. I know her too well to think she would countenance such impropriety.' He caught the look that passed between Agnes and Serena and was instantly on the alert. 'Well, what is it?'

'Gerald told his man he was heading for Nidderton,' said Agnes.

'Is that not where Mr Frayne is meeting the bishop?' murmured Serena. 'And bishops can issue licences for a speedy marriage.' She looked at Russ as he pushed his chair back, the legs scraping across the boards. 'You are going after them.'

'Yes.' He snatched up his hat. 'I do not think for a moment there is any truth in your outrageous supposition, but I need to be sure.'

'Splendid. And when you get back, brother mine, you may thank me properly.'

He was at the door, but at these words he stopped.

'When I get back, sister,' he said with menace, 'I shall arrange for you to be sent to a nunnery, you interfering baggage!'

The private parlour at the Bear was comfortable enough. A cheerful fire blazed in the hearth, but even with the shutters closed the sounds from the market square intruded. However, everyone was too grateful to have found accommodation to complain. Edwin had joined Molly, Fleur and Gerald for the evening, assuring them that he had seen quite enough of his ecclesiastical colleagues during the day and was happy not to dine with them. However, when the covers were removed, he declined Gerald's invitation to join him in a glass of brandy.

'I know it is not late, but it is time I returned to my own lodgings. Do not forget I have been up since before dawn.'

'So, too, have we,' said Molly, smothering a yawn. 'It has been a long day.'

'But a successful one,' put in Gerald. He reached out and caught Fleur's hand. 'We are both extremely grateful. To Molly, for agreeing to come with us, and to you, Edwin, for promoting our cause with your bishop.' He patted his pocket. 'I have the licence safe and tomorrow I shall make Fleur my wife.'

'And I shall have great pleasure in marrying you,' declared Edwin, rising. 'Now, if you will excuse me, I had best leave before I fall asleep at the table.'

Molly walked with him to the door, returning to find Gerald alone in the private parlour, sipping at his brandy.

'Fleur has gone out to, um, pluck a rose,' he said, using the familiar euphemism to indicate Fleur had gone out to the privy. 'She is afraid she will not sleep tonight, and I suggested she take a glass of something before we all retire.' He waved towards the bottles on the table. 'You see our host has provided some light wine, as well as the brandy. Will you join us?'

'With pleasure, Sir Gerald, although I do not foresee any difficulty in sleeping.'

'Nor I, but—' He broke off, frowning at the sounds of an altercation in the passageway. 'What the devil is going on?'

They both jumped to their feet as the door burst open and Russ came in, his greatcoat flapping open and a thunderous scowl on his face. He closed the door upon the still-protesting landlord and stood with his back against it, ignoring Gerald and glaring at Molly, who instinctively retreated behind the table.

'Aye, madam,' he barked, throwing his hat and gloves on to a chair, 'you may well cower away from me!'

'I say, old friend,' Gerald protested, 'there is no reason to be so angry with Molly.'

'Oh, isn't there?' Molly took another step away at his icy tones. 'She deceived me.'

'Because we did not tell you what was happening? That was my fault,' said Gerald. 'I swore her to secrecy'

'And why would you do that?' Russ rounded on his friend. 'Did you think I would call you out?' His lip curled. 'I would not waste my time. You are welcome to marry the jade.'

'No, no, Russ, you have it all wrong,' cried Molly, but her words went unheeded as Gerald moved forward, his face darkening.

'You go too far, Russington.'

'I haven't gone far enough yet!'

Molly watched in alarm as the two men squared up to one another. She flew around the table and pushed herself between them.

'You cannot start a fight here!' she said angrily,

one hand on each chest. 'Pray be sensible. You are friends.'

'Not any longer!' snapped Russ. He took Molly by the shoulders and firmly put her to one side. 'Out of the way, strumpet, and let me at him!'

For a brief moment chaos reigned. Molly grabbed his arm and Gerald protested as Russ tried to shake her off, but they all froze as a loud shriek rent the air.

'What is going on here?'

In the sudden silence Russ looked towards the door, where Fleur was standing with her hands on her pale cheeks.

'What the devil!' he exclaimed as she ran across the room and into Gerald's arms. Not that he really needed to ask. He looked back at Gerald. 'So you are not marrying Molly.'

'Molly?' Gerald blinked at him over Fleur's golden head. 'No, of course, I am not. She is here as chaperon. Fleur and I are to be married tomorrow, by licence.'

'Ah, of course.' Russ nodded slowly. 'I understand now. I owe you all an apology.'

He looked around for Molly. She had backed away and was now glaring at him.

'How *dare* you?' Her voice was shaking with anger. 'How dare you force your way in here and insult everyone in that brutish manner? You will go, this minute.'

'Not before you give me a chance to explain.'

'I have heard quite enough from you,' she threw at him. 'A jade, am I? A strumpet! You had best leave, before I summon the landlord to *throw* you out!'

'My love.' Fleur pushed herself out of Gerald's arms. 'I need a little air. Will you take me outside, please?'

'What, now?' asked Gerald, a note of surprise in his voice. Russ was looking at Molly, but from the tail of his eye he saw Gerald jump, as if he had been pinched. 'Oh, aye, yes. Of course.'

'No!' exclaimed Molly. 'Fleur, you cannot leave me alone with this…this *monster*!'

Ignoring her protests, Gerald whisked Fleur out of the room and closed the door firmly behind them. Russ knew they were giving him a chance to make his peace with Molly, but was it too late? She was still glaring at him, her arms folded as if to shield herself from attack.

He took a deep breath. 'I beg your pardon. Coming in here, what I said to you—it was very wrong of me.'

Silence. He tried again.

'I did not intend—that is, when Serena suggested you had run off with Kilburn I didn't believe her. I knew there had to be another explanation.'

'Ha! If that was so, why would you come chasing all the way to Nidderton?'

'Because I had to be sure. I could not bear the thought of your marrying Kilburn.'

'You were the one who said I must find myself a husband.'

She threw the words at him and he flinched.

'Yes, I know, but… I was wrong.'

'Oh? You think I am unworthy of a gentleman.'

'No!'

'You called me a jade.'

'I apologised for that.'

'And a…a strumpet.' Her voice positively shook with rage.

'I have said it was wrong of me. But I was angry. I have spent the whole day searching the town for you. I have called at every inn and hotel and tavern, trying to find you.'

'Why on earth would you do that?'

Molly's heart was pounding against her ribs so hard it hurt. Russ, too, appeared to be breathing heavily. He would not look at her, but was scowling at the floor.

She moved a step closer. 'Why, Russ?'

'Because I love you!'

It was as if the words were wrenched from him. He raised his head and looked at her.

'I could not let you marry Kilburn without telling you how I felt.'

She put one hand on a chair back to steady herself. It was what she wanted to hear, what she had dreamed of, but her anger still simmered and she was not about to throw herself into his arms.

'And what difference did you think that would make, if I *had* been about to marry Sir Gerald?' she asked him, her voice was dripping with scorn. 'Did you think I would cry off and marry you, because you are more fashionable than your friend, or perhaps because your fortune is ten times larger?'

'No! I know you too well to think you would be influenced by either of those things. I thought you cared for me.' He exhaled. 'I thought you loved me.'

'And yet you believed I might marry your friend?' She shook her head. 'For a man with such a reputation as a lover, Charles Russington, you are woefully ignorant of women.'

'Of women like you, yes.'

'I am not so very different.'

'Oh, but you are.' He gave her a rueful smile. 'You are good and kind and strong. A reformer. A woman of principal. Not at all the sort to attract me, and yet, from the first moment we met, I was lost. When I am near you, I cannot think properly. The polished address that I am supposed to possess all disappears. I admit it, I behave like a moonstruck schoolboy. I cannot help it, Molly, I have fallen helplessly, hopelessly in love with you.'

He had been moving closer as he spoke, his eyes holding Molly's, begging her to believe him. He went down on one knee before her.

'Nothing else matters to me but your happiness, Molly. I have never felt like this before, as if my very existence depends upon one person. Upon *you*. I want you in my life, Molly Morgan. I want you with me, at my side, as my wife, my friend. More than that, I want to be in *your* life, to help you with your charities if you will let me. I want to learn from your goodness.

'I cannot tell you how it will end, my love, but I give you my word I will try with all my heart to be a good husband to you, to love and cherish you for the rest of your days.' He reached out to take her hands. 'What do you say, dearest? It is a big risk, I know, but will you trust me to take care of you? Will you honour me with your heart and your hand?'

'Oh, Russ.' His face swam before her eyes. 'Oh, Russ, *how* I love you!'

She tugged at his hands and the next instant he was on his feet and pulling her into his arms.

'Say it,' he muttered, covering her face with kisses. 'Put me out of my misery, darling Molly, and say you will marry me.'

Darling Molly.

Her heart took flight at that and she answered him breathlessly. 'Yes, yes, I will marry you.'

With a growl of triumph, he captured her lips again, kissing her so soundly that her very bones turned to water. When Russ ended the kiss she sighed and leaned against him, eyes closed, and it was not until she heard a soft, apologetic cough that she realised they were not alone.

Gerald and Fleur had come in and were looking at them with unfeigned delight.

'So you have made it up,' remarked Gerald, grinning.

'Yes,' said Russ, keeping is arms tight around

Molly. 'Do you think the bishop would grant us a licence, too?'

'Undoubtedly. Frayne told us the fellow was pleased to be bringing one reprobate back into the fold, so I am sure he will be delighted to make it two.'

'Well, my love?' Russ looked down at Molly, who was still resting her head against his shoulder. 'Shall we be married in Nidderton? Perhaps Fleur and Gerald would delay their return to Newlands long enough to attend us.'

'I would like that,' she said softly. She added, blushing, 'Very much.'

Gerald clapped his hands. 'Then it is settled. Did I not tell you there was something in the air here? And, Russ, now you are here you can be my groomsman, tomorrow, If you will.'

'With all my heart, my friend.'

'Capital!' Gerald opened the door. 'Now, where's that rascally landlord? He must fetch us more glasses and we will celebrate!'

An hour later, after several toasts by the gentlemen and not a few tears shed by the ladies, Fleur announced she was going to bed. Molly would have accompanied her, but she waved her back to her seat.

'You have not yet finished your wine,' she said. 'I am sure Gerald will escort me to my room.

'With pleasure, my love. I am ready for my bed now, too. We have a busy day ahead.' He kissed Molly's cheek, then clasped Russ's hand. 'Goodnight, my friend. Fleur and I are delighted you will be with us for our wedding tomorrow and the news that you and Molly are to be married has made our happiness complete.'

With a final wave he took Fleur's arm and they went out, leaving Molly and Russ alone.

'Where are you staying?' she asked him.

'I left Flash at the Fox and Goose while I searched for you. I should be able to get lodging there for the night.'

'But it is late and you cannot be *sure* of getting a room.'

Molly kept her eyes lowered while the silence dragged on for a full minute.

'No,' he said slowly. 'They may be full by now.'

She studied her wine, turning the glass round and round in her hands.

'Fleur and I have separate rooms,' she murmured. 'You could share mine.'

She wondered if she had shocked him and looked up anxiously.

'Is that what you want, Molly?' He was watching her, a mixture of hope and concern in his dark eyes.

She rose and held out her hand to him. 'It is what I have wanted, ever since that night at Newlands.'

There was plenty of noise from the taproom but thankfully the stairs and corridors were deserted as Molly led Russ into her room. Pausing only to turn the key in the lock, he took her in his arms and kissed her.

'Are you sure about this, Molly?'

'Very sure.' Smiling, she cupped his face. 'I do not want to wait another moment for you.'

She drew him down to her, pressing her lips against his as her fingers slid into his hair and tangled with the silky curls. His tongue danced into her mouth, flickering, teasing, and she pressed herself against him as her body responded. Between kisses they began to undress one another, their fingers scrabbling with strings and buttons until they fell together, naked, on to the bed.

She gave a little mewl of pleasure as he put his mouth to one breast, while his fingers played with the other. She shifted restlessly as the lightness rippled through her body, but she resisted the pull of desire and concentrated on Russ's pleasure, kissing and stroking his hard, aroused body until she knew he was also at the tipping point, then she straddled him, taking him inside her, gasping at the delight of it and revelling at her power as he groaned beneath her. She bent forward to kiss him and he gasped as her breasts skimmed his chest. In one swift movement he caught her in his arms and rolled her over, taking control, never breaking the kiss.

He began to push into her, slowly and steadily, every movement a caress that took her closer to the pinnacle. Her response was instinctive, tensing around him, lifting her hips, feeling the heat building. When she would have cried out he stopped her mouth with a kiss, his tongue thrusting deep, and she felt her body melting beneath the onslaught until she was almost fainting with delight. He carried her higher, the ripples building into a flood. She was flying, soaring, almost delirious with the pleasure of it all. Russ gasped out her name and their bodies shuddered and bucked against one another. She felt the dam burst within her and clung on tightly as the final spasm took her over the edge and consciousness splintered. She and Russ collapsed together, sated, exhausted and cradled in each other's arms.

Gently, Russ drew the covers over them to keep off the chill air, and as he wrapped himself around her, Molly felt a glow of contentment. She snuggled against him and closed her eyes. The past was done now. She could look forward to the future.

Epilogue

One year later

The church of All Souls was full. Fleur and Gerald had already moved to the font with their baby girl, waiting for Edwin to begin the baptism. Molly felt her happiness growing as she gazed around her at all the familiar faces.

Agnes was sitting closer to the pulpit, as befitted the vicar's wife, and Molly was relieved to see that she was glowing with health as she approached the final stages of her pregnancy. Then there were her friends from Prospect House, filling their allotted pews, and in front of them were the servants from Newlands. Molly had watched in delight as Daisy Matthews, in her role as housekeeper, had proudly led them in, including her son, Billy, almost swaggering in his new livery as Sir Gerald's tiger.

Beside her, Russ lowered his head to murmur in her ear, 'Lady Kilburn is looking radiant today.'

Molly's gaze moved back to Fleur.

'Of course,' she whispered. 'She is very happy in her marriage.'

'And you, Molly—' his deep velvet voice sent the familiar ripple of pleasure through her '—are *you* happy?'

She glanced down at the sleeping baby in her arms. Their son, about to be christened as Charles Edwin Gerald Russington.

'Oh, yes. I could not be happier.'

She gazed up at him, her eyes shining with love, and Russ's heart swelled. He was overwhelmed with the pride and joy he felt for his family. He had never dreamt he would settle for life in a small town so far from London, but he was no longer a lost soul. Everything he wanted, everything he needed was here in Compton Parva.

He had come home.

Putting one arm protectively about Molly, he smiled down at her.

'Come along, then, my darling wife. Let us join Fleur and Gerald at the font and allow your brother to do his duty.'

* * * * *

LET'S TALK

Romance

For exclusive extracts, competitions
and special offers, find us online:

- facebook.com/millsandboon
- @millsandboonuk
- @millsandboon

Or get in touch on 0844 844 1351*

For all the latest titles coming soon,
visit millsandboon.co.uk/nextmonth

*Calls cost 7p per minute plus your phone company's price per
minute access charge